PRAISE FOR

THE FALL

"It's a thrill-a-minute story, with good here-and-now technology, and a striking scientific premise at its heart."
—*Wall Street Journal*

"R.J. Pineiro breaks the sound barrier with *The Fall*, one of the most original and electrifying science-based thrillers I have read in a long time. The opening chapter—the incredible "fall" itself—is mind-bending enough, but it only gets better, with cutting-edge science, vivid characters, and a plot that accelerates to a mind-warping climax. Highly recommended." —*Douglas Preston, New York Times bestselling author of The Kraken Project*

"Imaginative premise." —*Publishers Weekly*

"This alternate world sci-fi thriller is packed with high stakes and moves at a high speed." —*Kirkus*

"Jack's adrenaline is contagious - *The Fall* will keep readers on the edges of their seats, waiting to find out what crazy stunt Jack will perform next and to learn the fate of this charming, daredevil hero." —*Forces of Geek*

WITHOUT MERCY

"Constant action, sympathetic heroes, believable evildoers, and absolute authenticity on every page." —*Publishers Weekly*, starred review

"The authenticity of the story makes the tale particularly terrifying, especially at a time when real-life international relations appear unstable. A fine apocalyptic thriller right up the alley of Clancy and Thor fans." —*Booklist*

"A masterful thriller written by men of deep experience. Epic in scale yet swiftly paced, *Without Mercy* is as convincing as it is chilling. First-rate and very highly recommended!" —Ralph Peters, *New York Times* bestselling author

"The ultimate terrorist scenario, with authenticity steeped into every page. Col. David Hunt and R.J. Pineiro put their credentials on display in stellar fashion. Readers who enjoy Tom Clancy and Brad Taylor will find a new favorite." —Ward Larsen, *USA Today* bestselling author

WITHOUT FEAR

"Outstanding… This military adventure thriller deserves to become a genre classic." —*Publisher's Weekly*, starred review

BOOKS BY R.J. PINEIRO

* With Col. David Hunt
** With Joe Weber

AVENUE
OF REGRETS

A Novel

R.J. PINEIRO

Avenue of Regrets: A Novel
Auspicious Apparatus Press

ISBN-13: 978-1-7202154-4-8 (paperback)
ISBN-10: 1-7202154-4-8 (paperback)
ISBN-13: 978-0-9966628-7-1 (ebook)
ISBN-10: 0-9966628-7-1 (ebook)

The characters and events portrayed in this book are fictitious. Any similarity to real persons, living or dead, is coincidental and not intended by the author.

TABLE OF CONTENTS

For those who no longer walk among us,

Rogelio A. Pineiro
Linda Lory Wiltz
Julio Cesar Gomez
William Moser

Vayan con Dios.

AVENUE
OF REGRETS

A Novel

R.J. PINEIRO

"Only in the darkness can you see the stars."

—Martin Luther King Jr.

CHAPTER 1

I didn't always hate my life.

There was a time when I'd looked forward to getting up in the morning with the energy of a thoroughbred at the starting gate of the Preakness Stakes.

But as night falls, and I sip my third Mexican martini among complete strangers, my mind inexorably begins to drift to the event that propelled my life down this avenue of regrets.

My tired eyes contemplate the alcohol I consume to take the edge off of my transgressions while sitting in this crowded bar of a hotel in San Francisco after running an efficiency workshop at a local distributor of paper products.

Unfortunately, even this swirling green brew of cheap tequila, Cointreau, OJ, and lime juice fails to hold back the demons tonight—the seven-year anniversary of the worst mistake of my life.

Trying to blink away the past, I pop another jalapeno-stuffed olive in my mouth and chew it slowly while gazing around this watering hole. There are mostly casually dressed women of mixed ages wearing nametags from some convention sporting the acronym AFA.

Raul, a wiry Asian bartender with dyed purple hair, eyes the level of my drink while gliding by holding drafts, which he places on a tray at the other end of the bar. An aging blonde waitress wearing lots of thin turquoise and silver bracelets on both wrists picks up the load and starts to make her way through the packed house. The woman sports the hard looks of someone who's spent the better part of the past twenty years working tables. I have an appreciation for her kind, as I paid my way through school by mixing drinks at various clubs around The University of Texas in Austin.

I continue to stare at the AFA sign once more and wonder, given that I'm a minority here, if it stands for the American Feminist Association. In which case, given my distant past, I'd probably be better off having drinks sequestered in my room.

But soon, I muse that AFA stands for the Alzheimer's Foundation of America, and I'm unwittingly their latest case study. Although I am of sound mind, at least the last time I checked, I doubt even the worst form of dementia would shield me from my tragic wrongdoing.

On the lighter side, maybe all these women are members of the American Fertility Association and are searching for virile male donors.

I sigh and sip my drink, the only vice I have left after quitting smoking last fall—aside from coffee, which I began to drink by the gallon the moment I parted ways with the Marlboro Man.

To my right, the blonde waitress, scantily dressed in black, maneuvers carefully through this sea of intriguing female conventioneers while balancing the tray with apparent difficulty. For a moment I wonder if she is going to lose her load, but she quickly recovers.

I look towards the front desk and watch several flight attendants and a couple of pilots checking in.

Perhaps AFA stands for Association of Flight Attendants, but I quickly scratch that one, too, when an obese woman in a bright-red dress steps back and accidentally bumps into the petite waitress. Losing control of her tray, she deposits four cold ones down the black leather jacket of a conventioneer sitting at a table a couple dozen feet from me.

Mugs shatter on the floor. The waitress cups her face, her shiny bracelets rattling as she utters a scream in concert with the a cappella sung by her victim while the audience utters a long and low, "Ooooh."

"Damn temp," Asian Raul hisses under his breath while frowning, crossing his arms, and adding, "We get our regular back tomorrow."

Temp waitress or not, this is the most excitement I've seen all week, and it brings back memories from simpler days in school.

Martini in hand, I loosen my tie, rub a hand over the nicotine patch on my right shoulder in a worthless effort to get it to pump more chemicals, and shift on the barstool to watch the show under a sea of dimmed track lights.

Her face red with embarrassment, her long hair swinging as much as the loose skin under her arms, the waitress apologizes profusely and offers them free drinks while producing a wad of black napkins. The soaked victim displays far more control than I would have, calmly removing her jacket under the amused gaze of her drinking companions: a lady with a silver ponytail and ridiculously large earrings, and two women who remind me of aging hippies dressed in tie dyed dresses. A heavily tattooed man with a bucket and a mop appears from somewhere and starts to make his way towards the spilled mess. He wears the indifferent mask of someone who has done this countless times. But having been there myself, I can testify that there are far worse forms of spattered fluids to mop up in a bar than cold draft beer.

And just as quickly as it began, the event dissipates, and I slowly turn back to face the bar. Raul has a ball game playing on the monitor, and I stare at it while welcoming the alcohol haze numbing my senses, slowly drawing me to my special place.

I was happy once, and that's despite growing up with a father who'd beaten my mother to death after a decade of abuse—and who'd also sent me to the hospital a dozen times with broken bones and cuts while trying to protect her. I had managed to find a decent girl, father a great little boy, launch a promising consulting career, and build close friendships. In short, I had broken the cycle of abuse. I had been able to—

"What's your sign?"

I frown. A woman to my immediate left is talking to me. I'm not the type to strike up a conversation with strangers at social gatherings, especially at hotel bars. I just want to down a few "Mexicans" in peace, let the alcohol mix with the nicotine, head up to my room, and get a good night's sleep. Tomorrow I have to catch an early-morning flight back to Austin, where the weather app on my phone indicated temperatures continued to climb above record highs for early March.

Frowning, certain that seat was empty just a moment ago, I drop my eyebrows while slowly turning towards the owner of the voice, an attractive brunette in her forties holding a cosmopolitan. Her dark crimson fingernails match her lips. I have a feeling she turned heads a couple of decades ago, though her features seem a little off centered, suggesting she was in an accident or perhaps was physically abused. She reminds me of the women at Hill Country Haven, the shelter for battered women I run in Austin. My eyes momentarily drop to my right wrist, which is hugged by a lime-green rubber bracelet bearing our logo. We make them for less than ten cents each and give them out to anyone willing to wear one to help advertise our cause.

I raise my gaze. Neither the well-applied make-up, nor the silk scarf around her neck, nor the shoulder-length hair hiding her forehead and framing her face can conceal the slightly unbalanced features of a face exhibiting a fading tan. Fine wrinkles encircle her round brown eyes and slightly crooked mouth as she sips her drink, leaving an imprint on the edge of the glass.

How long has she been here?

"Pardon me?" I ask, finally making eye contact. There is an attractive delicacy and also the glint of recognition behind her stare.

"Your sign," she says, tilting her nearly empty drink at me.

At my silence, she adds, "Aren't you with the AFA?"

I desperately try to connect the dots between signs and AFA but all my alcohol-challenged mind can conjure is the American Fence Association.

As I'm about to embarrass myself, she adds, "The American Federation of Astrologers," and proceeds to finish her drink before tapping a fingernail against the glass while looking in Raul's direction.

Before I can help it, I lean closer and drop my voice a couple of decibels as I say, "For a moment there I thought it stood for Another Fucking Acronym." I guess the tequila is drawing me out of my introverted shell.

She tilts her head back and lets out a brief laugh, animation glinting in her eyes. "Good one."

I freeze. The laugh, the mannerism, even her intonation start to unveil painful memories. I instinctively force savage control to lock them down tight.

"So, you with them?" I ask, looking for any resemblance but finding not one feature that reminds me of—

"Do I look like a fortune teller to you?"

She looks like a former showgirl who, like me, life has banged up a bit but refuses to break. But there's something about her that reminds me of someone I've been trying desperately to forget. Suddenly, I have the urge to get up and celebrate the anniversary of my demise in the comforting solitude of my hotel room. I remember seeing a mini bar under the flat screen I can empty, never mind the inflated price I'll pay, which will be worth it to avoid this...

"So," she adds at my silence, "you never told me your sign."

Before I can reply, Raul returns with a fresh drink for her, setting the pinkish concoction in a martini glass on the counter while saying, "Cosmo for the lady."

"Cointreau instead of triple sec, right?" she asks.

"Just like the last one," he says, winking and hustling away.

I nod approvingly. That's how I used to make them.

She takes a test sip and nods, leaving another lipstick imprint on the edge of the glass. "Well?" she asks, looking back at me. "Are we sharing signs or not?"

"I thought that stuff went out with the Seventies," I say as my parting line. But the dark images of growing up in the late Seventies suddenly paint a picture of my drunken father beating my mother with my little-league baseball bat. I'm crying, hanging on to her, trying to protect her, trying to—

"Anybody home?" she asks, snapping the fingers of her right hand in front of me.

"Sorry," I mumble, adding, "Aries. I'm an Aries."

Gently stealing my drink and setting it on the bar top next to hers, she takes my hands, examines my palms, looks into the distance for a few moments, and says in an authoritative voice, "Aries. Unexpected encounters or unusual circumstances opening old wounds are likely to arise during this second week of March as Uranus aligns with the Sun. However, don't let worries or doubts get the best of you as situations may seem bigger than they really are."

I was never one to believe that zodiac stuff, but this is just too weird. Am I that easy to read? What must be a hopelessly dumbfound look on my face draws a devilish leer, which, like the rest of her, is a little crooked.

Taking a long breath, I retrieve my hands and gulp down the last inch of my martini, closing my eyes as the tequila scratches my throat and my fingers rub the nicotine patch very hard.

"Easy there, big fellow," she says, her grin broadening. "That was just a loose forecast. If you're really interested in unlocking the meaning of your horoscope I can hook you up with an accredited astrologer who can set up and interpret a mathematically-correct chart for you."

"I thought you said that you weren't part of the—"

"I just asked you if I *looked* like a fortune teller," she replies, giving me a slow feminine wink, complete with fluttering eyelashes and all.

I inhale deeply again under her amused stare and use my empty glass to signal Raul for my fourth—and hopefully last—Mexican of the evening.

He nods and gets to work.

"What's with the shoulder?" she asks.

I stop rubbing it and frown. "Nicotine patch."

"How long?"

"Six months."

"And how's that working out for you?"

"Good days and bad days."

She reaches in her purse a flashes a pack of Virginia Slims. "Tried three times. No good."

"I'm David Wallace," I say, extending an open hand, which she shakes firmly. "And you are?"

"I'm fascinated you haven't tried to pick me up yet. You're not gay, are you?"

"Not the last time I checked," I say as I watch Raul pour various shots into a stainless-steel shaker filled with ice.

"I'm not straight," says Raul, smiling and winking as he starts to shake my drink.

The mystery woman and I look at him somewhat incredulously, not certain how to react.

"Say," Raul adds, "you heard what happened when the gay guy tried to quit smoking and put a nicotine patch on his penis?"

She giggles and briefly looks away. I narrow my stare at this character.

Amid our silence, he says, "He went down to two butts a day."

We laugh in unison.

"Here you go, big boy," Raul says, grinning while delivering yet another beautiful drink topped by a perfect rim of salt and accompanied by another tiny silver tray with jalapeno-stuffed olives. The man's jokes might be lame but his bartending is top notch.

"*Gracias*, Raul," I say as he moves briskly to look after another thirsty customer.

"So," she says, "are you married?"

I close my eyes, though not at the realization that this woman is trying to pick me up.

I was married once.

I had a wonderful little boy.

I had a great career and good friends.

And I managed to screw it all up seven years ago tonight, so happy fucking anniversary to me.

And this conversation isn't funny anymore.

"Always gay or married," she says more to herself than me, disappointment filming her eyes as she finishes her drink, setting it down on the bar, and starting to turn away. "Never fails."

"Widower," I reply, the sadness bubbling through my façade quickly rearranging her quirky but enchanting features into a mask of compassion. Trouble is that what she sees isn't just sadness but also an overwhelming sense of guilt.

"I...I'm truly sorry to hear that, David," she finally replies, her fingernails softly tapping me on the wrist before offering an open hand. "I'm Kate Larson."

We shake again. "No worries, Kate Larson. It was a long time ago. I've learned to move on," I lie as the face of my deceased son, David, flashes in my mind.

Hold me, Daddy. Hold me tight.

I force the memory away as we hold the handshake while staring at each other in uncomfortable silence. For a moment, the clattering of glasses fades away, along with the rumble of conversations, and the rattling shaker as Raul mixes the ingredients of someone else's heavenly poison.

"So," I finally say, releasing her hand, "did you enjoy the convention?"

She nods. "It was good to get away from the heat for a few days."

"Heat from where?"

"Austin."

Now this is surreal. I mean, what are the odds of meeting what appears to be a decent and attractive woman my age in a bar across the country who also lives in Austin, and on the seventh anniversary of my life shifting to the dark side? Perhaps this roomful of astrologers is acting as some sort of cosmic antenna, radiating multiple megawatts of positive energy to pull me out of my self-inflicted state of misery. Could it be that someone high up thinks that seven years of darkness is long enough of a punishment? Maybe my luck is being reversed after burying the shards of my shattered life beneath gallons of booze and many a moonlit night.

Deciding that perhaps she's indeed some form of celestial lifeline, I open up and tell her I also live in Austin.

All of the sudden we're talking about our favorite bars on Sixth Street. We then switch to bicycling on the Veloway, kayaking on Lady Bird Lake, and hiking in the hill country—activities I have come to enjoy after pitching my last pack of cancer sticks.

The conversation inevitably leads to ways to beat the merciless triple-digit Texas summer heat.

"Say," I tell her, deciding not to be outdone by Raul by trying one of my favorite Texas summer jokes from my bartending days. "Speaking of heat, do you know how hot it is in Texas in August?"

She gives me a devilish smile that nearly makes me forget the damned joke. But I recover.

"So hot that you see trees whistling at passing dogs."

She flashes a smile, puts a hand on my forearm while leaning closer and whispering in my ear, "Better than Raul's, but keep your day job."

Her touch, combined with the smell of her perfume and the alcohol on her breath starts to—

"And by the way, what is it you do?" she asks, retrieving her hand while leaning back and taking another sip of her drink.

"My background is in consulting," I reply, "but I run a shelter in Austin for battered women. It's called Hill Country Haven, or HCH for short." I raise my wrist and show her my lime-green rubber bracelet embossed with ***HILL COUNTRY HAVEN – BE NOT AFRAID*** in orange. Mine, however is quite weathered, having worn it since we came up with the inexpensive advertising campaign four years ago. The orange tint has rubbed off from the words ***HILL COUNTRY HAVEN*** and ***NOT***, which I saw as a sign from above of what's coming to me for what I did to my family.

She runs a finger over the embossing and says, "Very noble of you, David. Though you should think about getting a new bracelet. This one's a little creepy."

I'm about to reply when her phone rings.

She produces an iPhone, answers, and listens for about thirty seconds, color draining from her face by the time she hangs up.

Kate looks as if she's just spoken to the devil himself.

"Is everything all right?"

"I…I need to go," she replies, looking about her with obvious concern.

She looks in the direction of the blonde waitress, who is serving drinks at the other end of the bar, and who looks at Kate for an instant before returning to her work.

Toying with her scarf while briefly biting her lower lip, Kate looks back at me and says, "It's been great...talking to you." She reaches in her purse and produces a business card. "If you ever need insight into the future—or the past—call this number. It's the AFA's hotline. Take care."

"Is there anything I can do?" I ask, not knowing what else to say.

She shakes her head and gives me a half smile while placing a twenty-dollar bill on the counter. "So long, David."

And just like that, she rushes off, vanishing as suddenly as she had appeared. I shrug and set the card down.

So much for a cosmic intervention on my dark anniversary.

I exhale, stare at the bar, and focus on the green concoction in my hand, gazing at my uncertain future in its emerald swirl. I think of the pain I have caused, of the people I have hurt, of the lives I have destroyed.

Of the sobering fact that perhaps there is no redemption for people like me.

Deciding I've had more than enough fun and alcohol for one evening, I pay Raul and stand with some difficulty.

As I'm about to pocket the AFA card and head out, I notice a note scribbled on the back.

**THINGS WERE NOT AS THEY
SEEMED 7 YEARS AGO.
CAREFUL WHO YOU TRUST WITH THIS.**

CHAPTER 2

The room falls away.

The conversations vanish along with the clanging behind the counter and the ball game on TV. I just stare at the handwriting, at the surreal message, my heart racing, my ears ringing as my blood pressure rises.

***THINGS WERE NOT AS THEY
SEEMED 7 YEARS AGO.
CAREFUL WHO YOU TRUST WITH THIS.***

What the hell does that mean?

What wasn't as it seemed back then?

I tragically lost my wife, my son, my job, my friends, and even my freedom while I was tried for a crime I didn't commit. And all because of a single mistake, one stupid night where a combination of long-working hours and the stress it put on my marriage led me to a tragic lapse of judgment. The past seven years have been one arduous climb out of that hole.

All of that has been very fucking real to me.

And what does she mean about being careful?

Who was she? How does she know what happened back then? Why did she look familiar? Why did she seek me out on the anniversary of that terrible night? And why did she leave so abruptly?

The questions choke me. I try to control my breathing, fearing the combination of alcohol and high-blood pressure will take me down in the middle of this group of astrologers.

Shoving the card in my wallet among my credit cards, I slowly stand.

"You okay there, big guy?" Raul asks. "Want me to get you a cab?"

"Thanks…I'm a guest here," I mumble, before thanking him for the drinks and heading out, though walking straight is a major undertaking demanding my full concentration.

Questions and anxiety assaulting my mind, I manage to reach the lobby with considerable effort. A pale guy with ash-blond hair wearing what looks like a security uniform speaks to a brunette behind the front desk. The borderline albino shoots me a bored glance before returning to his conversation. I walk past them without attracting further attention and turn towards the long corridor leading to the elevators.

As I focus on my balance, I approach a glass door marked *ICE & SNACKS*.

"Leave me alone!" a woman protests from inside the room.

I stop, peek through the glass door, and spot Kate arguing with a guy in a dark pinstriped business suit who looks like he just stepped out of an Italian Mafia movie. An Asian woman dressed in a ridiculously short miniskirt, knee-high boots, and a near-see-through white blouse chews gum loudly while watching the show. They stand in front of a rumbling icemaker flanked by vending machines.

"I saw you talking to him!" the Mafiosi lookalike says. "What the fuck did you tell him?"

Suddenly, he clasps Kate's hands and twists, forcing her to her knees, her face a mask of pain as she utters a barely audible cry. The Asian grabs Kate's scarf and turns it like a tourniquet, choking her.

"Hey! Let her go!" I shout, pushing the door open, startling them.

I immediately hear voices in the lobby a couple hundred feet behind me.

He releases her and turns to me; dark expressionless eyes on a tanned face regard me with indifference. The Asian also frees her and steps back, crossing her bony arms while glaring back at the intrusion.

Kate staggers to her feet, coughing, mascara running down her face, the contents of her purse spilled by her feet, her hands loosening the scarf, her terrified gaze finding me.

I was always the bullied, never the courageous type, and as I freeze in the doorway, in part to keep steady but also because I somehow feel safer with the door open, a voice urges me to run back to the lobby and alert the security guard.

The thug shifts his head slightly from side to side while gliding towards me, like a ghost, very light on his feet, his hair perfectly combed back, his suit impeccably pressed, and to complete the image, he even wears a chunky gold pinky ring.

He pauses and grins.

"Stop or I'm calling security!" I shout as he gets close. He cocks his head at my lame shout.

"I mean it!" I add. "Leave her alone!"

The man, sporting a prizefighter's face and a neck thicker than my thighs gets inches from me and simply crosses his arms.

Kate tries to come forward but the Asian slaps her and pushes her into a corner. Kate lands on her side next to the pack of Virginia Slims and other items from her purse.

"Hey!" I shout. "Don't you—"

"Now, Sport," he says with an eerie calm, his slightly bloated face and bulbous nose inches from mine. I can smell tobacco in his breath. "Why would you want to get in the middle of a personal chitchat between these lovely ladies and me? We're just cuddling, aren't we, girls?"

His gaze is steady, laser-like, burning into me, warning me, like the lightning preceding a thunderstorm.

"So," he adds, never looking away, "why don't you crawl back to whatever shithole you came from and let me finish my business here, yeah?"

I look over at Kate massaging her wrist and neck, using the scarf to wipe her tears. I see her pleading stare from behind the Asian blocking her way. She is obviously scared out of her mind, and the sight reels me back to the trailer home in Austin, back to my parents' bedroom as my father whips my mother raw. I feel the burning sting of the leather as it strikes my back again and again when I try to shield her, try to protect her—trying to prevent something that I was too young to prevent.

The same obsession to safeguard battered women that drove me to start the shelter in Austin suddenly comes alive as I retort with a steady voice that even surprises me, "It takes a real man to hit a woman...*Sport.*"

His expression tightens, except for his dark eyes, which remain lifeless, like those of a shark. "Listen," he says. "You have no earthly idea of the forces you're teetering with. I'm asking you one final time: Walk the fuck away."

But I can't. Kate has released the demons, and not just those from my childhood. The message on her business card has unearthed the sin from seven years ago that has left me an empty shell, with nothing to lose, with nothing to live for.

I snap, poking a finger at his chest. "And I'm telling *you* to haul your greasy ass out of this hotel and leave her alone."

I never saw him move, and in fact I don't believe he ever did. Except for his head, which he thrusts directly into my nose.

I'm not new to pain. Ten years of abuse before the sheriff hauled my father away taught me how to endure it. My father had beaten me with his fucking belt, had punched me with his bare knuckles, and had broken my ribs and my wrist with my own baseball bat while I was trying to protect my mother. But the head-butt, the first in my life, felt as if a freight train collided against me at full speed with the force of a thousand bat strikes. Wham. Hard. Unforgiving.

My knees give just as colors explode in my brain.

I hear Kate scream, hear shouts from the lobby, hear the Mafioso curse, bellowing a warning that echoes deep in my skull, resonating with the shouts of my father and the cries of my mother.

I collapse on the carpeted floor as a female shriek cuts through the darkness engulfing me.

Kate! NO!

But I'm unable to move, unable to scream or protest as the overwhelming pain spreads through my nervous system like sheet lightning, shutting me down hard, propelling me down a tunnel as gloomy as my life has been since that dreadful night long ago.

CHAPTER 3

It starts as a small light, flickering, like a distant star in the darkest night. A murmur accompanies it, reminding me of dinner conversation at a restaurant beyond a glass window. People are talking but I can't hear what they're saying.

The star grows in my personal cosmos, becoming a blazing sun, its blinding glow stinging, forcing me to close my eyes as the surrounding mumbling slowly become words, phrases, distinct voices.

"He's coming around," a man says.

"Let's give him some room, people," says a woman.

Slowly, with effort, I open my eyes just a dash and wait as my vision adjusts, as figures resolve in front of me.

It takes me another moment to realize I'm lying down on the carpeted floor of the hallway next to the glass doors leading to the vending machines. Three people are kneeling around me. Two male paramedics in their blue uniforms flank a woman in her forties dressed in jeans, a black T-shirt under a black jacket. Upon closer inspection I spot a silver badge shaped like a seven-point star hanging from a chain around her neck.

DETECTIVE
S.F. POLICE

"Mr. Wallace," she says very slowly in a deep voice that conveys the strength already broadcast by her wide shoulders. However, her large round eyes offer comfort. The ends of her lips curve down a notch, giving her what looks like a permanent scowl. Shoulder-length dark hair frames a stoic triangular face to go with the frown. Her nose is small and pointy, as is her chin, where she presses a dark fingernail while asking, "Can you hear me?"

I nod and manage a, "Yes."

"I'm Homicide Detective Marlene Quinn from the Personal Crimes Division of the San Francisco Police Department. Do you remember what happened?"

It takes me a moment, but staring at the glass doors and the humming ice machine bring it all back.

Nodding again, I close my eyes and breathe in deeply before reopening them, feeling life seeping back into my body. Unfortunately, the feeling of being alive includes a wave of pain in between my eyes.

"I was...attacked," I reply.

She jots something down on a small pad and then asks, "Do you know who attacked you?"

"No," I reply, raising my right hand and pressing the tips of my thumb and index finger against my eyelids.

"You have a bad concussion, sir," explains the attending paramedic to my immediate right, a fellow in his late forties or maybe early fifties with thinning dark hair. "This will help take the edge off," he adds, producing a syringe.

I cringe as he stabs me, but whatever he pumps into me warms up my shoulder while literally draining the pain away from my forehead.

"Where can I get more of that?" I ask.

He smiles.

"Mr. Wallace," she says as I quickly become alert. "Could you tell me what were you doing here and what took place?"

"Please call me David," I reply, taking a moment to enjoy my temporary painless state before spending a few minutes explaining my consulting trip to San Francisco, how I met Kate Larson at the bar, and how she was being mugged by the pimp-and-hooker dynamic duo.

"So, you've never seen the assailants before tonight, David?" she asks.

"Nope, but they seemed to know Kate. And when I tried to stop them, the guy head-butted me."

She writes down my statement before asking, "Were you attacked before or after the woman was murdered?"

I blink as the paramedics prop me up enough to see down the hallway, where I spot bloodstains on the walls twenty-some feet from where I fell. I tense when I also notice what looks like a body bag. A heavyset guy with white hair is kneeling by it, jotting something on a large clipboard.

"I...everyone was alive...though I did hear a scream as I passed out," I reply as my gut fills with molten lead at the thought of the bastards killing Kate and my failure to protect her.

I take a deep breath of regret.

Marlene nods somberly and makes another entry in her pad.

I point at the body bag. "Is that...did Kate Larson get..."

"We'll get to that," she replies, but without a hint of rudeness. "I have a few clarifying questions first."

"Anything I can, uh…do to help," I reply, though my mind suddenly gets tired again.

"Can you keep him conscious for just a few minutes?" she asks one of the paramedics.

"Not sure. We got him stable for now," he replies, "but we need to get him to a hospital pronto for X-rays and a CT. Pupils are dilated. Bad concussion. Could black out any moment."

Detective Quinn gives him a sideways glance and asks me, "David, do you remember anyone else aside from Kate Larson and her two assailants?"

I slowly shake my head. "There was the security guy by the front desk…but I was attacked before he got here."

She looks up and waves over a short, wiry, and balding man with a white mustache wearing a khaki uniform with the words **HOTEL SECURITY** embroidered over his left shirt pocket.

"David, this is Gabriel Gonzales, the shift security guard who found you. Is this who you saw?"

I stare into his aging eyes and shake my head again. "The guy I remember was taller, younger, and with very pale skin, almost like an albino, with ash-blond hair."

She offers no explanation while dismissing the guard before inscribing my answer in her pad.

"What does that mean?" I ask at her silence, my headache slowly returning. "If the guy I saw wasn't hotel security, then who was he?"

"That's what we're trying to figure out. You said your business is consulting but you run a shelter for abused women in Austin?"

"Right. I provide efficiency consulting to our suppliers and in exchange they donate stuff to our shelter. Works pretty well."

She slowly nods.

"Look," I say, "you could save yourself a lot of guess-work by just looking at the hotel security video." I point at the cameras hanging from the ceiling at both ends of the corridor.

"We're working on that. Thank you for the suggestion," she replies with forced politeness. "Anything you can tell us will only add to the information we will gather from the videos. Okay?"

I give her an embarrassed nod. "My apologies, Detective. I didn't mean to tell you how to do your—"

"Not a problem. You're hurt, confused, and under the influence of pain killers," she replies. "And please, call me Marley."

I nod.

She adds. "Could you point to the exact spot you stood when you were attacked by this…pimp?"

"Sure," I say. "It was right by the glass doors. I was holding one of them open."

"And do you remember if you staggered around before collapsing?"

Strange question. "I think I went down pretty hard."

"So you didn't run away, or stagger around before collapsing?"

"Nope."

"Are you sure, David?"

"As sure as I can be. It was pretty much lights out and down to the floor. Why is that relevant?"

"Could you confirm that the victim is the woman you met at the bar?" she asks, ignoring my question.

Given my experience dealing with cops seven years ago and recalling how they seldom provide answers during questioning, I just give her a resigned nod. But I can't suppress the squirt of acid spraying in my stomach at the thought of those bastards killing Kate and at my utter inability to protect her, just as I couldn't save my—

"Here," she says. "Let us help you up."

Marley and the paramedics help me to the side of the body bag halfway between the glass doors and the elevators.

My insides churn as I stare at the blood splashes on the pastel walls near the body. "I think I'm going to be sick," I mumble.

"Breathe deeply," says the older paramedic.

Marley adds, "Think happy thoughts."

Right.

As I fill my lungs, I notice a clear plastic evidence bag next to the body housing a bloody knife, presumably the murder weapon.

Marley taps the man I presume is the ME still kneeling by the side of the body. He looks up, regards me behind a pair of rimless glasses, sets the pen and pad down, and proceeds to unzip the bag.

In anticipation of a spasm, I tighten my jaw to avoid vomiting all over their evidence while I stare down at the victim's face. Her dead eyes are still open and fixated on the ceiling, a gash across her throat so massive it looks like she was nearly beheaded.

"Is this her? Is this the woman you met at the bar?"

My knees start to quiver and the paramedics catch me, holding me up enough for me to glare back at Marley and mumble, "The Asian woman…this is the Asian woman with…the man, the pimp who…attack…"

I can't complete the sentence as everything around me turns shades of light gray, then charcoal, and finally black, mercifully pulling me away from the scene.

CHAPTER 4

There is no amount of Vicodin sufficient enough to suppress the jagged pain stabbing my forehead, pulsating behind my eyeballs.

I gaze about the antiseptic interior of a colorless room in the ER of St. Francis Memorial while wearing a light-green hospital gown.

Although on the surface the bruise isn't larger than a quarter at the ridge of my nose, the bastard knew precisely how to hit me. According to the chief resident, who just left holding images of my noodle, the head butt had come dangerously close to ramming my nose into the frontal lobe. This is the area responsible for my basic motor skills, problem solving, memory, language, judgment, sexual behavior, and apparently bladder control because while I was out I pissed my pants.

And that could explain why my clothes are gone, and I'm left wearing this humiliating garment.

The CAT scan also revealed that while the nasal bones had not pierced the brain, they had bruised the surface of the frontal lobe, which explains the severe headache as well as the tingling in my limbs and the slight loss of sensation in my fingertips.

The good news is that the symptoms are temporary, that my nose isn't broken, and that I will be released in time to make my 6:00am flight.

It also means that as tired and groggy as I feel, SFPD Detective Quinn can resume her questioning.

She steps into my room after having a brief word with the chief resident.

Resembling more closely a competitive swimmer than a detective, she grabs a chair and pulls it near my bedside before straddling it, resting slim forearms on its back.

The chief resident told me that Marley got me checked out of the hotel, packed my bags, and is getting them delivered here within the hour.

It's one in the morning, almost two hours since I passed out at the hotel, so I'm hoping she's got news for me.

"How are you feeling?" Her bloodshot eyes gleam genuine concern as she puckers her lips, magnifying her natural grimace.

"Been better," I say.

But I've also been far, far worse.

She nods thoughtfully.

"Thanks for getting my stuff from the hotel, and also for checking me out."

"Of course."

"What's the word on the dead woman?" I ask.

"She had no ID on her. Her body is being processed now. We'll know who she is soon enough."

I sigh.

"But we now know who *you* are," she adds. "I read your case from seven years ago. I'm really sorry about your family."

I close my eyes as David's little face fills my mind. *Hold me, Daddy. Hold me tight.*

"Are you all right?"

"Just peachy," I mumble, reopening my eyes as my son fades away, realizing SFPD was bound to find out sooner or later in this age of super-connectivity. I look away while massaging my aching forehead with my fingertips. "So now what? Am I a suspect?"

She drops her brows at me. "Relax. Interesting case but all charges were dropped. I'm here to discuss *this* murder, and for the record, you're not a suspect."

"Glad to hear that," I say, recalling how the Austin Police Department tried to crucify me last time someone died around me. "But exactly how did you arrive at the conclusion that I'm not a suspect?"

Marley makes an effort to grin. "For starters, only an innocent person would ask a question like that. But just off the top of my head, you were too far from the victim, your prints were not on the murder weapon, and you had no trace of blood on you when security found you within a minute of the murder taking place. Whoever killed her would have been sprayed, just like the walls. And trust me, we really scrubbed your clothes."

"I guess that solves *that* mystery."

"What mystery?"

"Why I'm wearing this very liberating gown."

This time I get a full smile before she says, "Sorry. Your clothes are evidence now."

"Keep them. But I'd like to have my personal effects," I say, remembering Kate's note stuffed in my wallet.

Marley produces a manila envelope and empties it on the glass table next to my bed. "Everything we found on you. Please make sure there's nothing missing."

With effort I take a peek and spot my cash in a silver money clip, as well as my wallet, watch, phone, and some loose change. I open my wallet and quickly browse through it, verifying everything is in its rightful place.

"Looks fine," I finally say.

"I did take one of your business cards in case we need to reach you."

"Sure," I reply, realizing she didn't see Kate's note in my wallet.

As I'm about to tell her, Kate's scribbled warning flashes in my mind.

CAREFUL WHO YOU TRUST WITH THIS.

Instead, I ask, "Speaking of evidence, did you get what you need from the security video?"

"That would have been too easy. Cameras were not on."

"Broken?"

Marley slowly shakes her head. "Someone turned them off."

"Well, that's certainly convenient," I mutter.

"It sure is, but the question is convenient for whom?" she replies.

I squint my eyes. The pain in my head doesn't allow me to follow her logic. I suddenly find myself in desperate need of a cigarette. Fuck the patches and fuck the doctors.

"What do you mean?" I ask.

"According to your statement, the Asian woman was working with the guy who attacked Kate and who also knocked you out, right?"

"That's right."

"So," she continues, "my current working theory is that they unplugged the surveillance to do whatever they intended to do. But they didn't count on you intervening and on someone on Kate's side coming to her rescue and killing the Asian while your assailant got away."

"So you don't think Kate had anything to do with the murder?"

She gives me a cop shrug. "Based on your statement, she seemed quite helpless. Besides, the severity of the wound, its angle, and the fact that it was a single clean strike suggests someone quite strong, tall, and proficient with knives."

I nod. "She did look helpless, which is why I got involved in the first place."

"Although I can't prove it yet, I'm quite certain that someone joined Kate after you were knocked out," she says with conviction, before dropping her voice and adding, "Someone quite efficient, strong, and swift enough to fend off the pimp, kill the Asian, and get away before hotel security arrived less than a minute later. See where I'm going with this?"

Once more I just stare at her, too tired to follow.

She rewards my slow brain with a scowl and says, "It was the work of a professional, David."

I narrow my gaze. "Like an assassin?"

"Something like that."

A rush of adrenaline scours me at the thought of being tangled in something that involves professional killers.

"So," I ask after my aching neurons finally fire and I start to connect some dots, "do you think maybe this professional was the albino guy I spotted in the lobby?"

She tilts her head. "I'd love to question him. At the moment we're not sure who he was, only that he wasn't part of the hotel staff."

"But…I clearly remember him wearing some sort of uniform and talking to someone by the front desk."

"We know," she replies with a tilt of the head. "He was just asking directions—or at least pretending to do so. He didn't work there, but according to the front desk clerk he rushed in your direction when you screamed, and then he vanished—along with Kate and your assailant—before hotel security arrived. The clerk at the front desk remembers him well, and she'll work with one of our artists in the morning to produce a sketch. I'll email it to you when we get it. Meanwhile, if you're up to it, I'd like you to work with an artist to get us a sketch of the guy who attacked you. He's waiting outside."

"Glad to. Any word on Kate Larson?"

"Nope. And I checked with the AFA. No one there has heard of her."

I think of Kate's business card, and again I'm inclined to show it to her, and again, the warning pulls me back. I need time to think through the ramifications of her message.

Marley stands up and stretches. "Your bags should be here within the hour and—"

Her phone rings. She pulls it out of her back pocket, frowning while glancing at the caller ID before saying, "Marley."

She listens for thirty seconds as her face grows tense. "What the fuck?…How long ago?…Damn! I'm on my way!"

"What's going on?" I ask as she puts the phone away.

She stares at me for a moment, her face signaling she is still processing whatever it was she was just told.

"The Asian woman," she finally says as she heads for the door while running a hand through her hair. "Her body's missing."

CHAPTER 5

The flight home is uneventful, though the lack of sleep, my bruised brain, and the Vicodin haze are making the events of the past twelve hours seem like a strange and distant dream.

But as I store my tray table while gazing at the rolling hill country outside my window on final approach into Austin-Bergstrom International Airport, the sobering note scribbled on the business card reels me back.

THINGS WERE NOT AS THEY
SEEMED 7 YEARS AGO.
CAREFUL WHO YOU TRUST WITH THIS.

I stare at the Austin skyline under a mid-morning sun while thinking of my son and wondering what he would have looked like this year at age twelve.

The ever-present knot in my stomach starts to turn, to tighten, and I force my mind to think of Kate Larson.

According to Marley, who called me prior to boarding to make sure I made my flight, the body of the Asian woman went missing somewhere during transport from the hotel to the morgue. And no one had a clue, from the paramedics who loaded her body into the rear of their emergency vehicle to the team waiting at the other end to process it. And just like the disabled surveillance cameras and the killer's vanishing act, this continues to smell like the work of a professional.

And to add to the mystery, although Marley returned my personal effects, my lime-green HCH rubber bracelet was missing.

Why would anyone want to take that?

I close my eyes and try to wish the pain away, but it remains in place, like a splinter in my mind, taxing me as hard as Kate's warning.

The suburbs west of the city replace the hill country just before the plane flies over downtown Austin. My eyes find the tall Frost Bank building, where I used to work as a very successful senior consultant with the high-profile firm of Mercer, Martinez, and Salazar.

Those were the glory days.

Before I screwed it all up by sleeping with the wife of our best client.

I softly pat the bridge of my very tender nose while trying to wish away the past as the pilot executes a textbook approach, touching down a few minutes later.

Glad to finally be home, I deplane and painfully start to make my way toward baggage claim in seemingly slow motion—as measured by everyone else passing me by as if I were standing still.

I reach the main concourse, where airport planners smartly positioned a food court opposite the gates to lure hungry and thirsty travelers.

The smell of smoked brisket and sausage from the barbecue stand tickles my nostrils as a river of humanity flows around me hauling every conceivable model of carry-on luggage.

But not me. I'm a check-in kind of guy, especially on direct flights, and even more so when operating on reserve power.

I glance at my watch, and as I realize we've arrived almost thirty minutes early, I remember the pilot announcing a tail wind. This, of course, means that even at my present speed-racer stride I should grab my bag from the carrousel downstairs and make it to passenger pickup well before my ride gets here.

A hint of freshly-brewed espresso lingers with the aroma of barbecue hovering in this part of the terminal, and my eyes find the caffeine source an instant later.

My headache is getting worse, and I can't tell if it's because the pain killer is starting to wear off or because I have not had any coffee since yesterday afternoon.

Realizing I have a long day ahead at the shelter, I decide to cover both bases and make a beeline for the kiosk to order their largest latte to down my next dose of Vicodin.

The lady behind the counter starts to work the levers of the stainless-steel contraption while I rub a hand over my newly-applied nicotine patch and glance back towards the gate at the other deplaning passengers from my flight. As the PA system announces a flight boarding for Amarillo followed by another flight to Dallas, I momentarily marvel at the number of souls one of those jetliners can—

The hissing espresso machine fades into the background along with the voice on the PA system the moment I spot the swinging long blonde hair of a passenger walking away from my gate. She is looking away from me so I can't see her face, but her petite size, the loose skin on the back of her arms, and the dozens of turquoise and silver bracelets hugging her wrists remind me of—

"Here you go, sir," the barista says in a thick Hispanic accent, setting the steaming latte on the counter while pointing at the lids to the right of the kiosk. "That'll be four ninety-five."

I turn to her for just an instant, drop a five-dollar bill, snag the coffee, and take off after the mind-rattling apparition.

But she's already merged with the flow of people, appearing and disappearing in the swells and valleys of business suits, jeans, shirts, dresses, shorts, and lots and lots of carry-ons.

Ignoring the headache, I step up the pace, convinced it's her, remembering how Kate had glanced in her direction the moment she hung up the phone at the bar last—

Someone bumps into me from behind, propelling me forward, making me lose control of my lidless cup, spilling a good third into a passing traveler, a large man who raises his garment bag as a shield, fending off the wave of steaming coffee.

"Damn it!" he hisses, staring at the side of his dripping carry-on.

The person who I suspect bumped into me rushes by without uttering a word, blending with the crowd, vanishing from sight with amazing ease, like a ghost, though not before I get a glimpse of his very pale neck, ash-blond hair, and—

"Are you fucking blind?"

I'm face to face with a very angered and very large man holding a very soaked garment bag. He makes a fist with his right hand.

"I'm so sorry," is all I can utter as I stand there holding the remaining two thirds of my drink while automatically lifting my free hand to shield my face. "Someone bumped into me and—"

"Save it, asshole!" he shouts while shaking his head and checking his watch as he rushes past me. "I'm fucking late for my fucking flight!"

He snags a clump of napkins from the food court along the way and wipes off his garment bag as he disappears in the crowd while talking to himself under the disconcerting stare of those around him.

I turn back towards the last place I spotted her, but there is no sign of her or the guy who bumped into me, who for a moment reminded me of the missing albino from the hotel.

"Damn it," I hiss.

Exhaling, the past sixty seconds feeling eerily as surreal as last night, I step aside into a quiet gate area to gather my thoughts. I also take a moment to sip the remainder of my latte and down a Vicodin.

Am I just imagining things? After all, what are the odds that the blonde waitress would be on the same flight with me and was being followed by the mystery albino.

Get a grip, David.

I catch my reflection on a nearby mirrored column and realize I look like shit with my bruised and swollen nose, messy brown hair, and very pasty skin. My green eyes are terribly bloodshot as I narrow them at my refection and realize I need comfort food and lots of sleep to get some color back.

Suddenly longing for a familiar face, hoping the shelter sent my lovely assistant to pick me up, I start towards baggage claim while sipping what's left of my latte.

And I do spot a familiar face by the escalator leading to baggage claim, but unfortunately it's the face of the last person I expected to see today or any other day.

It takes me a moment, but clarity quickly returns with sobering force as I gaze into the dark stare of the leading detective in the murder case of Heather Wilson. She was the one-night stand that turned me into a murder suspect and triggered the destruction of everything I held dear.

The years have not been kind to Austin Police Department Detective Beckett Mar. He's aged significantly since the last time I saw him outside the courthouse following my acquittal. His short and stocky frame seems wider than I remember and continues to be crowned by a massive bald head that reminds me of a worn basketball, adorned with a bulbous nose laced with veins—an alcoholic's nose. Deep wrinkles crease his forehead while staring at me with beady eyes beneath thick brows.

"Long time, Detective. Waiting for someone?" I ask, barely able to suppress a frown as a chill crawls up my spine. The last time this man showed up unannounced was to arrest me for the murder of Heather and her husband, Bernard Wilson, founder of Premier Imports, my old consulting firm's most lucrative client.

He stretches an index finger at me. "Got word from a Detective Quinn that you might be up to your old tricks again."

I frown. The man is still impossible. "I guess some things never change," I mumbled to myself.

"Indeed," he replies. "Once a murderer always a murderer."

To this day Beckett still believes I killed Heather and Bernard, even after the DA withdrew the case when new evidence showed up at my trial.

"Is there a question in there?" I ask, the headache, my throbbing nose, my desire for a smoke, the apparitions, and the yet-to-kick-in caffeine conspiring to kindle my contempt for this man. "Or are you simply bored and figured you'd just come out and harass a citizen who's in great standing with this community...at least according to your boss' boss." I remind him how the mayor of Austin has already given me two awards for the humanitarian work we do at the shelter.

"How did you get that bruise?"

"Read the SFPD report. They actually have real cops over there making decisions based on real evidence."

"Is that how you want to do this?"

"Do what exactly, Detective? Are you going to arrest me for trying to prevent some lowlife from harming a woman?"

"When it comes to harming women you don't have the best record yourself. Or have you forgotten how your inability to keep your dick in your pants led to a crime of passion that also resulted in the deaths of your wife and son?"

Hold me, Daddy. Hold me tight.

And the demons are about to get unleashed right here right now in front of everyone. I clench my jaw hard and swallow them back down to the deepest recess of my gut before slowly breathing out through clenched teeth while the ends of the bastard's thick lips curve up a notch.

I hiss, "This conversation is over."

"This little chitchat is over when I say it's over."

"Then arrest me."

"I would, had you been found unconscious next to a nearly-beheaded woman in this town." He produces an image of the dead Asian, which I presume Marley had sent him. "But San Francisco is out of my jurisdiction."

"Lucky me. Can I go now?"

Leaning closer to me, he whispers, "People have a way of getting killed around you, and the murderers are never found. What does that smell like?"

"Like third-rate homicide detective work?"

He makes a fist and stretches his index and pinky fingers at me. "You go right ahead and fuck with the bull, David. Just don't whine when you get the horns."

I just stare back.

At my silence he adds, "You'll pay for what you did to Heather and Bernard Wilson, just like I'm going to do everything I can to help Detective Quinn nail your testicles to your forehead for this murder."

Deciding that it's best to keep it professional for as long as I can, I reply, "The evidence that led to my acquittal seven years ago was as clear as the evidence that proves I didn't kill the woman last night."

"O.J. Simpson was also found innocent, but in the end he got the horns…right up his ass, and so will you."

"I liked Heather," I reply even though at this point I can almost hear my attorney, Ryan Horowitz, screaming at me to just walk away. Beckett hasn't charged me with anything, meaning he's just fishing and I'm knowingly nibbling. "Why would I kill her?"

"See, that's just it. You had what everyone else didn't."

"And what's that?"

"Motive. Bernard found you boning his wife and you killed him, and then to cover your tracks you also killed her."

I was wrong in pursuing this. The man just doesn't know how to quit, even in the face of irrefutable evidence.

And while I might understand his obsession with the Wilsons' murder case because the killer was never caught and the whole episode hurt his career, I've had enough.

"If you do have any real questions, I suggest you direct them to my attorney. I'm sure you still remember Ryan. He was the guy who showed the DA just how fucked up your evidence was. Good day, Detective."

I walk past him and step onto the escalator down to baggage claim.

"I'll be in touch!" he shouts, looking down while pointing the pinky and index fingers of his right hand at me.

Bastard knows precisely which buttons to push. But so do I. And besides, I did nothing wrong last night. While I did sleep with Heather, and that led to the tragic death of my family, I did not kill her or her husband, and I've kept my nose clean since.

I toil around the crowded baggage claim searching for my carrousel while I get my breathing, my heartbeat, and my mind back in order.

I spot my flight number above Carrousel 3, where I'm met by my assistant, Margaret Black, one of the permanent resident-workers at Hill Country Haven. I co-founded the women's shelter about six and a half years ago—ironically using the proceeds I received from Evelyn's and little David's life insurance policies.

Margaret is a thirty-year-old who, like most women at the shelter, grew up in an abusive environment. In her case, she went from an abusive father to abusive boyfriends, reaching HCH three summers ago after having had enough.

Wearing a pair of black jeans and a lime-green crop top that exposes a small skull tattoo just above her bellybutton, she greets me with a cheery grin as I approach.

Her long hair is dyed as ebony as her lipstick, contrasting sharply with her very pale complexion. The words BE NOT AFRAID are stenciled across the front of her crop top above the Hill Country Haven logo in burnt orange. A large metallic cross hangs at the end of a thick chain around her neck.

"Hey, Marge," I say, glad to see a friendly face, and one which is also easy on the eyes.

Her grin quickly fades as she stares at my throbbing bruise. "What the hell happened to you?" she asks, the dark eye shadow shifting as she narrows her hazel eyes with obvious concern. Her eyeliner is as black as the mascara on her long lashes.

"Rough night," I reply, finding it difficult to concentrate from the throbbing pain. Rubbing a finger against my right temple, I add, "You should see the other guy."

"C'mon, David. What happened?"

"Bumped into a door."

"That's not even remotely funny," she replies, frowning while crossing her arms. Margaret is as tall as my six feet with long and slender legs. She is as stubborn as she is attractive, though in the heavily gothic style she adopted shortly after joining us as her way of breaking ties with her past life through a new look. Our resident therapist believes this is how many abused women mourn their lost years. But one day she should emerge from it just as most people emerge from periods of bereavement after losing a loved one.

She decides to block my way until I provide her with a reasonable answer.

"Okay, okay. I fell."

"David!"

"All right, all right," I say, touching her lightly on the shoulder. "I'll tell you everything in the car. Could you help me get my luggage? I've got a splitting headache."

She sighs, spins around, and marches towards the conveyor belt.

Ten minutes later we're riding in one of our aging lime-green Ford Aerostar minivans sporting bright-orange **HILL COUNTRY HAVEN — SHELTER FOR WOMEN** logos across the sides and rear. Above each logo we proudly display our message to those abused: **BE NOT AFRAID**.

"Well?" Margaret asks after clearing the airport parking toll booth and merging onto Highway 71 West towards IH-35 under a late morning partly-cloudy sky.

Momentarily steering with her right knee, she pulls out a pack of Camels and lights up.

I frown while looking at her inhaling deeply, and I quickly breath in as she exhales, getting a little taste of heaven.

She wears a pair of mirror-tint sunglasses, right hand resting on the large steering wheel, cigarette wedged between her index and middle finger, left elbow hanging out the open window. A black-leather thick bracelet with steel spikes adorns her left wrist. The opposite wrist is hugged by one of our bracelets.

She fidgets unconsciously with a silver band on her left ring finger in the shape of a skull with rubies for eyes to match the skull over her pierced belly button.

Margaret is very slim but muscular. In addition to assisting the nurses, she attends self-defense classes and should be getting her black belt later this year. She told me once that no man would ever hit her again.

Her case isn't an isolated one. Many women who finally take the leap and come to us become obsessed with self-defense.

Pain is an amazing motivator, and my throbbing headache makes me wonder if I should take a class.

I tell her about the incident last night but skip Kate's note and the airport episodes. I need to think that through before deciding on my next move. Maybe I'll have a chat with Ryan, who, in addition to being my attorney, is my Hill Country Haven co-founder and life-long friend.

Ryan defended me seven years ago when Beckett Mar threw the book at me, and he also handled the legalities of starting HCH while shouldering part of the start-up cost. He has been instrumental in issuing thousands of restraining orders and has helped as many women divorce their abusive husbands or cut ties with abusive boyfriends.

"Oh my God," Margaret exclaims while taking a drag and exhaling through her nostrils. "But the dead Asian was attacking this Kate Larson woman, right?"

"That's right."

"So perhaps the Asian woman had it coming?"

"I suppose."

She remains silent for a moment apparently thinking about my story. Then she asks, "But you said that the police cleared you of murder?"

I nod. "Yep. Someone else killed her after I was knocked out."

"And her body just disappeared?"

"Yep."

"That's creepy."

"Yep."

She slowly shakes her head. "And all of this started because you tried to stop a woman from being battered?"

"Yep."

Without warning Margaret pulls into a gas station, removes her glasses, and looks at me with a wet stare.

"What's wrong?" I ask.

"David…you're a wonderful human being who brings hope in more ways than you can imagine," she says, shocking me.

I'm trying to get my tired brain wrapped around the change in external stimuli from Beckett to Margaret. One wants to fry me and the other has me on a pedestal.

But Margaret isn't typically the soft type, especially with members of the male gender. Her father and boyfriends had beaten out of her every ounce of trust and compassion for the opposite sex. She told me once how towards the end of her last abusive relationship, her boyfriend and his friends gang-raped her after shooting her up with heroin. She contracted genital herpes from the episode, but unfortunately she was so out of it, she couldn't remember enough to press charges.

One of our pro-bono therapists told me that in a strange way her lack of memory was probably for the best. It was bad enough waking up naked and bruised in an alley and then learning from the ER doctor that she had the semen of six different men in her vagina.

But either way, she is mentally damaged from the experience and also forever dependent on medication to keep her disease in check. Herpes is forever.

I stare at Margaret in all of her mourning Gothic splendor. It's sad, really, that a young and attractive woman like her has little chance of ever trusting another man again. And what is even sadder is that Margaret isn't close to the worst cases we get at HCH. She's what we would categorize as a survivor, albeit emotionally and physically scarred for life.

"I don't deserve your kindness," she adds at my silence.

I don't like such compliments because flattery is instantly blocked by memories of that dreadful period of marital neglect that began about a year after our Caribbean honeymoon. Soon after David was born, I became a workaholic, surrendering my parental obligations and letting Evelyn shoulder the entire child-rearing burden. And it was this wedge I foolishly drove between us that not only had us on a direct course to a separation, but also led me so far from the straight and narrow as to cheat on her.

I feel color coming to my face as she puts a hand on my cheek. Her eyes flash compassion for another instant before the shields come back up. She abruptly switches to nurse mode, running her thumb and index finger over my bruise, softly pinching the ridge of my nose, which makes me wince in pain.

"Hey!" I scream, jerking away.

"It ain't broken," she says, slipping the glasses back on and driving off.

"Really?" I reply, softly rubbing a finger on the very tender spot she's just squeezed.

"You should consider enrolling in a self-defense class," she says, accelerating up the IH-35 ramp and merging with traffic.

"Never thought about it."

Truth is the same part of me that blocked her compliment welcomes the physical pain. It's hard to explain, but the worse the headache, the farther away the demons retreat. A volunteer therapist told me once that people with chronic pain on one part of their body would oftentimes injure another part just to divert the attention of the nervous system. I'm wondering if my aching mind is trying to do the same thing.

"So they didn't steal anything?" She draws from the cigarette and exhales towards the window.

"Nothing important."

"What do you mean?"

I show her my empty right wrist. "They took my HCH bracelet."

She makes a face. "That old worn thing? Why?"

"Strange, huh? But then again, everything that's taken place is pretty weird anyway, including the missing body. Why would this be any different?"

She shrugs. "Well, for what it's worth, I'm glad that damned bracelet is gone. None of us like the fact that it read **BE AFRAID** unless you paid attention."

She has a point, though I always saw the bracelet as a sign of what's coming to me.

"By the way," she says, "I'm not sure how you're going to do your interview now with that bruise on your face."

"What interview?"

"Channel Seven is coming tomorrow to do a piece on HCH. Remember Laurie Fox?"

I nod, remembering a fundraiser she covered about a month ago. "That's the first time a woman tried to pick me up." The comment, of course, makes me think of Kate.

She laughs. "Anyway, she's tried to schedule time with you since, though I'm not sure how much confidence you'll inspire about the security of HCH looking like *that*."

As always, Margaret makes a compelling point.

"Can we postpone for a couple of weeks? Let the swelling go down?"

"Would be the third time we pushed out her interview, but I can try."

"Thanks," I say while she finishes her first cigarette and lights up a second one. Margaret became a smoker at about the same time she went Goth.

She catches me looking and shoots me a sideways glance. "Want one?"

"Nope, but do you have to chain smoke?"

"Hey," she says, taking a drag and exhaling in my direction. "Told you not to quit."

"They kill people."

"You have to die of something, honey," she replies before blowing it my way again and smiling her great smile. "Sure you don't want one?"

"I've got my patch."

"Then why do you keep getting off every time I exhale?"

"I don't know what you're talking—"

"I think someone's following us," she interrupts, glancing at the rearview mirror.

Margaret would know. Her gang-raping boyfriend stalked her during her first year at Hill Country Haven, even with a restraining order. Ryan finally got rid of him by having one of his clients on parole rough him up. We haven't seen the bastard since.

"Are you sure?"

"I said *think*," she replies, pouting while switching lanes, the cigarette hanging from the corner of her mouth.

Our three vans get followed often by angered men who want their wives or girlfriends or daughters back, so over time we developed a technique to deal with this ugly reality of our business. But perhaps a combination of the Vicodin, the pain, the hangover, my nicotine and caffeine cravings, last night's events, and my airport experiences have me on edge because I'm suddenly quite worried.

I'm about to turn around when she says, "Don't. Then they'll know we know."

I frown because I know better.

"Are you feeling all right?"

"Just peachy."

She sighs and remains in the right lane of the highway, taking the next exit, Oltorf Street, while glancing at the rearview mirror.

"Did they follow?" I ask as my heart starts to race even though I've done this hundreds of times. Are we being followed because of last night, because of Kate's note? Or because my actions led to the death of the woman accompanying the pimp and now he wants retribution? Or could that be Beckett back there keeping an eye on me?

"Yep. They got off the highway."

"Terrific," I say, not certain how much excitement I can take in a twenty-four-hour period.

She shoots me a concerned glance while steering into a service station at the corner of Oltorf and the access road and pulls up next to the closest pump.

"All right," she says. "Time to force their hand."

I'm amazed at how cool she plays this out. I guess when life hardens you the way it has Margaret, it takes quite a bit to throw you.

"It's a black Chrysler sedan," she says, pressing a button on the console, which activates two rear-facing digital video cameras to capture the action.

Margaret then gets out and starts working the pump.

I grab a small notepad and a pencil from the center console on my way out. The plan here is to jot down their plate in case the cameras fail to capture it. We then turn the video clip and the tags into the Texas Department of Public Safety via Ryan Horowitz. If it turns out to be a husband or significant other whom Ryan has already issued a restraining order, we can press charges because our crafty attorney figured out a way to extend the restraining order's sanctuary to the vans even if the wife or girlfriend in question isn't aboard.

The vehicle slows down as it approaches the intersection, but I can't see inside because of its dark tinted windows. It never actually stops, cruising down the service road and proceeding onto the next entrance ramp to IH-35.

"Got the tag?" she asks.

I nod as I write it down, get back in, and we drive off.

She steers onto the access road before getting on the highway and proceeding to the upper deck to avoid all of the downtown exits of the IH-35 lower deck. "I'll get the info to Ryan ASAP. See which lowlife was following us this time."

I nod while staring out the window at the Austin skyline as we approach the downtown area, but my mind goes beyond the towering glass and steel buildings, remembering the heavily-wooded neighborhood northwest of the central business district.

Tarrytown.

Where Heather Wilson once lived.

Before some bastard choked the life out of her.

All of a sudden I have an urgent need to see Ryan.

CHAPTER 6

It takes me a long time to trust someone, which explains why those I do confide in I have known for a while.

And at the top of that short list is Ryan Horowitz.

His family had a trailer across from mine. But unlike my family, Ryan's was what I would consider normal. No beatings. No bruises, blood, or broken bones.

No midnight killings.

Ryan had been at my side when bullies harassed me in school, always acting as the older brother I never had, and in some bizarre way even as the father I wished I had.

Ryan had been at my side when the paramedics carried away my mother in a body bag, her face beaten to a pulp with that damned baseball bat.

Ryan had been at my side when the cops charged my drunken father with murder and when a judge sentenced him to life without parole.

Ryan had kept in touch as I made it through the Texas foster care system, connecting again at the University of Texas, where he was finishing his senior year when I started undergraduate school.

When the world turned its back on me in the wake of the deaths of Heather and Bernard Wilson, Ryan became my only ray of hope. He was the only person on the planet that made me believe I did have a chance to avoid rotting in jail for the rest of my life for crimes I didn't commit.

And as the dust finally cleared, it was Ryan who challenged me to put my recently collected life insurance money to good use by co-founding Hill Country Haven with him in memory of Evelyn, David, and my mother.

"There's a very thin membrane separating purity from the worst form of depravity," Ryan says in his even-pitched voice sitting behind the weathered metal desk in his office on the first floor of HCH's building in north Austin, just west of IH-35 on Palmer Lane. He points to the open manila folder on his lap.

I briefly look at the large framed poster behind him. It's from an old HCH campaign depicting a woman seen from above hugging herself in a dark room. Above her is our logo in orange as well as the words **BE NOT AFRAID.** Below her reads, **HAVE THE COURAGE TO BE GOOD AGAIN.**

At the bottom is our toll-free hotline plus information stating that we will come and pick you up any day any time.

I came up with the main theme after an old religious song of the same title. The slogan beneath it was Ryan's idea, though for me it carries a different meaning.

"Know what I mean?" he adds, focusing his deep-blue eyes on me while running a hand through his short brown hair. He is dressed casually, especially for an attorney: a pair of faded jeans, one of our T-shirts, and dark loafers, no socks. The neck of the T-shirt looks like it's nearly strangling him as he retains the husky build from his years playing rugby in high school and at UT, where he got his nose broken a couple of times, lending it its slight curve. A fine scar traverses his chin, which he split open during a division championship in his senior year. Ryan is probably the only person in this building who displays evidence of physical damage who wasn't abused.

I rub my patched shoulder while dropping my gaze to the pack of cigarettes on his desk. Ryan has smoked for as far back as I can remember, and it was Ryan who gave me my first cigarette when I was thirteen. When I kicked the habit six months ago he thought I would not last six hours.

I frown, not only because the recent events have piqued my desire to smoke again—and I happened to be surrounded by damned smokers—but also because Ryan has always been calm, composed, cool, even when faced with circumstances that would make other people tremble. So, him telling me stuff like this makes me wonder just how extreme the case he is reading is.

His UT Law School ring shines in the streaming sunlight as he raises his hand and rubs his scarred chin, which makes him look more like a street fighter than an attorney. He returns his gaze to the folder, visibly upset, preoccupied.

I've already told him about last night. Although he was initially pissed I didn't contact him right away, he was glad I was not accused, proud that I had stepped in to stop a battering, relieved I didn't incur a long-term injury, and joked that it was about time I got a new HCH bracelet. He was momentarily perturbed about the missing body, but soon shrugged it off.

I also told him about the sedan following us from the airport, and he said he would look into it, guessing that it would lead to yet another restraining order violation.

And he had quickly returned to business as usual.

Let's face it, after seeing what we see here every day, a murder across the country and my little bruise rank pretty darn low.

But I have not yet told him about Kate's note or the airport incidents with the blonde, the albino, or with Beckett Mar as Ryan seems a bit too preoccupied with his case.

Deciding to wait for the right moment, I gently massage my right temple in an attempt to lessen the headache while contemplating the slightly peeling lime-green walls and matching linoleum predominant across the entire building. It glows this afternoon as shafts of burnt-orange and yellow-gold pierce through the windows behind his desk. For some strange reason, Ryan's T-shirt is also glowing, making him look somewhat reverent, even superhuman with his muscular arms and powerful chest and neck.

An interior designer picked the color scheme way back to make the place as cheery as possible, though after six and a half years of heavy use, it could use a face lift.

As I'm about to get up and leave him to his work, someone knocks on the door.

"Come in!" Ryan shouts without looking up, leafing through the document.

"Got the order ready, Boss," reports Dana Knox in the very deep voice she has from her days as Dan "The Fort" Knox, a former professional wrestler and bodybuilder.

Dana is even huskier than Ryan, the dark skin of her muscular, vein-laced arms protruding beyond the short sleeves of a very tight green and orange T-shirt also glistening in the late afternoon sun as she steps up to the desk and holds out a piece of paper for Ryan, who looks it over without taking it.

Dana wears a pair of tight jeans and burgundy cowboy boots to match her heavy lipstick. Long black hair with orange highlights drops over the breast implants she financed from old wrestling championship earnings. And, like the rest of her firm body, the C Cups seem to defy gravity.

"Hey, handsome," she says, tenor-like, looking my way while Ryan keeps reading. She smiles, exposing the space in between her front teeth. Dana bears a green **BE NOT AFRAID** tattoo across her right forearm because her wrists are too damn thick for one of our bracelets.

While the rest of us wear T-shirts and wristbands, Dana certainly lives the HCH brand to the fullest.

"Need some boxing lessons, Boss?"

Before I can reply, she adds, "Wait, don't tell me, I should see the other guy, yes?"

Ryan grins at that.

I smile without humor.

"Just busting your balls, Boss," she says, a radiant smile flashing across a face that evokes images of Michael Strahan all made up on a Macy's catalogue cover. Dana is certainly an acquired taste, but once you get to know her, you realize she's a wonderful human being, very tough—and terribly strong, which got her the shelter's highest-risk job: guarding our entrance. She also expedites paperwork between the courts and the Travis County Sheriff Department to get restraining orders served. In spite of the court orders to keep abusers away from the premises, at least a half dozen angered significant others try to break into the shelter each week to claim their beloved.

I guess so they can abuse them some more.

But first they have to get through big Dana—or the other very tough lady guards protecting our very own pearly gates.

While Ryan and Dana review the papers, I glance about the office, admiring Ryan's framed decorations from his days with the U.S. Army Rangers. He went to college through the GI Bill, which meant he had to go through the Army's ROTC program as an undergraduate at the University of Texas before going to Ranger School at Fort Benning, Georgia. Ryan went on to serve three tours in country, one in Iraq and two in Afghanistan, before returning home a decorated hero, and heading straight to UT to get his law degree.

"Looks good," Ryan finally says. "Make sure the sheriff serves the bastard before the sun goes down."

"Consider it done, Boss," she says, her booming voice echoing in the room.

I met Dana one early morning at the emergency room at Seton Medical Center five years ago while visiting a former shelter resident who had been beaten up by a new boyfriend.

Dana ended up there shortly after she had transitioned from Dan to Dana following SRS, sex reassignment surgery. Turns out her former wrestling buddies had nearly killed her. She had multiple lacerations, broken ribs, a broken nose, a dislocated shoulder, and she had a bad concussion from multiple blows to the head.

I told her about our shelter, and she joined us the instant she was released.

"Can I get you anything, Boss?" she asks me.

I slowly shake my head, again, feeling pretty humble and even somewhat embarrassed by my little bruise. "I'll be fine. Thanks."

As she leaves, Ryan returns to his papers and mumbles, "It's a very thin membrane, David. A very *fucking* thin membrane."

"What the hell are you talking about, man?"

"Adelia Sanchez," he says, reading the case file. "Twenty-seven. Four months ago a neighbor called APD at three in the morning after hearing screams coming from her house. By the time the cops arrived, Adelia's boyfriend had bailed, leaving her in a pool of her own blood from multiple razor cuts to the breasts and groin area...plus, she was found with a mouthful of flesh carved out from her face."

I lean forward. "What?"

Ryan pulls a color image from the file and tosses it across the desk.

I look at it and immediately feel the urge to vomit. She doesn't look human. Patches of crimson skin on her forehead and cheeks mark the spots where the skin was torn off, in some places still hanging from her face in a *Dawn of the Dead* sort of way.

"Dear Lord," I mumble, holding back the nausea. "What sort of sick bast—"

"*And* she was four months pregnant."

I take a deep breath, then ask, "How is the—"

"Lost it. The boyfriend kicked her repeatedly in her abdomen before cutting her up. According to the police report, he'd told her to get an abortion, and when she resisted, he decided to kick the baby out of her."

"What happened to him?"

He shakes his head. "Cops caught him trying to flee to Mexico, but the prosecution fucked up and the bastard got off on some technicality yesterday. Adelia, who's still recovering from reconstructive surgery, is upstairs scared out of her mind. Dana's on her way to court to file a restraining order."

Ryan produces another picture. "This is Adelia before the attack and this is the picture we took last night, when she came running to us after the bastard was released."

I just stare at the images, Ryan's words echoing in my head.

There is a very thin membrane separating purity from the worst form of depravity.

The pre-attack Adelia was a beautiful Latina, amazing cat-like eyes, a great smile, high cheekbones, and silky, light-olive skin. The one from this morning looks like a zombie from the television series *The Walking Dead*. Her face is a patchwork of scars and discolored skin as the surgeons did what they could to transplant skin from the back of her thighs.

"Marge is upstairs with the nurse sedating her now," he adds.

I hand the pictures back to him and look away, the bright surroundings failing to do their work. The horrible images superimpose on wherever my stare lands. And then the same sinking thought that grips me every time I think of such abusive bastards strikes me across the face with the power of a hundred head butts: Am I headed for the same hell as they are? Is the pain I inflicted on my loved ones in the same league as Adelia's boyfriend? As the bastards who raped and beat Margaret? Or the ones who sent Dana to the ER? Or as the thugs who killed Heather and Bernard Wilson?

As my own father?

At least my father didn't kill me.

I close my eyes as the image of my little David staring up at me with stretched arms looms in my mind and—

"So," Ryan says, clasping his hands. "What's up?"

I wipe the sweat from my brow even though it's quite cold inside his office. I'm having another one of my hot flashes, but it has nothing to do with male menopause. My sins boil me from the inside, creating a year-round personal Texas summer, perhaps a taste of things to come in the afterlife.

He closes the file and sets it on top of a pile labeled **PROCESSED**, which is twice as tall as the one labeled **INCOMING**. On average, we get about fifty cases a week, which Ryan handles with the help of his "paralegal" team made up of residents he trained himself, such as Dana and Margaret. Texas happens to be one of the states where a formal education isn't required to legally work as a paralegal.

I hesitate for another moment, before reaching into my pocket and producing the business card, which I hand over to him.

Ryan reads the front and frowns. "Please tell me you're not getting into this fortune-telling crap."

"The other side, genius."

He drops his eyebrows at me, flips it over, and just stares at it for a while, color suddenly leaving his face.

Yep, that's precisely what I thought, too, pal.

In some strange way I feel relief just by sharing this disturbing piece of news with him.

"Well?" I say after giving him a minute. "What do you think?"

"I…" He pauses, closes his eyes, and pinches the bridge of his nose for a moment before resting his hands on the desk. "As your attorney," he continues, clearing his throat twice in the process, "I suggest you…forget about this."

We lock eyes for a while. I can see that he's as serious as the day he fought off bullies beating me up in the field behind the trailer park.

"Why would I want to do a thing like that?" I finally ask. "There's even a dead woman invol—"

"Because," he interrupts, swallowing, taking a deep breath, regaining his composure—which in itself has already triggered alarms in my aching head. "It's been seven years, David. Seven *long fucking* years, and I've been with you every painful step of this winding road you've traveled to get on with your life. And in the process you've done a lot of good for a lot of people. Why would you want to go back down that dark hole you've finally crawled out of? Why would you want to look back and reopen old wounds?"

I try to remember what Kate Larson told me back at the bar while reading my palms—something about new encounters reopening old wounds.

But the problem is that those wounds never healed. If anything, new information on what happened back then might be my chance of mending, and the bizarre events associated with last night only add credibility to Kate's note.

I stare at the person I love as a brother and say, "If there's more to the story that could help me get things straight in my head, then I have to know."

Ryan closes his eyes again while leaning back in his chair. I've seen him like this before, as he mentally prepares a counterargument.

I let the litigator have his private moment of self-counsel.

In a way I don't blame him for suggesting that I forget about last night. He's doing what he has done all of my life: protecting me.

Ryan saw what I was like at my lowest, and his helping hand was what allowed me to climb out of the hole I had dug for myself. His advice isn't only as my attorney, but also as a close friend who doesn't want me to fall back down into that pit.

But Ryan doesn't get that the demons never left; that they are alive and tearing into me every single night, chipping away at my sanity, reminding me that there is no atonement, no penance, for what I did to my family.

I stare at the poster behind him, at the words that so often I wish to believe.

HAVE THE COURAGE TO BE GOOD AGAIN.

I sigh as little David's large brown eyes stare at me out of the deepest corner of my mind, realizing there's simply nothing I can do to make amends, and Ryan can't protect me from the brutal reality that my actions resulted in the death of my son and my wife.

No one can…unless things were not as they seemed.

"Look," he says, a hand toying with the pack of cigarettes. "Your case was…different."

"Really?"

He drops the pack on the desk and shows me his open palms. "That's not what I meant. The circumstances certainly made it different, but there was something else about it that bothered me."

"What?"

Ryan crosses his huge arms and lowers his gaze. The litigator-prizefighter is again considering, pondering, contemplating his approach, searching for the right words to make his point.

"You're not in court, Counselor," I say.

He just breathes deeply and looks away.

"Is there something about the case you haven't told me, buddy?" I press, getting a bit worried now.

"Sort of," he finally says.

"And that would be?"

"How you got acquitted. The way the evidence showed up to get you off the hook."

During most of the trial it looked as if I was going to hang. Beckett Mar had everything pointed at me, from DNA and my fingerprints to my lack of an alibi, and in his opinion, the perfect motive. The prosecution's case, led by Assistant DA Sebastian Serrato, looked airtight. I thought I was done for, and so did Ryan. Then, wham, two pieces of evidence make it to Ryan's office: the mismatch between my hands and the shape of the bruises on Heather's neck, and the security video that showed me leaving her house when I said I did, showing Heather still alive, and at least a full hour before the murders were committed.

"And in addition to being cleared for Heather, it didn't hurt that Bernard's body or the weapon that caused all of that bleeding mysteriously vanished," Ryan adds. "No corpse meant no murder charge against you for him."

For a moment the comment makes me think of the gash across the missing Asian woman's throat before my thoughts turn to Bernard Wilson's body, which was never found, though his blood—along with my fingerprints—had been everywhere. And that all makes me remember the way Heather Wilson was found: strangled, bruised, and tied naked to her bed with my semen in her vagina and elsewhere on her body.

But the new evidence had forced Serrato to drop all charges against me, and the judge sent the jury home. Case closed.

At the time I had been too relieved to worry about how that evidence reached Ryan. I was just damn glad it did—at least the selfish part of me that didn't want to rot in prison for the rest of my life, or even face a lethal injection. But Kate's note—and the new murder and associated missing body—had suddenly made it relevant to rethink everything that took place.

And the apparitions this morning plus Beckett harassing me only kindled the fire.

"What I'm trying to say," he adds, "is that there was something unusual about the whole sequence of events in that trial."

"But nothing substantial enough for you to put your finger on?"

"Something like that."

"And doesn't that make this note plus the strange murder and subsequent body-snatching even more significant?"

"It makes it significant all right—significantly *dangerous*."

"Why?"

"Because," he said, leaning back, rubbing his scarred chin again. "The way I read it—and mind you this is pure speculation on my part—someone wanted you framed, but then something must have transpired that made that someone back off and get you acquitted."

"You mean Beckett Mar?"

Ryan gives me a half smile. "Beckett had no clue. He was a puppet, and so was Serrato. Someone else was pulling the strings, making you look guilty before suddenly back-pedaling."

"Why would anyone want to do that?"

"Well it wasn't because of your charming looks."

I'm a little dense at the moment, so I ask, "Then, why?"

He frowns in the way a big brother does at the naiveté of a younger sibling. "Someone wanted that case closed, and fast, David. So they did."

This is too surreal, dragging me back to my many sessions with Ryan during the trial, which seems like a hazy dream now, a collection of loosely-sequenced scenes. I truly had not thought much about the way I was acquitted, only that I had been. I was too consumed with grief and guilt to care about the *why* of the thing. Evelyn and David had died in a tragic car accident following my arrest, so my mind just wasn't up to par.

"Why would someone want that case closed?" I ask.

"The hell if I know. One moment Serrato claims that you took advantage of Heather when she was drunk, and when Bernard showed up, you killed them both, but managed to hide his body and the murder weapon. Then Serrato suddenly decides that this had been consensual sex, that you had no reason to benefit from her death, and that you left before Bernard showed up, before Heather was strangled."

I consider that for a moment.

I often think about who killed Heather Wilson and just as importantly, why someone had done such a thing. Was it Bernard? Someone else?

I suddenly get the itch to go chat with Beckett Mar even if it leads to more verbal abuse. He knows stuff he isn't telling me. I could also seek out the smooth-talking Sebastian Serrato, who first swore to fry me then quickly left the courtroom without even glancing my—

"Don't do that," Ryan says.

"Do what?"

"That look in your eyes…don't."

"What look?"

"Don't pursue this. Keep moving forward."

But I can't.

I won't.

And Ryan knows it.

The bizarre events of the past twenty-four hours have opened a door to the past, to the hope of finding peace, perhaps even making amends. Something is most definitely going on and the temptation to find out what it is overwhelms Ryan's sensible advice.

HAVE THE COURAGE TO BE GOOD AGAIN.

I have to go through that door.

I have to go back and learn anything that can be learned and deal with the consequences as they come.

But do I have what it takes to see it through?

I've never been the courageous type.

I was always the bullied, the abused. Ryan, on the other hand, was the protector, the war hero, the great litigator. And this one consistent solid figure in my life is telling me not to go down this potentially dangerous rabbit hole.

BE NOT AFRAID.

"Ryan, I need to know," I finally reply, wondering just what the hell I may be getting myself into but refusing to let fear get the best of me.

Besides, what do I have to lose?

Perhaps that's what courage really is: the sobering realization that you have nothing left to lose, liberating you to take chances and find your truth.

"All right," Ryan says, his blue eyes on me as he leans forward, plants his forearms on his desk, and crisscrosses his fingers. "Tell me, wise guy, exactly what are you going to do?"

That's a good question to which I don't have a good answer. Perhaps I go track down Beckett and Sebastian, but in reality I'm not even sure what I'm going to ask them. I'm not a cop. I have no detective schooling. I'm a free-lance efficiency consultant by training and the director of a shelter for battered women by choice.

His eyes narrow while the edges of his mouth curve up, stretching the scar on his chin.

"What?" I ask.

"You don't have a plan."

I say nothing.

He continues. "You have no *fucking* idea what to do, do you?"

I just stare back.

"Tell me, David. What's going to be your first move? Seek out a retired DA prosecutor? A busy APD detective?"

I remain silent as he pulls a drawer open and rummages through a pile of business cards. In the digital age, Ryan Horowitz still relies on paper to keep track of his contacts.

"What are you doing?"

He doesn't reply as he continues searching, his fingers finally plucking a dark-green card from the stack.

"It's Serrato's current information," he says. "I don't have Mar's but I'm sure he's still with APD. Call the station."

I'm about to tell him I have already spoken to Beckett but instead just catch the card he tosses at me.

DR. SEBASTIAN SERRATO.
UNIVERSITY OF TEXAS SCHOOL OF LAW

"Serrato's teaching law at UT?"

Ryan shrugs. "I heard from a former professor of mine that he's actually pretty good. He's teaching first year Criminal Law."

"Great. I wonder if they discuss my case in his class."

"What are you going to tell him, David? That some mystery woman from some astronomical society—"

"Astrological."

He frowns and points an index finger at me before adding, "Are you going to tell him she gave you this note at a bar in San Francisco? And that you saw her later getting beat up by some pimp in the company of another hooker? Would you also like me to get you the contact info for Detective Mar so he and Serrato can laugh at you together? And by the way, could you tell me when that is so I can bring the popcorn? This should be better than reality TV."

He tosses Kate's card back at me.

"And what makes you think they want to talk to you anyway?" he continues before I can point out to him that I've already spoken to Beckett. "The case ruined their careers. Serrato had aspirations to run for office and ended up teaching first-year law students. Mar never made it past detective. And all because of you."

"Bullshit," I reply. "Don't blame me for their demise, especially Beckett's. The bastard showed up at my house on a Sunday morning with a half dozen police cruisers flashing lights, guns, and badges to arrest me right in front of Evelyn while waving the rape and murder flag. Then he cuffed me and walked me out in front of all of my neighbors. Evelyn was so distraught that she lost control of her car on the way to her parent's lake house and—"

"Stop looking back, or you're going to fall right back into the shithole."

I stare at the one person who sacrificed so much for me. Seven years ago Ryan had to resign from the prestigious Gardner & Gardner firm, which recruited him straight out of law school and where he was already a partner, to handle my case. At the time, G&G's largest client was no other than Premier Imports—Bernard Wilson's company. Ryan was the legal firm's point person, spending a lot of time in New Orleans managing the legalities between the local casinos and Premier's bank, The International Bank of Texas, that financed them. Said another way, my old consulting firm as well as Ryan's law firm worked for Bernard Wilson. So when I fucked his wife and got accused of killing them both, Ryan had to resign in order to defend me.

"And I doubt Serrato or Beckett will talk to you anyhow," Ryan adds.

"Beckett already did," I say.

Ryan plants his palms on his desk as he leans forward. "What? Where? When?"

"At the airport. He was waiting for me by baggage claim."

"And?"

"And he wasn't laughing."

"What did he want?"

"Who knows. I think he was just fishing. SFPD called him about last night, and that gave him an excuse to poke me a little. But you're right. He continues to be pissed and still believes I killed the Wilsons. He did show me a picture of the dead Asian woman from last night, told me he knew I was guilty now just as I was back then, and said he would be in touch. Perhaps I should touch him first."

"What did you tell him about last night?"

"Not a thing. Screw him."

As he opens his mouth to reply there is a knock on the door.

"Come in!" Ryan shouts while staring at me.

"Ryan," says Margaret, inching the door open and sticking her head in the room, silver cross dangling from her neck, dark eyes encased in black mascara focusing on us. "Your five o'clock is here, and I'm off to do rounds."

I get up to leave and pocket Kate's card as well as Serrato's.

"We'll continue this conversation over dinner," Ryan says, narrowing his gaze at me. "Meanwhile don't go making any phone calls or visits yet. Okay?"

I turn for the door.

"David? No calls or visits okay?"

"Fine," I blurt out as Margaret stares at me then at him.

A tall woman in her mid-thirties I've never seen before steps in as I walk out with Margaret. Her left wrist is in a cast and she wears dark sunglasses that fail to completely cover the large hematoma surrounding her left eye. Her upper lip is swollen, and she also has bruises on her arms and neck.

"Who's that?" I whisper as Margaret follows me to my office a few doors down the bright hallway. We house an average of two hundred women at any given time with a monthly turnover of about twenty-five percent, making it nearly impossible to know everyone all the time. Margaret, however, is quite the efficient assistant, making it a point to know everyone and keeping me informed when I need to be.

"She caught her husband in bed with another woman and when she tried to leave him, he used her as a punching bag and told her if she called the cops he would cut her face up. Must be related to Adelia's soon-to-be-ex-husband."

Once again I feel quite embarrassed to show my little bruise in public.

"What was that all about in there?" she asks.

"Ryan being Ryan," I say, shrugging.

"You were never a good liar," she replies. "Anyway, I have two things to tell you. First, I spoke with Laurie Fox, and she reluctantly agreed to push the interview out, but only by a week."

"It'll do. And the second thing?"

"Somebody dropped this off for you," she says, handing me an envelope. "Said it was important."

"Who?" I ask as I reach for my door while eyeing the small envelope. My name is written across the front of the—

I stop midstride.

The handwriting.

I pull out Kate's card and place it side by side with the envelope.

It's a perfect match.

"Hey, what's that?" Margaret asks, pointing at Kate's scribble from last night. "Oh, my God! What does that mean? Is that what you were discussing with Ryan? Who gave you that?"

"Marge. Listen," I say, putting a hand on her shoulder. "Who dropped off this envelope?"

"Some blonde. I saw her from the hallway as she left it at the front desk but didn't leave a name, and she was gone by the time I stepped out to find her."

"Old or young? Short hair or long?"

"On the older side but slim. Hair was long and curly. Why?"

I feel a chill while staring at my name next to her note, Ryan's words echoing in my head.

Someone wanted that case closed, and fast, David. So they did.

I tear it open while marching into my office with my lovely assistant in tow.

"Don't you have rounds?" I ask.

"It can wait," she replies, glued to me.

Realizing I'm not going to shake her that easy, I just sit at the edge of the desk, tear open the envelope, and unfold a small sheet of paper. Margaret plants herself shoulder to shoulder by me, the side of her face almost pressed against mine. So much for privacy.

I ignore her and read the scribbled note.

And stop breathing.

"David? What does that mean?" she asks. "What the hell does that mean?"

I feel as if an elephant has planted its massive ass on my chest.

The room vanishes as my vision tunnels, as Margaret's voice fades in the darkness swallowing me. But I can see my hands; I can see the note, the second message from Kate Larson.

**WANT TO KNOW WHAT REALLY HAPPENNED?
SIX PM TONIGHT. HEATHER'S PLACE**

CHAPTER 7

If I had told Ryan I was going to follow up on this new note from Kate, he would have tried to talk me out of it, just as he had started to do with Kate's first message.

And besides, I don't have a plan, just as I don't have any earthly idea who lives there now. Last I heard, the place was purchased by a private party the year after the double murders.

So I'm doing what I've done on those occasions when we had disagreed: do it anyway, risk getting in over my head, and then rely on Ryan to rescue me should things spin out of my control.

On this unusually toasty late afternoon in March in sunny north Austin, my partner in crime is no other than the delightful Margaret Black, who just happens to have rounds near The Drag, a long strip of eclectic shops, restaurants, and bars on the west end of the University of Texas, also known as Guadalupe Street (pronounced gwad-a-loop) between 19th and 29th street. Heather's old place in Tarrytown is just northwest on 35th street but Serrato lives on the outskirts of the UT campus, so I

71

figured we'd swing by Heather's before making rounds and hit Serrato's afterwards.

At Hill Country Haven "rounds" is the activity of using the vans to drive around the areas populated by homeless in the hope of finding an abused woman on the run—or any woman on the run for that matter, including teenage girls, whose numbers have grown exponentially in the past two decades. The dark alleys projecting west from The Drag are a traditional hangout for the city's increasing number of panhandlers, which university students living in the area, as well as business owners, refer to with affection as Drag Rats.

Margaret drives one of the vans down IH-35 and gets off on 38th Street heading west towards Tarrytown, where we're going to do our little business at the Wilson's former residence before I accompany her to do rounds.

I'm sitting next to her holding my notes and pondering what I'm going to find out from this enigmatic Kate Larson and whether or not Serrato will give me the time of day.

"Hey, so let me get this straight," she says in her classic driving pose, left elbow hanging out the window, a cigarette wedged in between the index and middle fingers of her right hand resting on the wheel. I stare at the dark lipstick on the filter as well as the half-inch-long cinder at the end of the cigarette. I'm about to ask her to flick it outside but decide against it.

It's useless with her.

Margaret pretty much does as Margaret pleases.

She takes a drag, exhales through her nostrils, and adds, "This Kate Larson comes up to you at a bar, starts conversing, gives you the first note, then you find her getting beat up by someone you guess was her pimp and a fellow hooker, then you get head-butted by the pimp, the hooker is killed, then her body vanishes, and now you get another note from Kate."

"I don't think Kate was a hooker, Marge. And she said she was from Austin."

"Did she proposition you?"

"I told you, I don't think she's a hooker. I think she was someone special—someone who, by the way, did appear damaged and reaching out for help."

"Right."

I stare at the pale profile against the passing streets through the smoke between us.

"A woman comes up to you and makes conversation at a bar in San Francisco," Margaret says. "She's attractive, even exotic, and moments later she's getting beat up by what looks like a pimp? C'mon, David, you're not thinking with the right head anymore. She was probably getting beat up because she didn't produce for her pimp because you turned her down." She draws from the cigarette and exhales through her nostrils while her left fingers fidget with the skull ring. I can almost swear its little red eyes are staring at me.

I'm not sure how to respond.

"Want to know what I really think?" she adds.

"Please."

"David, honey, you need to get laid. And pronto." She blows the smoke in my face and smiles with her dark lips, the black mascara stretching as her grin broadens.

I just stare at her.

"Excuse me?"

"If you can't tell a hooker when one's staring you in the face, it's time to get some. Maybe then that blood can go flow back up to your head and you can start thinking straight again."

I'm at a loss for words.

She continues without missing a beat. "Because while there may be something there, while she could potentially have some information that could be pertinent to what happened seven years ago, your comment that she was… what did you call her? *Something special?* And then what? She was going to help you while holding hands and singing Kumbaya…well, that's certainly on the naïve end of the scale."

"Me having sex has nothing to do with—"

"When was the last time?"

"What?"

"The last time you got some?"

I cross my arms and rub the nicotine patch on my shoulder. "I'm not going to answer that."

She pulls again from the cigarette, exhales, and says, "That's what I thought."

I say nothing.

"There's no patch for that, you know." She grins while pointing at me with the cigarette. "Only the real thing will do."

"Are you offering to help out in that department?" I ask in a bold move that I know is going to backfire. Margaret may be damaged, may be abused, may be completely untrusting of the male gender, but she is one savvy woman. She's street smart, and also quite witty. Even Ryan has difficulty sometimes winning an argument with her.

She laughs out loud in a way she seldom does, before stretching a thumb towards the large cross on her chest. "*Me?* My dear, dear David…forgetting for the moment that you're my boss, the fact is that you couldn't possibly handle me."

"What?"

"I'm too much woman for you."

"What the hell does that mean?"

She keeps driving as a devilish leer forms on her dark lips. She crushes the cigarette in the ashtray between us, and I take a moment to admire her profile. She has what any guy would call a nice pair, not too large and not too small, and which push her black tank top a couple of inches off her very flat belly, where the little skull with the matching makeup lives. A swan-like neck partly hidden by her dark hair connects a face with a Barbie-like profile. Margaret looks like one of those women who never quite lost her baby looks, which she keeps hidden beneath the dark make-up in bereavement of her abused years—if you believe our pro bono therapist. But that's where the niceties end. Beneath the skin she's one tough cookie, hardened by a life that no human being should ever have to live.

"Now you're staring at my boobs," she says, catching me with the corner of her right eye. "You definitely need to get you some."

"But you're off the table, yes?" I ask, fascinated at the way Margaret can make me forget about my problems through her own bizarre sense of humor.

"Face it, David, what are you going to do with me? You need a nice miss from the suburbs who's sweet and from a respectful family, and who will marry you and give you a nice baby and…" She stops, then adds, "I'm sorry. I didn't mean to—"

"It's all right." I take a deep breath as she looks my way, the smugness long gone, leaving her with the same compassionate face she flashed at me when picking me up at the airport.

I stretch my hand and pat her on the shoulder gently. "You of all people have absolutely nothing to be sorry for."

We remain quiet for a few moments, and then she says, "Careful, David. You may not be as tough as you think."

"Tell me something I don't know," I say, pointing to my bruised nose, whose throbbing has lessened through the day as I continued popping Vicodin every four hours.

"You dummy. I'm talking tough here," she replies, shifting driving hands and touching me on the left temple with the fingernails of her right hand. "And here," she adds, lowering her hand to my heart, touching my chest.

And that's probably true, but I still need to find out what Kate might know about what took place seven years ago.

"We're almost there," she announces, driving down from 38th street to 35th.

I stare at the majestic trees planted long ago on both sidewalks stretching their branches over the street, meeting in the middle, creating a sort of tunnel that shades this most prestigious neighborhood of an eclectic architecture of gracious houses, small condo buildings, townhomes, and old churches. Everything is nestled among some of Austin's nicest and most peaceful parks with lily ponds and pools, nature trails, white-tail deer, and the Austin Museum of Art. Heather and Bernard Wilson lived on a quiet street overlooking a green belt.

As my mind evokes images of their house, a white van drives in the opposite direction and my eyes land on the driver, a pale man with silvery hair that reminds me of—

"Here we go," she says, reading Kate's note and the map app on her phone before looking at house addresses on mailboxes or painted on sidewalks.

The van is gone before I can get a good enough look, but I could swear that it was the same guy from the hotel last night and the airport this—

"Earth to David. This is the house number according to the note."

I blink the sight away and nod slightly while glancing at the street. I don't have to look at house numbers. There are some things in life that you just can't forget.

Heather's house is one of them. I desperately need a smoke now but my foolish pride keeps me from bumming one.

"That one," I say, pointing to a red-brick two-story colonial-style mansion on our right. It has a beautiful garden and a narrow and short gray cobblestone driveway projecting from the street to a rotunda in front, before continuing towards the back of the house, where presumably the garage is located. Large windows flanked by black shutters overlook us as Margaret steers the van towards the main entrance.

"No cars here," she says. "Maybe they're in the garage."

I'm fighting serious flashbacks now and my fingers are really aching for the comfort and relief that the stupid patch can't quite deliver.

As the sun starts to settle and David's little face looms in my mind, my stomach fills with acid while I stare at the place where everything that went wrong with my life began.

I glare at the double doors beyond two steps connecting the circular driveway to a covered portico.

On the other side of those wooden mahogany doors extends the foyer where a very lonely and very drunk Heather Wilson, long ignored by her husband, threw her arms around me and pulled me into that irresistible embrace that led me to take her right there against the wall, and again in the kitchen, before finally making it to the bedroom. It had been a wild night, but unlike my trial, which memories are vague at best, I remember every detail of that encounter with uncanny detail, as if it was—

"Enjoying the daydream?"

I blink.

Margaret has her arms crossed. "Are you just going to stare at the place or are you going to ring the bell?"

Good point.

We step up to the large double doors under the portico, and I stab the button to the right of the doors with my trembling index finger, hearing a pleasant but short tone echoing inside the house.

A minute of bile-erupting anticipation passes by.

Nothing.

"Again," Margaret says, but again, no one answers the door.

I turn around, inspecting the grounds, the quiet street beyond, seeing no one.

I check my watch. It's exactly six in the evening, just as the note said, and precisely where the note said to be.

"Maybe she's late," Margaret offers.

"That, I seriously doubt."

"Why?"

"If Kate Larson has something to say to me, and she has waited seven long years to do so, she would *not* be late."

"I guess," she says, making a fist and giving one of the doors three hard knocks.

To my surprise, it inches forward.

"It's not locked," I say.

"Really?" she replies, pushing it open and sticking her head in, screaming, "Hello! Anybody home?"

Before she gets a reply or I can stop her, Margaret is already in the foyer.

Isn't that trespassing?

My heartbeat starts intensifying a headache that the Vicodin has tamed but had not completely eliminated. I close my eyes for a moment, breathe in, and force my legs to follow her into the exact spot on this planet where my life took its worst possible turn.

Margaret is shouting again from the edge of the roomy foyer, her voice echoing inside the spacious interior with its twenty-foot ceilings.

I have difficulty breathing, and not because of where I'm standing, in the place where the beautiful Heather Wilson stripped off her clothes, unbuckled my pants, and latched herself onto me, dragging me to the bottom of the dark abyss of marital betrayal in my tragic momentary lapse of reason. Although Evelyn and I were on the verge of a separation, my actions were still inexcusable on so many levels.

I'm standing on the dark wooden floors of the same foyer under the soft-white glow of the same ornate chandelier. But my narrowing vision lands on a table a few feet from us, where I notice the framed pictures monopolizing its granite surface. They're all of my former boss, Gustavo Salazar, his wife, and two teenage kids whose names escape me.

I drop my brows, thinking that my eyes are playing tricks on me. This was Heather and Bernard Wilson's home. What's Gustavo doing here? Did he buy this place?

And if so, why would he ever do that knowing that his best friend and his wife were murdered here?

I get closer, inspecting pictures from various locales around the world, and also taken in different years as judged by the height of the two kids, a boy and a girl. There's one in front of the Eiffel Tower, another on a beach, another at a ski resort. And they all have matching silver frames except for the one in the middle bordered in dark wood and placed there apparently in a hurry, almost shifting the other frames aside to make enough room.

And it is at this moment that I realize I may have made a profound mistake by coming back here, by not listening to Ryan, by insisting in marching back into my dark past in a foolish search for an absolution that doesn't exist.

Right there, in plain view, is a five-by-seven of a smiling Bernard Wilson standing next to Gustavo.

"David? What's wrong?"

I have a lump in my throat and can't seem to cough up any words as I continue to stare at the backdrop, at the impossible Austin skyline behind them. Squinting, I try to make sure my mind isn't playing games.

"David? What's wrong with that picture? What do you see? What's it telling you?"

THINGS WERE NOT AS THEY SEEMED 7 YEARS AGO.

But it isn't those two posing together for a photo that rakes my intestines like a sizzling claw. It was no secret that the imports and exports magnate had a close friendship with my boss, which made it all the more difficult for me when I ended up sleeping with Heather—and even more so when I became the suspect in her murder.

What exacerbates the drilling in my head, the pounding in my temples, is the two of them standing in front of the many high risers built along the shores of Town Lake in recent years.

In *recent* years.

My eyes focus like a laser on the four tall condominium buildings on the west end of the downtown area that have only gone up in the past two years, as Austin's population continued to explode, creating huge demands for living space.

Two years ago.

The long missing Bernard Wilson was alive and well in Austin.

Two. Fucking. Years. Ago.

Someone wanted that case closed, and fast, David. So they did.

I grow dizzy, the room turning into a swirl, like a cyclone in my confused mind.

"David! Talk to me! What's going on? What is it about that picture?"

Unable to speak, I find myself reaching out for the only other soul in this room as my knees quiver, as blood drains from my aching head—as the demons emerge from the underworld that has been my life since the last time I stood here.

Closing my eyes, I let it all go, surrendering myself to her embrace, to her body pressed against mine in the silence of this foyer. And this time, I'm the one latching on, seized by unquenchable desperation.

I feel her cheek pressed against mine, arms wrapped around my numbing body, a hand caressing my back, my head, her fingers running through my hair, just as Heather Wilson did a lifetime ago, just as—

"Stay where you are!"

The familiar voice behind me jolts me away from the painful flashback, from the realization that I was hugging Margaret tighter than I have ever hugged anyone in a long time.

"Now turn around slowly," the voice adds. "Hands up where I can see them."

Slowly, I turn around and raise my hands. Margaret does the same.

Right there, in the middle of the entryway, is APD Detective Beckett Mar accompanied by a very young and very tall brunette dressed in dark slacks and a black blouse, her badge hanging from her belt.

Their weapons are drawn.

CHAPTER 8

"There's no law against hugging," says Margaret, reacting before I can. She doesn't know Beckett, and she certainly doesn't know we just had a sparring match earlier today.

I blink away the flashback and force my mind back to the surreal present, my eyes shifting between Beckett and the framed picture.

"What the hell are you doing here?" he asks, holstering his sidearm.

His much younger, taller, and thinner companion, who looks as if she graduated from the academy yesterday, regards Beckett with obvious confusion while also putting away her weapon.

"I could ask you the same question," I reply. "In fact, I could argue that you're stalking me."

"Yes, but again, I'm the cop, and I get to ask the questions. From what I can tell, unless you now live here, you're trespassing."

"Door was open when we got—" Margaret starts.

"Little Miss!" Beckett interrupts. "The grown-ups are talking."

"The hell I—" Margaret tries to reply.

"Hey!" Beckett snaps his fingers. "You will know when I want your opinion, Miss Skull, because I will be handing it to you."

He then turns his lovely personality back to me and blurts, "This is pretty sick, David. Even for you."

"What is?"

"Trying to fuck someone else on the same spot you fucked Heather Wilson."

"Take a break, Beckett," I reply. "You don't have to be a prick every second of every day."

He makes the little bull horns sign with his left hand and points them at me. "Keep it up."

"All right," I say. "Like Margaret was trying to explain to you before you cut her off *and* insulted her, the door was open, so we called out for anyone first. Then we stepped into the foyer."

"Why are you here?" he presses, keeping the index and pinky finders of his right hand trained on me while his younger partner looks on.

"We got an invitation to come," says Margaret, somehow feeling the urge to defend me.

Beckett shifts the horns toward her. "This is serious police business. Last warning, Miss Skull. One more word from you and my partner will cuff you and throw your Gothic ass in the back of the car until we can figure out what to do with you. Clear?"

Margaret crosses her arms. "Sure."

Beckett gives her an exasperated look, before turning to me and asking, "An invitation from whom?"

"From the same person who apparently also invited you," I reply.

"And who might that be?" he asks.

"I was hoping you would be able to tell me that."

"You think this is all one big fucking joke?"

"Nothing about the past seven years can be categorized as even remotely funny, Detective, from Heather's tragic murder to the vindictive way you arrested me in front of my family and neighbors, to my wife being so upset that she lost control of her car and killed herself and my boy, and the ensuing nightmares that haunt me to this day."

He lifts his shoulders and says, "I wasn't the one cheating on his wife and shitting where he ate. Now who sent you the invitation?"

"I'm not really sure."

"What does that mean?"

"It means," Margaret replies, "that he's not sure who sent him the invitation. Are you stupid or pretending to be stupid?"

"That's it," Beckett says, looking at his partner and tilting his head towards Margaret. "Cuff her and throw her in the car."

"Is that really necessary?" I ask, deciding to level with him. "I was planning to reach out to you today regarding the note I got to come here in spite of Ryan's warning—and in spite of the way you treated me this morning at the airport."

"This guy was at the airport?" Margaret asks me. "Where."

"This is Margaret Black," I say. "She's my assistant at HCH, the shelter that—"

"I know about HCH," Beckett interrupts while signaling his associate to stay put. "Who sent you the invitation?"

My rebellious assistant glares at me with her fiery raccoon-like eyes and says, "You're not obligated to tell them anything. If they were going to charge you, they would have done so by now, and they would have also read you your rights. They haven't even identified themselves as police officers for crying out loud. The way I read it, they're just fishing."

"And the way I read it," says the female detective, speaking for the first time with a deep and authoritative voice, "you're beginning to piss me off."

Beckett grins at that.

Margaret tightens her fists and retorts, "And I'm just getting warmed up."

My strange mind starts to wonder who would win the cat fight.

"You don't really want to go there," says the female cop, her face turning red as Beckett continues to grin, apparently seeing how his young partner handles herself.

"May I have a minute, please?" I say.

Beckett gives me a slow nod.

I put my arm around Margaret as she keeps hers crossed, guide her out of ear shot from them, and whisper, "It's okay, Marge. He's just as surprised to see me here as I am to see him, and it's also pretty obvious that this Kate Larson wanted us to meet here. I need to know what's happening, and I was planning to call him anyway."

"Why didn't you tell me he was at the airport this morning. What did he want?"

"He just wanted to let me know that SFPD called him. Now, please trust me on this one. *Please?*"

She cups her lips with a hand as she whispers into my ear, "Okay, I trust you know what you're doing, but I sure in the hell don't trust cops...especially those two. So far you've been doing all the talking. He hasn't told you dick. Call Ryan."

"In a moment," I reply, before turning to Beckett. "Did you also get a note?"

He considers my question and slowly nods.

"Who is she?" I ask, tilting my head towards miss no-name.

"My partner, Detective Claudia Brand."

Her dark hair is pulled back tight in a bun, which accentuates her tall forehead above a pair of brown eyes briefly glancing my way with indifference. Her cheeks are still red as she burns Margaret with her stare. To her credit, Margaret simply glares right back.

I quickly review my options, including asking him if he's going to charge me with anything and to be allowed to call Ryan, who would be here in a flash. But something tells me that getting lawyered up isn't going to get me the answers I so desperately seek. And that something also tells me that Beckett is on the same boat trying to figure out what this is all about. Perhaps we can help each other.

So, despite of everything Ryan has ever taught me, and despite the way this man has treated me, I decide to open up a little and convey an abridged version of what I told Detective Marley Quinn, plus I throw in Kate's first note.

Beckett listens without interrupting while Margaret takes my hand in a silent show of support. Claudia is busy scribbling in her notepad. They will compare this statement to the one I gave Marley last night and look for discrepancies. Standard procedure.

"So that certainly explains the bruise on your nose," Beckett says as if he never read the SFPD report. "How did you get the second note?"

"Some woman dropped it off at the shelter."

"Was it Kate Larson?"

I slowly shake my head. "This one was older and blonde." Something tells me to hold back for now the little fact that she was in all likelihood the woman I saw last night waiting tables and this morning at the airport.

"And where are these notes with matching handwriting, Mr. Wallace?" Claudia asks, addressing me directly for the first time.

"Please call me David."

"Please answer the question," she replies.

"With Ryan at HCH," I lie, the same little voice in my head telling me to hang on to them for now.

"Who's Ryan?" she asks.

"Ryan Horowitz," replies Beckett for me. "The attorney who got him off on technicalities seven years ago."

"Let's not go there again today. I didn't kill her."

"You don't really believe that."

"Don't tell me what to believe. I'm innocent."

"Many people who knew the Wilsons would disagree."

"I slept with her but I didn't kill her."

Beckett shakes his head. "David, David, David. It was no secret that Heather married Bernard, twenty years her senior, because of his money and power. It was also no secret that Bernard kept mistresses in other cities, including Monterrey, Mexico, one of Premier Import's largest satellite offices. The night of the murder, Bernard was supposed to be out of town. A lonely and neglected Heather Wilson got inebriated at that company party and asked you for a ride home. You took advantage of her. Then Bernard walks in and catches you fucking his drunk wife. So you killed him, probably in self-defense. But then Heather wants to call the cops, so you panic and also kill her. One of these days you'll have to tell me why you only disposed of one of the bodies."

I remain calm as he drags the pre-trial version of the story he fed into the DA to get a warrant for my arrest. "I know what I did and didn't do, and I did *not* kill Heather or her husband."

"Whatever helps you sleep at night, pal. Oh, wait. You can't with the nightmares and all, right?"

"Go to hell."

"I'll be there soon enough, but so will you. You'll burn for what you did in this room."

That's actually the first thing he's said today that I agree with.

"That's harassment," Margaret says, squeezing my hand. "Are you sure you want to keep that up?"

"Are you sure you want to spend the night in jail, Miss Black?" Claudia asks.

"What are you charging us with?"

"We can hold you for forty-eight hours without pressing charges, and we can also arrange special roommates for you," she says.

I certainly don't like the sound of that.

"I'm sure that will go well with the media," Margaret replies, calling their bluff without checking with me first. "APD holds Hill Country Haven workers without charges and thus prevents the rescuing of battered women in downtown Austin for two days. APD declines comment. Laurie Fox from Channel Seven would have a field day with that. Are you sure you want to explain that one to your captain?"

The two ladies exchange another round of contemptuous glares.

"That's enough," says Beckett, before asking me, "So, Ryan advised you against investigating this on your own?"

"He urged me to leave the past in the past."

Beckett pushes out his lower lip and nods. "You should listen to your legal counsel."

"Ryan isn't the one losing sleep every night."

"You keep saying that…losing sleep every night," Beckett says. "That doesn't sound like an innocent man."

"That sounds like a man who has to know if there's even a remote chance of understanding what really happened seven years ago, because contrary to what you choose to believe—or at least make me think you believe—I did not kill anyone. But having consensual sex with Heather plus your rape and murder accusations did stress Evelyn enough to lose control of her car, resulting in—"

"I also don't get why your wife would have been stressed out about you cheating on her. If I remember correctly the two of you were splitting anyway, right? So your act of infidelity would have been just more ammo for her lawyers to nail your balls to your forehead."

The man is impossible.

He puts up a hand, frowns, and adds, "All right, so you decided to come here."

"I did," I continue. "And this is a nerve-racking place for me, but I had to know if there was any validity to Kate's claim. So I decided to check it out before accompanying Marge to do rounds."

He drops his brows over his inquisitive beady eyes. "Rounds?"

I take a minute to explain.

Margaret adds, "Basically what you're going to keep me from doing by holding me for forty-eight hours."

Beckett and Claudia look at each other and decide to let it go.

Beckett then says, "Anything else you wish to share with me?"

"Sure. The memory of my dead son haunting me every night. My guilt. My despair. My anger. My craving for a cigarette? You choose."

"You actually quit smoking?"

I frown and nod.

"When?"

"Six months ago."

He reaches into a pocket, produces a pack of Marlboros, and lights one up while winking and saying, "Good for you."

I just stare at him blowing the smoke in my direction. Bastard.

"So, anything else you wish to share with me aside from your personal problems?"

"Such as?"

"For starters, exactly what happened when you got here?"

I exhale while rubbing my nicotine patch and say, "When we arrived, we found the door open and stepped into the foyer while calling out for anyone in the house. And that's when you found us." I decide to hold back my suspicion that Gustavo Salazar owns this place, and a little voice tells me to check with Ryan first before telling the cops about the picture of Gustavo and Bernard, especially the way Beckett wants to fry me. I simply don't trust this man.

Claudia jots everything down in her little pad while Beckett keeps staring at me.

"What do you plan to do now?" he asks.

I think of Ryan asking me the same question. "I don't have a plan."

He pouts and regards me for a while, trying to read a reaction. I work hard at giving him none, before I look past them when spotting two uniformed APD officers approaching the house, palms resting on the handles of their holstered weapons.

"Misery loves company," I say, pointing in between them.

They look in unison and Beckett flashes his badge before motioning for Claudia to go speak with them. I overhear something about responding to a silent alarm.

He then turns to me and asks, "Tell me, David, why do you think someone would ask you and me to come back to the scene of the crime seven years later?"

"That's what I hoped to find out by coming here."

He keeps studying my face and is about to reply when Claudia calls him over.

Beckett makes his little horn sign to point at us. "Stay where you are. Don't look at anything. Don't touch anything. Don't do anything. In fact don't even *think* anything. Be right back."

As he leaves, Margaret leans over and whispers, "You didn't tell him about—"

"I need to consult with Ryan first," I reply, before glancing at the table again to make sure my mind isn't playing tricks on me.

Yep, that's Gus and Bernard, and those are definitely the Town Lake condominiums that went up a couple of years ago.

And my amateurish detective mind starts to pull together a scenario: The blonde waitress works with Kate Larson, and they broke into this place to let me know that Gus had bought the house and also to show me that Bernard is alive.

But why not just meet us and tell us what's going on? Is it because people are after her like in San Francisco, and she fears for her life? And why is Bernard alive and well and in contact with Gus, but he never went to the police?

The throbbing in my head intensifies as I glance at the front door, noticing Beckett and Claudia conversing with the officers while repeatedly turning their heads in my direction.

Staring at Beckett makes me wonder why is Kate also sending notes to him, the guy who wants nothing more than to crucify me? Is it possible that Ryan was right and Beckett, as well as Sebastian Serrato, are good guys misguided by bad information?

Beckett points at me with his index finger before curling it twice, motioning me over.

"Stay back a second," I whisper to Margaret before I go and meet them just past the entrance, beneath the covered portico.

"We need to run," he says. "New homicide and we need to beat the media."

"What about the house?" I ask.

"The security company told us that the owners divide their time between Austin and Grand Cayman. They're not due back for a couple of months. The company is sending someone over with a key to lock up. These officers will hang here until they do."

"Who are the owners?" I ask, testing his willingness to share information.

"We're checking right now."

And I guess I must have asshole written on my forehead. I realize then that Beckett is either that lousy an investigator or he doesn't want to tell me. In any case, I just nod, remembering hearing about Gus retiring from MM&S the year after Heather's death and moving to the Cayman Islands. Apparently he also purchased his old business associate's home.

"Are we free to go?" I ask, wanting some time to think about everything before confronting Sebastian.

Beckett sighs, then says, "For now, but this isn't over. Don't leave town. I'll find you later."

We're in the van a minute later heading toward The Drag.

"The picture," I say. "That was Kate sending us another message."

Instead of replying, Margaret pulls over into a gas station.

"What are we doing?"

She reaches behind her. "I shoved this under my bra strap."

I stare at her with a mix of surprise and admiration as she produces the picture frame.

"How did you know I—"

She winks and hands it over, before driving off and saying, "You kept staring at it, so I figured it was important, and I wasn't about to let those bastards have it."

Clutching the frame with both hands, I inspect it carefully now, trying to make sure I wasn't seeing things. It's definitely Bernard and Gus standing on the south shore of Town Lake with the recently-built downtown condos in the background. Unless it was digitally altered—and Ryan knows a guy who can help us with determining that—my old client is alive and well.

I open the frame and pull out the picture, and that's when I see the now-familiar handwriting across its back.

SHOW THIS TO SEBASTIAN SERRATO.
TRUST NO ONE ELSE.

CHAPTER 9

On the way to The Drag I explain to Margaret the significance of the picture as well as the note scribbled on its back.

"So you're going to show it to Serrato?" she asks.

"Yep. He was the prosecuting attorney back then, and besides, I was going to swing by his place after rounds anyway. Now I have something tangible to show him."

"That Bernard Wilson is alive?"

"Unless the picture is doctored."

"This whole thing makes your old associates look pretty damned guilty."

I suddenly remember the albino who keeps popping up everywhere I go. I tell Margaret about him.

"So you saw him at the hotel lobby, then at the airport, and a while ago driving away from the house?"

I shrug. "I think it's the same guy, and if he is, I guess he must be Kate's associate."

"Well, it looks to me as if they're manipulating you into doing their dirty work."

I nod, but realize I have no choice in the matter. I have to know what happened, and Kate knows that and is using me to help her unravel whatever this is—but I'm not really complaining.

It's already after dark on a weeknight and mobs of UT students are exiting the campus heading to their apartments with a short stopover at the many stores lining the west side of Guadalupe Street.

And among them are also professors.

Headlights crisscross in the night, their glow mixing with neon signs from tattoo parlors, specialty bookstores, and gift shops packed with UT paraphernalia, to furniture rentals, homemade jewelry, local fashion shops, a couple of pawn shops, and the dozens of local eateries and bars catering to a hungry and thirsty college crowd.

I massage the ridge of my nose with the tips of my thumb and index finger and stare at the picture, thinking of my old boss at Mercer, Martinez & Salazar, and his best friend Bernard. "I have to agree. They do look *very* guilty… unless…"

She glances my way. "Unless what?"

"Bernard didn't actually kill her but feared those who did and maybe Gus is helping him hide out. Remember, the police found Bernard's blood in the house."

"Maybe he was trying to defend Heather and got wounded in the process but managed to get away and is terrified of showing his face."

"Well, the fact that he never surfaced again led the prosecution to declare that he was first missing then presumed dead. But after my acquittal all leads went cold. Heather's murderer was never found and neither was Bernard's body. And now here he is, with my old boss at MM&S and apparently as happy as can be."

I continue staring at the photo. Two old friends posing for a shot on a sunny day in lovely Austin.

Two old friends with a big fucking secret.

A secret that Kate Larson and her albino co-conspirator are nudging me to help solve while being hunted probably by the same people who Ryan indicated wanted this case closed and forgotten.

The big questions are who and why?

And also, why me? Why was I first framed and then quickly acquitted? What forces conspired to try to take me out of the equation and then release me? And why am I being dragged back into it now, seven years later?

"Hmm," I mumble, while staring at Gus and Bernard's smiling faces.

Margaret looks my way as she pulls into a dark alley two blocks west of Guadalupe.

"What?"

"Well, looking at these two hanging out together suggests that perhaps something was not quite ethical either at Premier Imports or at MM&S."

"Or at both."

"And I was the consultant going through Premier's business processes to improve their efficiency," I say, thinking out loud. "Could it be that I was about to stumble onto something they didn't want me to see?"

"Like what?"

"I wonder if this is why Kate's asking me to show this to Serrato. As the prosecuting attorney he may have been privy to information on my old case that no one else saw. Maybe Kate's trying to get him to open up by showing him that Bernard is alive."

I briefly close my eyes and shake my aching head while Margaret comes to a stop in the middle of the very dark and seemingly deserted alley.

I'm about to tell her to blow off doing rounds tonight and go straight to Serrato's home, but I doubt a couple of hours of helping the homeless will make a difference. Besides, it's probably too early to catch the UT professor at home.

I peer into the darkness around us. After so many years driving the streets, we're a known entity among the forgotten, the abandoned, and the abused.

Among the Drag Rats.

Slowly, as my vision adjusts to the darkness, shadows start to shift along the edges of the wide alley, in between buildings, behind rows of dumpsters.

Many pairs of eyes flashing in the dim moonlight begin to emerge out of this murky world. Suddenly, I see them, mostly women, young and old, many sporting bruises visible through the dirt and mire filming their faces.

But they come, slowly, with hesitancy at first, pausing a dozen feet from the van.

"Show time," says Margaret, getting out.

I put my conspiracy theories on ice and crawl in between the front seats to the rear and slide open the side door from the inside.

For this trip we have removed the van's middle seats to make space for boxes packed with donations to give away. Some of our volunteers and residents help making sandwiches, and we get tons of canned stuff, bags of chips, and sodas donated by many grocery stores in the area. Some of it has just expired, which isn't good enough to sell but it's still quite safe to consume. And for these poor souls who survive on the leftovers thrown into trashcans by area restaurants, what we have qualifies as a gourmet meal. A box contains dental care kits, each with a disposable toothbrush, toothpaste, and floss. A couple of local clinics donate them each month. There are also three boxes with other toiletries, including plastic combs, small packs of tissues, plus the indispensable hand and body lotion, which is always a bestseller. We also have clothes donated by private individuals or local stores—especially T-shirts and socks. The homeless don't have access to laundry facilities, so they have to change often, dumping their old clothes.

I handle the boxes of food and sodas while Margaret passes out the non-consumables.

One interesting thing about the homeless is their politeness. Within thirty seconds a couple dozen women and a handful of guys quietly form a single line down the alley, and I begin to hand out food and drinks.

First in line is a woman well into her fifties with hair so dirty it's hard to tell its color. She gives me a smile beneath a layer of dirt, revealing equally brown teeth. She is dressed in an overcoat and sandals.

"Thank you, sir," she says, taking a can of soda and a sandwich, and selecting a dental kit, a new T-shirt, and a hand towel, before disappearing into the night.

We nod, smile, and wish her well.

They know we run a shelter, but they have their own reasons to stay in the streets. At the top of the list is fear of a significant other breaking in and dragging them out. There are a couple of shelters in town where that has happened recently, and it gives the rest of us a bad rep. In our six and a half years operating HCH we had only one such incident, and that was during our first few months in business. We have since tightened our security. Unfortunately, the general perception is still that the dark alleys offer better sanctuary than our guarded walls.

The body odor is the other thing that strikes when you first start working rounds at HCH, but you eventually learn to ignore it. Most of these souls haven't bathed in weeks.

An emaciated girl in her late teens is up next dressed in soiled jeans and a weathered UT sweatshirt. She has very short hair, almost shaved, exposing skull sores. Her eyes are as sunken as her cheeks and also bloodshot. But it's her mouth that grips me as she attempts to smile. Her teeth are either missing or rotten, adding to her gaunt look.

She wears the mask of a crystal meth addict, and for a runaway female teenager it also means prostitution to pay for the habit. They truly become sexual slaves, engaging in anything their "drug daddies" order them to do, from S&M to bestiality in order to get another hit. This girl was probably a freshman at UT last year with pony tails, chatting away on a cell phone at the local frozen yogurt stand. She probably either dropped out or ran short of cash to pay for tuition, room, and board, and could not secure a student loan. Rather than getting a normal job with normal pay, she decides to answer an ad for modeling or exotic dancing, taking the first step down to this netherworld. Soon, the modeling and dancing leads to propositions for sex, which at first are quite lucrative as she is young, attractive, and disease-free. But soon the realization that she has become a hooker sinks in, leading to depression, which pushes her to alcohol and drugs to escape the reality of her life. The result of the destructive drug-prostitution cycle is precisely what stands in front of me reaching for a can of soda, a sandwich, and one of the black T-shirts donated by a local furniture store. The meth, crack, and heroin suck the life out of them and within a year the same pimps who inducted them into this world dump them for fresh ones, leaving them to rot in alleys like this one.

But we don't judge at Hill Country Haven.

We just try to help any way we can, and we never, ever, ask anyone to come with us even though we have plenty of room.

The girl just nods and walks away, replaced by a woman perhaps just a little older than Margaret with a terribly bruised face. Purple blotches cover her left cheek and chin. Her right eye is almost swollen shut. Her left one is bloodshot. Her nose looks far worse than mine and is crusted with dry blood.

She wears a robe and slippers, and her face, aside from the bruises, isn't dirty. She has probably been out here for a couple of days hiding from an abusive husband or boyfriend.

Margaret glances my way, and I know she's found her first target for the evening.

With practiced ease, she pretends to go to the rear of the van while I handle all the boxes, which in reality isn't hard at all. But we always have at least two people for safety as well as to work the special cases, such as this battered woman who takes a can of sardines, a soda, and a tube of body lotion.

As I continue to distribute the goods, Margaret goes after her mark.

I serve in total twenty-seven people, all women save for three old men who claimed to be disabled veterans.

Closing the side of the van, I check on Margaret, who's still talking to the woman in the pink robe. She now has called an alley friend, a girl in her early twenties also bruised up but otherwise new to the streets based on her appearance. Her long blonde hair is in a ponytail. Her jeans and T-shirt are a little wrinkled but otherwise clean. Her face, however, sports a purple lump from her right ear to the right side of her lips. Her light-blue eyes are red and swollen from crying. Damage aside, she's actually quite pretty and attractively built, and that puts her at extreme risk of turning to drugs and prostitution.

Margaret is attempting to take on two salvageable targets at once.

I arrive just in time to watch her work her magic.

"Have you ladies seen Deborah?" Margaret asks, pulling out a photo and instantly personalizing a bruised woman in her late twenties. Short brown hair frames a face marked by heavy bruising around the eyes and left cheek. Tracks of dry blood connect her busted lips to her neck.

They look at the picture for a moment, and then slowly shake their heads as expected. Deborah has been missing for five years.

Margaret frowns. "That's too bad," she says. "Deborah used to live at Hill Country Haven, where we were teaching her accounting, but her boyfriend talked her into moving back in with him just to beat her up again. She called our hotline indicating she would be hiding in The Drag. She wants to get back to a safe and clean bed, a warm bath, and steady meals tonight, so we're trying to find her."

Their eyes blink with interest when she mentions the hook words: safe and clean bed, warm bath, and steady meals. Almost in unison they cross their arms, but it's the older one who speaks first.

"This shelter…does the police have a record of who lives there?" she asks with a bit of effort. In addition to her swollen lips, the inside of her mouth and tongue are inflamed. She reminds me of a woman at the shelter last year whose boyfriend, apparently angry at her spending too much money on gourmet coffee, decided to wake her up one morning by pouring a pot of freshly brewed coffee on her face and mouth, causing first-degree burns on her skin as well as her tongue, palate, and throat.

Margaret and I shake our heads in unison, and I take the opportunity to speak for the first time. "We have an anonymity exception with the State of Texas due to the nature of our work. What that means is that your identity is protected at all times. You don't have to tell us your real names. In addition, we have a legal service on site that can assist you in changing your name if you choose to do so. Some of our residents do that when enrolling in school or if they get employment following one of our training programs."

The ladies exchanged a glance, apparently considering that. The younger asks, "Is it an all-female staff?"

"It is all female aside from me, who runs Hill Country Haven," I say, "and our attorney and co-founder, who handles restraining orders, separations and divorces, name changes, and other related legalities that our residents require."

"So the guards are also women?" the same young one asks.

I can't quite tell which answer would make her feel better. On the one hand, she could fear male security having their way with female residents. On the other hand, she could be concerned about the security female guards would provide against a determined husband or boyfriend, who could also be bringing his drinking buddies along to drag his girl out kicking and screaming. We need to be very careful in our responses now. One bad answer and they burrow back into their lairs.

Margaret answers first. "All female, but don't worry. Our security staff is well trained and carry Tasers and pepper spray. No one is getting through."

"Ever?" the older woman asks.

"One time," I say, abiding by an honesty principle at Hill Country Haven to build trust, though in some cases, like what we call the *Deborah Hook*, we need to stretch the truth a bit for a good cause.

Margaret elaborates. "It was over six years ago, right after we opened. We have since tightened our security and have not lost a single resident involuntarily."

"Can you take me?" asks the older woman, her voice cracking, her hands shaking.

"Welcome to Hill Country Haven," Margaret says, extending a hand.

The woman takes it as tears well in her eyes. "My name is Kathryn."

Margaret smiles. "Hello, Kathryn."

"Welcome," I add. "Tonight you will sleep without fear."

As I say this, a white BMW with tinted windows and shiny spinners cruises down the alley, the heavy bass echoing against the walls of this dark world within one of America's most prosperous cities.

Although we don't know who it is, we certainly know what it is. The luxury vehicle stops twenty feet from us and the rear left door swings open. A tall and handsome Hispanic man dressed in a starkly-white T-shirt, dark jeans, and black cowboy boots emerges and points at the girl, who looks at us before slowly backing away from us and towards him.

I exchange a glance with the pimp, who regards me with complete indifference as he pulls out a wad of bills and uses them to lure the girl over.

"Wait, honey," Kathryn says. "You don't want to go there. Come with me. It's going to be all right."

She shakes her head. "I just need some cash to get out of town," she mumbles. "Besides…this shelter looks too good to be true."

"No, honey," insists Kathryn. "I have a good feeling about them, and I have heard others talk about this place. We'll be safe."

Margaret and I exchange a glance as we watch the girl struggle between the forces of good and evil. But we can't interfere. We can answer their questions, but we can't convince anyone to come. They must do this voluntarily. HCH is all about providing freedom of choice to those who may have never been free to decide on their own, and it starts with their decision to join.

"I really need money fast to skip town," she insists, continuing to retreat, arms crossed, as the pimp flashes her—and us—his finest nice-guy smile of gleaming teeth. "They can help me."

I stare at the devil enticing yet another soul down the road to perdition. I think of the meth addict and for an instant almost shout that she was making a paramount mistake. These people will suck the life out of her, and in a year there will be nothing left except a gaunt shell.

But I can't.

I just stand there and watch the pimp put a handful of bills in her hands before hugging her like you would a long-lost friend. These guys can be seriously charming bastards, knowing exactly what to tell a lost girl, before helping her into the rear of the sedan, waving at us before closing the door, and driving off.

Margaret's eyes find mine again and we sigh, knowing what's in store for someone like her. The pimps know, as we do, that these runaways won't go to the police for fear of their abusers tracking them down. And all of these girls think they can do this for a few weeks or even a couple of months to get enough cash and leave, but what they don't realize is what's waiting for them. After luring prey to their dens, the lions usually tie them to bed posts and shoot them up with heroin for a couple of weeks straight while raping them to break them in. They exit this indoctrination nightmare already addicted to heroin and willing to do anything for their next hit. There is no accumulation of cash for them, no escape, no future; only the drugs their young addicted bodies crave in exchange for tricks.

A young and cute thing like that can easily bring in a few thousand a night, at least for several months, until the life destroys them and they end up here like the toothless girl behind the dumpster gumming her sandwich.

But we saved one so far this evening, and that is a victory. And as cold as it sounds, we learned long ago to let go of those who don't wish to be saved. Besides, we don't really have room for everybody, so the math, unfortunately, works.

We're back in the van a minute later. Kathryn sits quietly in the rear, eating from a bag of potato chips.

We make three more stops in the area over the course of two hours, handing out roughly two-thirds of our supplies before we reach a small apartment complex three blocks from campus. Kathryn is by now sleeping in the rear seat alone. We found no other ladies willing to join us this evening.

Next to the apartment building is a row of small duplexes, eight in total with manicured front lawns under large oaks.

Margaret parks the van in front of the farthest one by the corner, and I get out. "I'll just be a minute," I tell her, before glancing at our sleeping passenger.

I take the picture of Gus and Bernard with me as I step away from the van, walk across the narrow lawn, and onto the small porch, noticing lights inside.

Gathering my thoughts, I ring the doorbell and listen to the short chime inside.

A pause, then I hear clicking footsteps on the other side of the door.

"Who is it?"

"David Wallace," I reply.

Another pause, then, "What do you want?"

"I need a moment of your time."

"Go away."

"There's something I must show you."

"There's nothing I want to see. Please leave now and never come back."

Staring at the dark door, I say the one thing I hope will get him to talk to me. "I have proof that Bernard Wilson is alive."

Slowly, the door inches open, and I stare at Sebastian Serrato's long and narrow face. He glares back at me with dark eyes behind rimless glasses. His brown hair and closely-trimmed goatee are now streaked with white and more wrinkles crease his face. Otherwise, he seems to have aged better than Beckett. Maybe it's the academia life.

"Dear Lord, man," he says, "what in the world are you doing here in the middle of the night?"

"I need to speak with you about my trial."

"David…that was a long time ago. What are you doing digging up the past?"

"Listen, Sebastian," I say, staring into the eyes of someone who once swore to send me to death row. "I'm really sorry to bother you so late, but something has happened in the past twenty-four hours that's forcing me to look back at the case."

He studies me for a moment before peering up and down the street. "What?"

I take a couple of minutes to recite an abridged version of what happened in San Francisco, at Heather's place, my chats with Beckett, and then show him the photo Margaret stole.

He grips it tightly while breathing deeply. "Jesus, the condos…"

"Precisely," I say. "Now turn it over."

He does, reading Kate's note.

"It's the same handwriting from the other two notes, Sebastian. This woman thinks you can be of help. How?"

"Go away, David," he says, handing the picture back to me. "Go away and forget you ever saw this."

"I can't do that. I need to know what really happened."

"You should care more about what's *going* to happen if you don't drop this. Now please go away before someone sees us. I'm not supposed to be talking to you."

"Has someone threatened you?"

"Does Ryan know you're talking to me?"

"Not yet. But what's that got to do with—"

"I can't help you," he interrupts. "Now, I need you to please go before—"

I hear a buzzing sound by my left ear, like an angered hornet, just as my world turns red while Serrato grabs his neck and tries to scream.

I stagger back in shock.

His eyes bulging behind glasses sprayed with blood, his mouth wide open, foam and blood exploding through it, Serrato drops to his knees before collapsing on the lawn.

"David!" Margaret screams as a figure emerges from the shrubs next door and fires repeatedly at a vehicle with its lights off accelerating away in the night. In an instant I spot the long muzzle of a rifle vanishing inside the car's rear window as tires spin furiously, burning rubber while speeding away.

What the fuck?

I drop on the lawn while watching Margaret also duck behind our van as the mystery man races down the street, firing round after round at the departing vehicle.

In an instant, as the shadowy figure rushes beneath a street light, I spot his ash-blond hair, his pale skin reflecting the gray light.

"Wait!" I shout at the mystery albino man. "Don't leave! Please!"

But he's gone just as sudden as he'd appeared.

"David!" Margaret screams again.

"Sebastian's been shot! Dial 911!" I scream as I put a hand behind Serrato's head, his dying eyes finding mine in the night.

"Who did this, Sebastian? Who shot you? Help me find them!"

Crimson froth oozes from his mouth and nose while blood pulses from the side of his neck. He is choking on his own blood. Margaret rushes over with her cell phone glued to her ear while shouting the address.

A figure dashes away from the van. For a moment I think Kate's friend is back, but then I see the pink robe. It's Kathryn, who obviously doesn't want any part of this.

I try to apply pressure to the wound as Serrato glares at me.

"New Orleans…Preston…smuggle…" he hisses as he coughs more blood, and his eyes roll to the back of his head.

"What does that mean?" I ask at the mention of Bernard Wilson's son, Preston, who now runs Premier Imports. "What happened in New Orleans with Preston, Sebastian? What are they smuggling?"

He coughs again, spraying blood and foam on my face as he goes into convulsions while Margaret continues to speak with the 911 operator.

"Stay with me, Sebastian! Stay with—"

"He's gone, David," Margaret says, placing a hand on my shoulder while kneeling on the grass next to me, retrieving the bloodstained picture of Gus and Bernard from the lawn.

"He's gone."

CHAPTER 10

The first vehicle to approach the duplex is a sedan topped by a small blue and red flashing light above the driver's window. The 911 operator informs Margaret that it is a detective's vehicle who happened to be nearby.

Just under five minutes have elapsed since Serrato took his terminal breath, and I used the time to gather my thoughts and also to phone Ryan but it went straight to voicemail. I urged him to call me ASAP, as I'm getting the feeling APD isn't going to treat me gently.

The sedan cruises towards us, its headlights cutting through the darkness, stopping a dozen feet from our van's front bumper, where I'm sitting next to Margaret with a towel wiping my face while she continues to speak with the 911 operator.

The front passenger door swings open, and Beckett Mar's massive head looms out of the vehicle like a rising full moon. He holds his badge high in the air.

"What the hell is going on, David?" he asks as he steps away from his vehicle. Claudia also gets out but remains by the sedan.

He approaches us slowly as an ambulance and two police cruisers reach our street, alarms blaring.

"What happened here?" he asks, kneeling by me, his beady eyes a foot from mine. Flashing red and blue lights stain the street. Neighbors finally get the courage to venture out of their homes. Uniformed officers unroll yellow police tape to keep the growing number of onlookers from contaminating the crime scene.

I lower the hand towel, which is smeared with blood.

"Are you all right?" he asks before I can reply.

"Not my blood," I say as Margaret thanks the operator and hangs up.

Beckett motions Claudia and her handy little notepad over to take my statement, which I can provide in less than a minute.

A CSI van pulls up and three technicians hauling silver cases duck under the police tape and approach the victim, snapping pictures all the while.

As the stroboscopic flashes from the forensics team gleam like lightning, momentarily washing the emergency lights, I decide to disclose everything to Beckett except for the picture and the multiple sightings of her albino friend. Margaret had already cleverly hid the picture in one of the sandwich boxes.

"So," Beckett says, "after I last saw you, you did your rounds for a couple of hours, distributed meals to the homeless, and then decided to come by and shoot Sebastian Serrato? Why did you wait so long to kill him?"

"Excuse me?"

"You have to admit that you have plenty of motive to do so."

"Wait a mome—" Margaret starts.

Beckett snaps his fingers in front of her face. "Hush, little lady. My patience is wearing thin with you."

Margaret settles back against the grill of the van.

"You already have my official statement of what happened," I reply. "If you wish to charge me with his death, go right ahead, but it's not going to help you find the real killer or solve the case from seven years ago."

He studies my face just as he did back at Heather's old place, before saying, "What do you think Serrato meant when he told you," he pauses to look at Claudia's note pad and adds, "that you should care more about what's going to happen to you if you don't drop this? And that you should go away before someone saw you speaking to him?"

"I'm not really sure."

"Take a guess. Amuse me."

I was going to try to stay clear of any sort of guesswork, but Serrato bleeding out all over me certainly put me in a slightly more cooperative frame of mind.

"Look," I start, "something very strange happened seven years ago. One moment I was going to fry for a murder I didn't commit and the next I'm exonerated. Someone decided to close the case fast, and they apparently did. Now some mystery woman is trying to pry it open by feeding me these fucking notes and manipulating me into doing her dirty work and also letting me take all of the risk. That bullet could have easily hit me…or, hell, even been meant for me."

"I'm still waiting for you to tell me something I don't already know."

"All right. Serrato's final words—'New Orleans, Preston, and Smuggle'—they ring a bell with me…at least the first two."

"Explain."

I look away for a moment before replying, "Okay. You probably remember that Mercer, Martinez & Salazar had substantial consulting contracts with Premier Imports, which was run by Bernard Wilson and his only son from his first marriage, Preston, and that I was the senior consultant for general and administrative processes, or as we called it back then, G&A?"

Beckett nods while Claudia jots down the essentials.

"All right. Just before you arrested me seven years ago, I was in the middle of mapping the business processes between Premier's Austin headquarters and their largest satellite office in Latin America, located in Monterrey, Mexico. In fact, the company celebration we were having on Sixth Street the Friday I slept with Heather marked the completion of a project where we identified improvements in the transportation process of goods between Austin and Monterrey. With me so far?"

He nods again.

"That Friday we had an executive readout of the project but unfortunately Bernard was in New Orleans on some business trip related to his banking activities there, so Preston attended in his place. I presented our proposal to increase operating margins by as much as four percent, and since this particular area of Premier's operation averaged a revenue close to a half billion dollars, that four percent translated into twenty million dollars that dropped straight to Premier's bottom line. The next steps were to perform an analysis of the interfaces between Premier Imports' operation and its wholly-owned subsidiary, the International Bank of Texas, which basically paid for the costs of transportation of goods, handling fees, import-export taxes, etc. I strongly suggested to Preston extending the process improvements to connect with Premier's operations in

New Orleans, where Bernard had acquired interests in the local casinos at bargain prices during the post-Hurricane Katrina months. Preston loved everything and gave us the green light to proceed while tripling the MM&S retainer. Gustavo was ecstatic when I called him shortly after the meeting and indicated he would kick off the process to make me a partner."

"So you had reason to celebrate that Friday night," Beckett comments.

I nod. "Little did I know I was celebrating my demise."

He grunts while lighting up a cigarette. "So you think Serrato was trying to tell you that your consulting project was about to expose you to the ugly side of Premier Imports' business in New Orleans? Perhaps something connected with the casinos and a smuggling operation?"

I nod again while frowning and staring at the burning end of his smoke, then add, "But there was something else that bothered me that Friday night."

"What's that?"

"Heather, who had just returned from New Orleans after accompanying Bernard on his business trip, decided to join us and got quite drunk, which was uncharacteristic of her. In fact, I still remember how somber she had been all evening, which made me wonder just what had happened in New Orleans that week that pushed her to drink like that."

"You must have been close to her in order to notice such mood change," he says, hoping I would open up on my relationship with Heather since the case was thrown out of court before the prosecution could dive into such details.

"Yes," I reply. "I had gotten to know Heather in my initial months consulting at Premier, where she was in charge of the building's interior design. She was beautiful, lonely, and had an underlying fragility that naturally drew men to her. Bernard Wilson's priorities, however, had been on making money, and he paid no attention to her. But I did. I listened to her stories about growing up poor in New Orleans. She told me how she financed her bachelor's degree in interior design from Tulane University through the proceeds from dozens of beauty pageants and modeling."

"Short story is that you were in a loveless marriage, on the brink of a divorce, and had fallen for the young wife of your firm's best client."

I look away and painfully remember how Evelyn and I had drifted apart. After rubbing my damned patch, I regard him through the coiling smoke and mumble, "Yes."

"All right, David. Let's see what the CSI team finds out when they go through the crime scene. I won't charge you if they support your story," Beckett says, standing in front of the vehicle with his arms crossed, the headlights behind him turning him into a silhouette.

Margaret and I slowly get up, and I'm about to thank him when he adds, "But I think you might want to come with us."

"Come where?" I ask.

"It won't take long," says Beckett.

"I don't know where it-won't-take-long is."

"We've found something we think you may want to see," he replies, using the cigarette as a pointing device.

"What's that?" Margaret decides to chime in as Claudia puts away her notepad.

Beckett frowns at her but answers anyway. "It's best that you see it."

Beckett's doing the cop thing again.

Margaret takes my hand and says, "You've already told this man enough for one night. Not another word until you consult with—"

"Of course," Beckett interrupts, taking a final drag and throwing the butt by his feet before crushing it with the toe of his shiny black shoe. "Get your lawyer if you wish."

I lower my brows at the comment. "Do I need one?"

He shrugs. "Only if you're guilty."

"Guilty of what?" Margaret intercedes on my behalf. "You've just told him that you believe his story about—"

"This isn't about Serrato, Miss Black."

"Am I a suspect for something else then?" I ask.

He shrugs again. "That also depends."

"Depends on what?"

"On what you say and do when we show you what we need to show you."

"Are you charging him with anything at this time?" Margaret asks.

Beckett shakes his head.

"Then please leave us alone or we'll file charges against your department for harassment of two volunteer workers doing a humanitarian service for the city of Austin."

Beckett grins while nodding. "Pretty good, Miss Black. Looks like Mister Horowitz has been teaching paralegal classes at the shelter."

"Then you should know this is definitely starting to border on harassment," she replies. "Either charge him with something or leave us alone."

"Sure," Beckett says, amusement glinting in his narrowed gaze. "But I figured I was doing you a favor."

I feel my headache returning. "What do you mean?"

"We found Kate Larson," he says.

I'm at a loss for words.

"That's the homicide we responded to this afternoon, Mr. Wallace," adds Claudia. "We're holding her at the morgue."

I inhale deeply and feel blood draining from my head. I tighten the grip on Margaret's hand to steady myself.

"Yep," says Beckett, his grin making his face look even wider. "I thought you would be interested in seeing what we found on her during her autopsy an hour ago."

"What…did you find?" I hear myself ask even though at the moment I'm having an out-of-body experience.

"Sorry, pal," Beckett says, winking. "You either come with us to the morgue, or…have a nice evening." He turns to leave, and so does Claudia.

I'm trying to grasp the magnitude of what they've just told me. Kate Larson is dead. They're holding the body at the Travis County Medical Examiner Office, which moved recently from its long-time location on Sabine Street in downtown Austin. And apparently, Kate has got something on her that they want me to see—something every ounce of sanity left in me is urging me to see.

"Wait," I say as they're about to get in their vehicle, before turning to Margaret. "Have Ryan meet me at the morgue."

CHAPTER 11

Every large city has at least one morgue, and that morgue is operated by the Office of the Medical Examiner. In Austin, it is located on 7723 Springdale Road, near the intersection of Highways 183 and 290.

The Travis County Medical Examiner Office, as its official name implies, services not just the city of Austin but all of the smaller satellite cities that fall inside of Travis County. As director of HCH, I have had the unenviable task of coming down to this uplifting place at least a half dozen times a year to identify the bodies of former HCH residents who'd left for one reason or another and were found dead with no next-of-kin but with something on them connecting them to us.

We come north on Springdale Road and turn into the parking lot of the TCMEO's new 55,000 square-foot facility, certainly an upgrade from its old location, which is now a sobriety center. There, I stare at a new concrete marker outside a glass and steel building displaying under gray lights the seal of Travis County above the words,

TRAVIS COUNTY MEDICAL EXAMINER OFFICE

We park in front, and I follow them up the steps to the lobby, where two APD uniformed officers behind a counter look up from a small flat screen that's playing some ball game I can't recognize.

"Evening, fellows," Beckett says, flashing his badge. Claudia does the same.

The officers eye them, then me, and return to their game after one of them presses a button on their console and the magnetic locks on the doors to our right disengage.

We proceed in silence towards the morgue, which is located in the rear. It consists of enough refrigerating units to accommodate up to 100 bodies.

But we don't go into the actual morgue. We step inside one of the observation rooms adjacent to the morgue, where a large glass partition separates a small area of the morgue sectioned off with privacy curtains to keep outsiders from seeing anything but the body of their loved ones.

Beckett, who stands to my immediate right while Claudia remains a respectful distance to my left, has apparently arranged to have the body of Kate Larson carefully draped from head to toe on a medical cart already parked in front of the glass partition. But he didn't bother to request the privacy curtains, allowing me to see the large morgue, a rectangular room lined with body coolers. A technician stands stoically next to the cart ready to do the honors. The only part of the body I can see is her right toe, where a green tag is attached with a plain silver wire.

I stare at it wondering if I recognize it, though I probably wouldn't be able to identify my own toe.

"According to the medical examiner," Beckett starts in his police voice, "cause of death was strangulation after forced sexual intercourse. Her blood-alcohol level was well above the legal limit. Time of death is estimated at four in the afternoon, give or take thirty minutes. She was found naked, tied to the bed in a hotel room by the airport. There wasn't much more in the room except for her clothes, two empty wine bottles, and a pair of half-full wine glasses."

I swallow hard, the word strangulation flashing in my mind. She was found just like Heather: drunk, naked, tied to the bed, and strangulated after having sex.

Beckett continues. "She has a record, David, from California and Louisiana. Prostitution. That's all we know for the time being but our CSI team is still working the hotel room and she's headed back to the medical examiner's table for more analysis. We're also sharing all information pertinent to this case with Detective Marlene Quinn from the SFPD since her prints identified her as Kate Larson, currently a registered resident of San Francisco, California."

The word 'prostitute' makes me think of Ryan and Margaret, who mentioned that possibility.

Searching for the strength to go through with this while staring at the blanket covering the body of someone who opened the doors to my gloomy past, I give Beckett the nod.

He in turn nods to the technician, who pulls the cover from her face.

My legs turn to jelly when I see her.

Beckett catches me on my way down, running an arm around my back to steady me, allowing me to see a face I no longer wish to see.

"Easy there, pal," he says.

Claudia moves closer and also helps me stand.

In all my years performing body IDs, the cops never get it wrong. They never do. If they tell you your mother is dead and ask you to come to the morgue to perform an ID, you can pretty much bet your ass that it'll be the body of your mother that gets unveiled.

But not tonight.

For the second time in the past twenty-four hours, I'm led to believe that the Kate Larson I met at the bar was killed, and for the second time someone else is lying under the blanket.

She isn't the Kate Larson I met in San Francisco.

She isn't the woman who has passed me all of those strange messages; the woman who I unknowingly rescued at the painful price of a head butt.

"Is this her?" asked Beckett.

I muster the power to slowly shake my head. Then, as blood floods back into my head, I add, "She isn't the person I met last night."

"But her fingerprints--"

"I don't care. That's not whom I met at the bar."

Strength returns to my legs, and I'm able to stand on my own again. Beckett and Claudia sense it and slowly let go of me.

I stare at her hard and lined face, at the wrinkles around her eyes, at the long and blonde curly hair, at her thin but flabby arms. I remember the skin of her arms swinging along with her hair as she deposited four cold beers down the back of that lady conventioneer, just as I remember her walking away from me this morning at the airport.

And of all voices colliding in my confused mind, I hear Raul's, the bartender.

Temp Waitress. We get our regular one back tomorrow.

"David? Who is she?"

"I…I'm not really sure."

"What does that mean?"

"It means I don't know. But I *do* know she's *not* the Kate Larson I met last night."

"But your reaction when you saw her," Claudia interjects. "You've seen her before."

As I'm about to reply, the doors to the identification room burst open. It's Ryan Horowitz, briefcase in hand, followed by Margaret.

"Not another word, David! Not another fucking word!" Then he turns to Beckett and Claudia. "And you two. What the hell do you think you're doing?"

Completely unmoved by his outburst, Beckett simply shrugs. "We're just talking, Counselor. He came here of his own free will."

Ryan looks at me. "Is this true, David?"

I nod.

He looks back at Beckett. "Are you charging him with anything?"

"Nope," Beckett replies.

"Then why is he here?"

I hate being referenced in the third person, so I interject, "I came here, Ryan, because he told me they had found Kate Larson…dead."

Ryan stops, visibly rattled by what I've just said. Blinking, he rushes past us to take a look at the body. Then, inhaling deeply, and quickly regaining his composure, he says, "That's…that's the woman who gave you the—"

"It's not her," I reply with more calm than I feel. "She's the waitress at the same bar last night."

"Who?" asks Beckett.

"The waitress at the bar," I repeat. "Where Kate and I met. She was waiting tables." I then look at Ryan and add, "They claim she's a prostitute."

Ryan raises his right eyebrow at me, flashing an *I told you so.*

Beckett and Claudia look at each other, apparently not knowing what to make of the fact that she was the waitress, which doesn't surprise me because I don't know what in the world to make of it either. Though I seem to remember Kate had looked in the direction of the waitress right after receiving the upsetting phone call. And of course, there was also the comment made by the bartender, Raul, about her being a temporary worker. And let's not forget that I'm pretty sure I saw her this morning at the airport, and that she fits the description of the woman who dropped the note at our front desk earlier today.

But I don't say anything else. I think Ryan is right. I need to do some thinking.

"Well," Beckett says, "you may not know <u>this</u> Kate Larson, but she definitely had stuff from you."

"And on you," adds Claudia with a confusing devilish grin.

"I...don't understand."

"She was wearing this," Beckett says, producing an evidence bag housing a collection of turquoise and silver bracelets...plus a Hill Country Haven green bracelet.

And it is at this moment that my legs start to quiver again when reading the orange words, ***BE AFRAID***, through the clear plastic. My eyes go back and forth from her body to this very personal warning which I'm guessing was sent by whoever is behind the conspiracy I am being manipulated to investigate.

BE AFRAID.

BE AFRAID.
BE AFRAID.

"Detective Quinn reported that nothing was stolen from you last night," Beckett states, "except for a Hill Country Haven bracelet. Is this it?"

"Looks like it," I say with difficulty while trying to figure out how she ended up wearing it. My initial thought is that the killer put it on her to send me a warning to back off. But if so, how did he get it? Did the pimp steal it before the Kate Larson I met was rescued?

My headache is getting out of control once again as each discovery only results in more questions than answers.

"So you're saying this is yours?"

"I'm saying," I reply, my hand pressed hard against my patch as I try to squeeze out every drop of chemical relief, "that it looks like the one I lost last night after I was attacked."

Beckett accepts the answer and hands the evidence to Claudia, who gives him a manila envelope.

"There's something else we wanted to share with you tonight, David," he says, pulling out a glossy black and white photo from the envelope and handing it to me. "We found this, and a dozen others like it, under the mattress in her hotel room. That was quite the night you had back then."

"Nice butt, Mr. Wallace," adds Claudia without the slightest hint of amusement in her voice or on her face. "You fuck like a king."

"I think David must have read the Kama Sutra," says Beckett.

"Maybe even contributed a chapter or two," Claudia adds.

"That's quite the hammer, pal," Beckett jokes, shaking his head.

Margaret flashes me a wide-eyed stare while her lower lip drops a bit. Ryan just rolls his eyes and looks away.

I ignore them all while staring at the image in my hands, immediately knowing exactly when it was taken seven years ago.

It is a photo of me with my pants down to my ankles pinning Heather Wilson against the wall in the foyer of her former home in Tarrytown. Her pale legs are wrapped around my waist as I'm entering her. Heather's hands are gripping my shoulders, her mouth wide open, eyes closed.

And written across the bottom with a permanent marker in the now-familiar handwriting of the still-at-large Kate Larson read the words,

WE MUST AVENGE HER, DAVID.
HELP ME AVENGE MY FRIEND.

CHAPTER 12

"Is it possible she was planning to blackmail you?" Ryan offers.

Margaret, Ryan, and I are sitting at a table in the rear of the Star Bar, a watering hole on Sixth Street, having a much-needed drink.

And make that two for me.

Although I wasn't charged with anything for either Sebastian Serrato or Kate Larson, Beckett requested that I remain in town while they let the CSI team do its handiwork on the victims and the crime scenes. Another CSI team had been deployed to dust the home of Gustavo Salazar. Beckett already knew he owned the house and shared that with me after shocking me with the bracelet and picture as his way to soften me up to see if I would tell him anything else. I pretended I knew nothing else, and Ryan requested that I be allowed to go home, having seen enough excitement in twenty-four hours.

"I don't see how or why," I reply, downing my second Mexican martini and flagging down the waitress for a third one as my craving for a cigarette skyrockets even after placing a fresh patch on my right shoulder. "I mean, everybody knew I slept with Heather, including Evelyn, Bernard, Gustavo, Sebastian, Beckett—and the entire nation for that matter. Who was she going to show the photos to? And why? What did she have to gain by doing so?"

I shake my head and stare at the picture of Gustavo and Bernard, which Margaret already wiped clean of Serrato's blood.

"He's got a point, Ryan," says Margaret, sitting next to me while holding a pack of cigarettes she can't smoke inside the bar. Ryan regards her from across the table, frowns, stares at his own pack of cigarettes, and settles for a consolation sip from his Shiner Bock. "Lover boy here doing Missus Wilson is old news."

Ryan regards us with quiet confidence and says, "David, you are now an established member of this community. Even the mayor knows you. Whether you like it or not, you've done a great thing in recent history. People have really forgotten about what took place back then. Those pictures would have harmed you."

"How?"

Now he gives me the older-brother sigh, his voice turning a bit condescending. "HCH depends heavily on contributions, on donations. Even our electric bill's a donation from the Central Texas Electric Co-op, as is our water, our sewage service, and our garbage pick-up. Then we have the furniture stores giving us their old inventory, the shoe stores donating last year's models, as well as dozens of other retailers. And then there's the long line of professionals donating their time, from general practitioners, gynecologists, and dentists, to therapists and psychiatrists. And they do it because they believe in HCH, and just as important, they believe in and respect its founders, especially you.

Whether you like it or not, the fragility of your reputation ranks up there with people in public office. Those photos would have hurt your standing in the community and it would have adversely affected HCH's operations."

"All right, all right," I say, conceding. "But if we assume for a moment that blackmailing wasn't her intent, why would she have them, and why the inscription?"

"To help you remember," Ryan says. "In case you've forgotten or in case some of the warnings—like Serrato's assassination and the bracelet—start to discourage you from continuing to shake the trees and see what falls out."

"What do you make of the guy who fired at the departing vehicle?" Margaret and I told Ryan that after we left the morgue, and how I thought I also saw him by the Wilson's residence. "He seems to be appearing in multiple places and based on his timing he probably was the one who planted the photo in Gustavo's foyer."

Ryan slowly shakes his head. "Sounds like this Kate Larson has a team working with her."

I continue to stare at the picture while feeling like that lost teenage girl in the alley stuck between the forces of good and evil. I finally toss it his way and ask, "Could you have your guy make sure it isn't doctored?"

He nods and pockets it, before adding, "I also have a new surprise to throw into this: the license plate of the car following you from the airport this afternoon."

I had completely forgotten about that, and the look in his eyes makes me lean forward, planting both forearms on the table. "What?"

"According to the DPS, that license plate is blocked."

"What does that mean?" asks Margaret as I frown and look away.

"It means that the vehicle in question is involved in something critical enough either at the state or federal level that requires it to be blocked in the database."

"Someone high up doesn't want us to know who was following us this morning," I add.

We sit in silence for a moment, considering just what sort of force I'm going up against.

"One thing I find strange is that you're still alive," says Margaret.

I tilt my head. "Killing me would certainly take the wind out of this investigation. And the killer could have easily done that this evening. But instead only Sebastian was killed to keep me from finding out what he knew. Why?"

"From where I'm sitting," says Ryan while toying with his pack of cigarettes, "I would say that someone's not only manipulating you into doing their detective work for them, feeding you clues so that you probe and also take the heat, but they're also protecting you from getting killed to keep you investigating."

"How? And Why?"

"I don't know." Ryan returns the shrug before drumming a finger on his smokes.

"Irrespective of *how* or *why*, the people manipulating you know you will continue to probe because you simply have to know what happened," adds Margaret, unconsciously toying with her own pack.

These two need to step outside, get their fix, and stop screwing with their cigarettes or I'm going to start twitching.

"So in essence they're taking advantage of my emotional baggage and are manipulating me."

"In the end, these things are always about money," says Ryan. "Follow the money and you get to the core of the matter."

"And money means business," I say, thinking of Serrato's warning again, of the potential smuggling of something involving Preston Wilson, Bernard's son, and their operation in New Orleans. "Following Bernard's alleged death, Preston took over Premier Imports and according to Serrato he could be involved in the smuggling of something connected to his operation in New Orleans."

I sip my martini while remembering Preston, the Harvard Business School wizard who used to shadow Bernard to all of his meetings as the elder executive groomed his only son to run the billion-dollar empire. Preston was smart all right, certainly living up to his Harvard MBA reputation. But he also had his old man's mean streak, the ruthlessness that combined his nose for business with an obsession for driving competitors into bankruptcy.

During my time dealing with Premier Imports, I saw Bernard, and later Preston, emasculate vice-presidents when they made mistakes. I saw them pound employees into the ground to increase output. And perhaps that's why Bernard and Preston always liked me, as my job was to seek innovative ways to increase efficiency, to improve margins, to lower cost, to get their employee base to do far more with far less.

I make a mental note to dig up the details from my last consulting job at Premier, which still reside in a back-up memory stick that we kept as part of a defense I never quite needed due to my unexpected acquittal.

"What do you remember from your New Orleans assignment while at Gardner and Gardner? Anything that jogs your memory given Serrato's final words?" I ask Ryan.

He considers that for a moment and says, "No. All I remember from those days was a lot of boring legalities and endless meetings between the International Bank of Texas and the Louisiana government to get the casinos operational in the wake of Katrina so Bernard and Preston could capitalize on their investment. Serrato's final words are very interesting, but they don't jog anything. Everything I handled for Premier via my old law firm was one hundred percent legit. No smuggling or funny business. Only tons and tons of legal work, for which Gardner and Gardner was paying me a small fortune, especially because I had to spend almost a full year in New Orleans dealing with state and local officials and bankers to get the casinos operational."

I continue drinking while staring at Ryan's very tired face, remembering how my downfall forced him to quit his lucrative job. At the time, Ryan had been dating some local girl I never met named Sheila in New Orleans during his year-long assignment, but she passed away unexpectedly. Although he doesn't speak about her, I know Ryan cared greatly for her because he was visibly upset for a long time, and he never dated again. In a strange way, our love-lost tragedies—albeit mine was self-inflicted—only help strengthen our brother-like relationship.

By the time I finish my third martini, I can barely keep my eyes open, so we walk out of the bar and into a refreshing evening breeze.

Ryan and Margaret light up in unison the moment they step away from the premises. I stand there barely awake as they get their fixes before we get into Ryan's car and drive to my apartment located across the street from the shelter.

Margaret heads to her room at HCH and Ryan drives off to his home a mile away. I stagger down the walkway leading to the outside steps of the apartment complex I have called home since founding the shelter. I've often thought about living at the shelter but that would be in violation of one of our cardinal rules. The moment the doors close for the evening, HCH is 100% female.

I muster the strength to make it up the stairs, my mind nearly gone, my eyes half closed. I reach the second floor landing and give our well-illuminated margarita-green and orange sign across the street a passing glance. The words BE NOT AFRAID shine like a beacon against the dark sky.

I fumble with my keys, find the right one, and insert it in the keyhole of my own haven, the place I use to retreat from a life that sometimes feels like someone else's.

I unlock the door, flip the foyer light, and freeze.

The place is in shambles, from my old vinyl collection littering the living floor, broken picture frames, and books piled by fallen shelves, to the upturned sofas and end tables.

BE NOT AFRAID.

Those words suddenly echo in my mind as I calmly close the door and wade my way to the kitchen, where I see more of the same: pots, dishes, and broken glasses everywhere, though for reasons that escape me the bastards left my wine bar lining the left side of the kitchen alone. The contents of my well-organized pantry form a pile next to the stove. In the bedroom I find the mattress off to the right and the box spring on its side. There is a knee-high river of clothes flowing out of the closet, and from the looks of it the bathroom is also in serious disarray.

But my sleep-deprived, physically-bruised, and chemically-altered mind has stopped caring. I need to sleep, and I need to do it now. My eyelids are shutting down for the night. My legs are giving out from under me. My tunneling vision focuses on the mattress, still right side up, with the pillows still on top.

While popping a Vicodin to make sure I will be out for the count, I make a beeline for the pillow-top and collapse face up.

My eyes stare at the slow-moving ceiling fan.

I focus on the blades, follow their circular motion as my mind also starts to spin, pulling me away from the mystery messages, from the killings, from the reality that the past isn't as it has seemed all these years—from the faces of people I had hoped never to see again. The whirling motion also draws me away from the reality that some motherfucker just tore through my personal space either searching for something or just to issue another warning.

In spite of it all, the remote possibility of redemption for what I did—or thought I did—seven years ago, worms itself through my wired senses, managing to hold back the demons.

For the first time in a very long, long time, I am not afraid, even while immersed in the chaos of my apartment, and I peacefully drift into deep sleep.

CHAPTER 13

Something stabbing me in the ribs awakens me.

I open my eyes but the light pierces deep into my mind, like a splinter ripping through my brain.

I use my hands as shields while slowly coming around and—

The stabbing returns and I jerk away from it while mumbling something I don't even recognize.

"Rise and shine, Boss!" a deep male voice pounds my eardrums. The acoustic energy traverses my mind, colliding somewhere in the middle of my aching brain with the beams of light raking my optic nerves.

"Damn," I mumble, lacking enough hands to cover my eyes and my ears, finally opting to shield the latter while slowly squinting.

My room is bright from sunlight shafting through the windows, but the view of the ceiling fan is blocked by the massive black head of Dana Knox. Her blonde hair swinging over her implanted breasts, Dana's bright pink lips part into a huge grin nearly broken in half by the large space between her front teeth.

"Helluva party, Boss."

I slowly come out of my chemically-induced sleep feeling groggy, even cranky.

"What…time is it?" I ask.

"Almost two in the afternoon. We missed you at staff and at lunch. Ryan finally sent me over to see if you were still among the living."

With some effort I sit up and for an instant, in that weird state immediately after waking up, I'm momentarily taken aback by the mess around me, before my mind remembers.

"You live like this, Boss?" Dana asks, sitting in bed and joining me in my visual inspection of the place. "And silly me thought you were OCD being an efficiency consultant and all."

She is dressed in tight jeans, pointy red cowboy boots, and her classic two-sizes-too-small HCH T-shirt. Today her fingernails match the color of her lips.

I stare at the tattoo around her wrist and at the matching message on her T-shirt and frown. I'm certainly not afraid this morning, but I'm sure as hell getting rapidly pissed that somebody decided to turn my personal space into a dumpster.

"Somebody broke in," I say. "Found it like this."

"Oh," she says, helping me to my feet and holding my left arm to make sure I remain standing. "Want me to call the cops?"

"Not yet," I reply. "At the moment I need a shower and a latte."

She offers to run to the coffee shop down the street, and I tip-toe around stuff to get to the bathroom, where at least the soap is still in place, and I can find a clean towel.

I let the hot water hit my back for a while, keeping my eyes closed while I massage my temples with my fingertips, breathing deeply, trying to decide what my next move will be, then musing at my own foolish belief that I'm actually in control of anything.

I shut off the water and dry off while heading for my closet to search for something to wear amid the mess.

As I fish out a clean pair of underwear, blue jeans, and an HCH T-shirt, Dana walks in the room with a large coffee, catching me with my clothes in my hands. "Sorry," I mumble, covering myself.

She grins and then says, "You have nothing to be ashamed of, Boss. Let's just make that our little *big* secret."

I frown at this added invasion of my privacy, before getting dressed, taking the latte, and a bag of nicotine patches from the box in my closet. I also snag the pre-scription bottle of Vicodin out of my pants from last night as well as the two notes from the Kate Larson who keeps cheating death.

Locating a chair in the small dining room adjacent to my sacked kitchen, I sit down to have a breakfast of champions.

"Looks nutritious," offers Dana, sitting next to me while I apply a patch to each shoulder before opening the bottle of Vicodin. "All food groups represented?"

Through the intense throbbing, which seems worse than yesterday, I force a smile before downing a pill with a sip of latte.

"I heard you've been popping those like candy since you returned from San Francisco."

"And?"

"That stuff is addictive."

"And?"

"I know how hard it is later."

"From your wrestling days?"

She nods. "Before long I couldn't function without them. It took me six horrible weeks in rehab to kick the habit."

"Well, I don't intend to be on them for very long, but at the moment they're my best friend."

"Just remember what I told you."

"Let's also make this our little secret, shall we?" I say, pointing at the mess around us. "I don't want anyone to know just yet that this happened."

"Don't worry, Boss. This mess, your Vicodin habit, and...the *other* thing," she says, while staring at my groin, "are safe with me." She winks and folds her massive arms beneath her equally firm breasts. And I finally notice she has decided not to wear a bra today so her nipples point straight at me through the green fabric.

Sweet Jesus, it's way too early for this.

"But, seriously, why not call the cops?" she asks. "Someone broke into your—"

"Because," I interrupt, "I know which cops will be sent my way, and they're only going to hit me up with more questions. Today it would be nice to actually get some answers instead."

She considers that for a moment, then says, "Your place your call, Boss. You should at least tell Ryan."

"I will," I reply, sipping my coffee, closing my eyes as it warms my chest.

"What about calling the cops so you can also call your insurance company in case something's missing?" she asks.

"Well, given what has taken place in the past day and a half, I don't get the feeling this was a robbery. Besides, my flat screen and the rest of my electronics are still here," I say, pointing to the hardware luckily bolted to the wall. "They were looking for something else."

"What?"

"I don't know, Dana, and that's precisely why I'm not calling the—"

Dana's phone rings to the tune of Shania Twain's, *Man, I Feel Like a Woman.*

I try damn hard not to roll my eyes.

Dana winks again as she fishes her phone out of her back pocket. Like her lips and nails, it's also pink.

She looks at the caller ID and says, "Ryan."

I nod.

She answers, listens for a moment, looks at me as her smile fades, then says soberly, "We're on our way right now," and puts the phone away.

"What?" I ask, not certain if I want to hear the answer.

"You've got visitors."

"The cops again?"

"Nope. The FBI."

CHAPTER 14

If there is one place on Earth where I'm probably still considered persona non grata, it would be the FBI Austin Field Office.

That's the old stomping grounds of Evelyn's father, Jackson Feen, former SAC—Special Agent in Charge—of that office, where I met Evelyn shortly after MM&S was awarded a contract by the FBI to improve their administrative processes in Texas.

The Federal Bureau of Investigation.

I walk across the street and suddenly solve the mystery of the black Chrysler sedan with untraceable plates that had followed Margaret and me yesterday from the airport.

It's parked in one of the guest spots by the double doors leading to our lobby.

For a moment I try to remember the names of the agents in Jackson's staff from back in the day, and one immediately comes to mind: Assistant Special Agent in Charge (ASAC) Jessica Herrera, Jackson's second in command. I worked with her closely during my time running efficiency workshops at Jackson's office, and we got to know each other quite well.

It was Jessica who introduced me to Evelyn.

It was Jessica who helped me smooth things over with Jackson, at the time a single parent, when he learned I was seeing his only daughter.

It was Jessica who stood at our wedding as Evelyn's maid of honor.

It was Jessica who convinced Jackson to pay for that incredible honeymoon in the Caribbean.

And it was Jessica who wanted to burn me at the stake when I cheated on Evelyn, and when my actions not only led to her tragic death and to the death of my son, but also resulted in Jackson Feen leaving the FBI and dying a year later from alcohol abuse.

Dana follows me into the lobby but remains by the front desk with three other ladies chartered with guarding our premises. The first is Patricia Norton, a tall and powerful ex-Army Ranger and prison guard who caught her second husband sexually abusing her teenage daughter. Patricia shot him once in the balls and once in the head. Although the DA's office didn't prosecute, the State of Texas wasn't as benevolent in the matter and fired her without benefits. And even Uncle Sam disowned her despite the years she served in Iraq and Afghanistan before she became a prison guard.

Next to Patricia stand Janice Smith and Lucille Wesson, both hardcore lesbian bikers dressed in black leather and extensively tattooed. Smith & Wesson, as they're known at HCH, possess between them more guts than what you would find on a slaughterhouse floor. About a year ago three angered husbands crashed through our doors in an attempt to "rescue" their spouses. Smith tasered the one who looked like the ring leader, making him piss his pants and thrash on the floor like a fish out of water. Wesson grinned at the other two and reached for her own Taser. I've never seen guys run so fast.

I continue on to Ryan's office, pause a moment in front of his closed door, give it a polite double knock, and go inside.

Ryan, as I had properly guessed, is sitting down with my old FBI pal, Jessica, who immediately turns around. There is a second agent, a man, also sitting down but who remains facing Ryan.

Last time I saw Jessica in that courtroom, her glare conveyed medieval torture for what I did to her best friend and her family.

Today, she seems distressingly civilized, which makes my confused mind consider pulling the five-fire alarm.

"Hello David," she says, stretching a hand at me. "How have you been?" She is a petite Hispanic with short hair and dark-olive complexion whose diminutive size should never be confused with her ability to bring down thugs twice her weight. Jessica Herrera is as tough as they come, and she would make a great addition to our lobby security team. In classic FBI style, Jessica, as well as her mystery colleague, are both wearing dark-blue suits.

We clasp hands firmly as she says, "You're doing some good work here, David."

Now I'm really worried. A compliment is the last thing I expected from her. I'm the guy whose act of fornication resulted in the demise of the Feen clan.

"May I ask what this visit is about?" I say while staring at the back of the head of the mystery blue suit still facing Ryan.

"David," says Jessica, "this is Special Agent Max Caporini from our San Francisco office."

I look at Ryan, who slowly rolls his eyes as Agent Caporini stands up and turns to face me.

Everything around me suddenly fades away as my vision narrows onto the face staring back at me.

I breathe in deeply while taking two steps back in complete shock.

The pin-stripes and gold chain have been replaced by a dark-blue suit, a white shirt, and a dark tie hanging from a perfect knot. His hair is still combed back, his prizefighter face is still tanned though he now has a nasty cut on his left cheek. His eyes are no longer indifferent but glint in dark amusement as they land squarely on the spot in between my eyes, where he head-butted me two nights ago.

"Sorry about that, Sport," he says, stretching an open hand in my direction. "You left me no choice. I had to protect my cover. No hard feelings, huh?"

I barely hear him as my blood pressure shoots to infinity and beyond, triggering a ringing in my ears that also rockets the throbbing behind my eyes from the blow I took from this motherfucker.

My mind whirling faster than a cyclone on steroids, propelling my thoughts to the periphery of my consciousness, I try to fight back the all-too-familiar feeling of blood saturating my head, turning everything into shades of red.

I breathe deeply again and again as my full vision returns, as the ringing recedes, as I reach deep into my reserves and pull out the determination to remain standing, to not let this or any other surprise take me down again.

Logic returns to its rightful place in my bruised noodle as I stare at this man, wondering what else happened while I was sleeping.

"Agent Caporini was only doing his job, David," explains Ryan, obviously watching my hesitation to come near this guy.

Although I hear him, my mind is trying to process the myriad questions pounding me, but as I finally open my mouth, all I can think of saying is, "Did you have to hit me so fucking hard?"

Caporini exhales heavily and retracts his peace offer, saying to Jessica, "I told you he wouldn't accept it, and frankly, I don't blame the guy."

As has been the case for the past thirty-six hours, every time I think this situation can't get more bizarre, it does. And as it also has been the case since San Francisco, my level of courage has been steadily increasing as I come to terms that there is really not much anyone can take away from me that I haven't already lost. And along with courage, I am growing more suspicious of everyone around me.

I shift my stare from Ryan, to Jessica, to Max—The Butthead—Caporini while breathing deeply. I'm trying damned hard to arrest the surge of anger flooding my senses, making my head teeter and spin. I suddenly remember I'm holding a cup of steaming coffee and resist the temptation to throw it at him. Doing so would probably qualify as a federal offense. The bastard can knock me out, can inflict Vicodin-popping pain in my brain—can even make me piss my pants and get away with it. But if *I* touch a fucking thread on the fine suit of this bastard my ass goes to jail.

Instead, I slowly lift my right hand and calmly bring the lid to my lips, taking a sip, closing my eyes as I swallow.

"Does anyone want to tell me what this is all about?" I finally ask while doing another round of staring before sitting down in the middle of the three chairs facing Ryan's desk. The FBI agents flank me as they take their seats.

"Why don't you start by telling us precisely what the woman who approached you told you?"

"With all due respect to the Federal Bureau of Investigation, I believe I'm entitled to some answers, especially after taking an undeserved beating."

"And you need to start cooperating with the agency of the United States government chartered with protecting your freedom," says Caporini.

"Look, David," Jessica starts.

"Oh, I remember now. You're the agency whose motto is…what was that? Fidelity, Bravery, and Integrity?"

They just stare at me.

"Problem is," I continue, glancing in Ryan's direction while sensing the Feds burning holes in my aching temples. "At the moment it feels to me more like Flogging, Battering, and Intimidation."

Ryan leans back and smiles while crossing his arms.

"David, look," Jessica starts again. "We would like to know exactly what the woman who approached you at the bar discussed with you."

"What's her name?" I ask.

"That's classified," she replies.

"What about the Asian woman who was killed?"

"Also classified."

"Who came to Kate's rescue after you knocked me out, killed your Asian friend, and almost got you too?" I point to the inch-long bandage on his left cheek.

"Sorry, David. That's also—"

"I get it. One way street only." I look at Ryan. "Do I have to tell them anything?"

"Entirely at your discretion."

"Can I call SFPD Detective Marlene Quinn and let her know that the artist rendition of the bastard who attacked me is this character?"

Ryan shakes his head. "The FBI trumps the SFPD, and APD for that matter. Only the FBI can decide if and when to share information with local law enforcement."

"What can these two do to me if I just can't remember?"

"Nothing officially," Ryan says. "As far as I can tell, you—or HCH—have not been involved in any crimes or violations of federal law, including but not limited to terrorist-related activities, cyber-based attacks, public corruption, organized crime, white-collar crime, significantly violent crimes, drugs, conspiracies, mail fraud, sexual exploitation of minors, bank robbery, or illegal gambling. Did I leave anything out?" he asks.

Jessica and Butthead don't reply.

"In layman's terms," Ryan continues at their silence, "you haven't done anything that can remotely qualify as a federal offense, so you can end this conversation at any moment."

"And unofficially?" I ask.

He shrugs. "I guess they can try to throw some made-up charge but it won't stick. You haven't done anything wrong. If anything, you were wrongly attacked by an undercover officer and you've already cooperated with the SFPD in the matter."

"Why are you here, Jessica?" I ask. "And why were you following me yesterday morning when I got into Austin?"

"Try not to release information in the process of asking a question," Ryan says.

I frown.

"We're in the middle of a long investigation," Jessica says, crossing her shapely legs and resting her hands on her dark-blue knee-length skirt. "It's imperative that we locate the woman who approached you in San Francisco."

"Why?"

"I'm afraid we can't release that information without compromising the case," Caporini replies.

"Why?"

"Because…it can compromise national security."

"And why's that?" I probe.

"David, this isn't one of your efficiency workshops where you get to ask questions about our operations," Jessica interrupts before Caporini can answer. "This is a serious federal investigation and you're bordering on obstruction of justice."

Jessica apparently remembers how I approach a problem in my consulting business by asking multiple questions to reach the root cause of an issue before brainstorming solutions. Unfortunately, her warning pales in comparison to my current state of mind. Ignoring her, I ask, "How did the body of the Asian woman disappear from SFPD custody?"

"David…neither of us can answer that," she replies.

"Then I guess we have nothing to talk about."

"Look, Sport," Caporini says, "I'm taking a huge risk by coming here. I've been undercover for the past two years, during which time I may have seen my wife for maybe two weeks. We were on the cusp of a major break in my investigation when…the woman you met at the bar went missing three months ago, and she resurfaced two nights ago to meet with you. She's the best link we have to cracking this case, and the FBI needs your assistance to locate her. Do you really want to get on the Bureau's bad side?"

"I've been there." I glance at Jessica. "It ain't so bad."

"David," Jessica adds, "we just need to know if there's anything she might have told you that Agent Caporini could use to find her. He flew in last night from San Francisco and is heading back this afternoon to continue his investigation."

I shrug and say, "What does any of this have to do with—"

"Damn it, man!" Butthead explodes, his nose turning red. "Don't you get it? We're talking about a *federal investigation*. And by the way, I could make a case that you interfered with the investigation back in San Francisco and again now by withholding relatable information."

"*Relatable*," I say. "That's a big word there...Sport."

"Here's a big phrase for you," he replies. "Criminal indictment for obstruction of justice."

"Are you making an official charge, Agent Caporini?" Ryan asks.

"No," Butthead says sitting back. "I'm just bonding with a civilian."

"Well, you suck at it," I say.

"Please be reasonable, David," Jessica pleads. "All we want to know is what she told you."

"I have a question," I say to her. "Did you guys flip a coin to decide who would play bad cop or is this guy always the asshole?"

"Watch it, Sport," Butthead says, leaning forward. "You have no idea the kind of trouble you could be in."

"Are you threatening my client, Agent Caporini?" Ryan asks.

The Fed sinks back in his chair and slowly shakes his head.

I regard him for a moment as he looks away in obvious exasperation. From this angle, with those sagging cheeks and tiny mouth he really looks like an ass with ears under his caricature-like combed hair.

A butthead indeed.

Before I know it, I manage a grin.

"What Agent Caporini is trying to tell you," says Jessica, briefly narrowing her gaze at my half smile while playing her role, "is that you're now on the radar screen of the same forces the Bureau is combating."

"Thank you," Butthead whispers while still looking away from me.

I stare back, certainly not liking where this is headed.

"Allow me to translate," says Butthead, looking me in the eye again. "You're this close from some bastard pumping a couple of slugs into your sorry ass."

"Doesn't sound as bad as some butthead head-butting me," I say.

Ryan rubs his scarred chin while watching this very carefully, like a litigator waiting for the right moment to object for the benefit of his client.

"Do you think this is funny?" Butthead shouts, his face inches away.

The last time he was this close I ended up in the hospital.

"Back away from my client, Agent Caporini!" Ryan snaps, an index finger pointed directly at the Mafiosi-lookalike. "Or this little chitchat is over."

Butthead runs a finger over his new scar and complies while winking at me.

"David, listen very carefully," Jessica takes over. "The Bureau believes you're at high risk of becoming a target. This is the main reason why my San Francisco colleague is here. These people are very dangerous. They killed his partner two nights ago at the hotel and have now also assassinated a former state prosecutor. You're lucky to have survived this long."

I guess that means the dead Asian was also undercover FBI, which also explains her body vanishing to keep SFPD from meddling with their top-secret investigation.

But the warning about me being a target, coming from the mouth of the FBI, and in particular Agent Jessica Herrera, does carry some weight. For a moment I think of Sebastian and the dead waitress, of the mess some lowlife has made of my apartment, and I'm wondering if that's just the start of better things to come.

My little voice, however, tells me to keep my apartment to myself, as well as the notes I got from Kate and the cameo appearances of her handy albino associate. If I didn't share them with Beckett and his stoic partner, I'm sure as hell not going to share them with the government agency who hates my guts for what I did to one of their own. At least with SFPD and APD I know I didn't kill any cops—or indirectly assist in their deaths. Jackson Feen, on the other hand, was admired and respected by everyone in the Bureau, from the smallest satellite office to its headquarters in Washington, D.C.

"You're still not helping me connect the dots," I reply. "What does any of this have to do with me? I'm just the director of a shelter for—"

"Is he really that stupid?" Butthead asks Jessica.

"Please refrain from addressing my client in that manner," Ryan says, staring hard at him.

"I thought you said he would be reasonable," Butthead tells Jessica, ignoring Ryan. "Perhaps we should just let the Darwinian process take place here. I'll return to San Francisco and continue my investigation, you head back to your cases, and Mr. Smart Mouth here becomes a statistic. Of course, *after* he gets tortured in inconceivable ways."

The room goes quiet as I consider that.

"They'll start with your fingernails," Butthead decides to add in case I didn't get it. "Then comes the isolation wounds. Do you know what that is?"

I just swallow while Ryan, who is supposed to be interceding or objecting or doing whatever it is that lawyers do in situations like this, is listening with apparent interest.

At my silence, Butthead adds, "That's when they pluck out your eyeballs, cut off your tongue, and pour acid into your ear canals. Then they feed your eyeballs to you. How's that for starters, Sport?"

"David, I'm really quite worried about you," Jessica says soothingly.

Man, she should get an Academy Award because the Jessica I learned to know and fear way back would have already sliced off my genitalia, grilled it, and fed it to me with a side of eyeballs.

"Please believe me when I tell you," she adds, "that I only have your best interest in mind when I urge you to tell us everything you know so we can reach closure as fast as possible and prevent any harm coming to you. I really care about you."

And I really think pigs fly.

"You passed out when I bumped into you," says Butthead. "That was just a love tap compared to what's coming your way."

"You've made your point with my client, Agent Caporini."

"Fair enough," says Butthead, looking at me to see if I'm close to cracking.

Staring him squarely in his ass face, I say, "I would like to know why the FBI thinks I'm a target."

Butthead's grin vanishes as his eyes grow indifferent, reminding me of San Francisco right before he knocked me out. I'm obviously getting to him as his bulbous nose and cheeks turn a darker shade of red and a vein starts to throb across his forehead.

He finally replies, "As you wish, Sport. That way you can add blindness, deafness, and muteness to your pigheadedness."

"That's enough," Ryan says.

"Does that mean you're not going to tell me how I'm connected to what's happening?" I ask, though the thought of eating my own eyeballs starts to erode my earlier determination to keep pushing for answers.

"What do you think is happening here, David?" Jessica asks.

I take a deep breath and look at Ryan long and hard before getting the sudden urge to cooperate, at least a little, especially if doing so may increase the odds of keeping my eyeballs in their sockets and out of my mouth.

I say, "The mystery woman told me that things were not as they seemed seven years ago."

That certainly draws a reaction from them. They snap their heads at each other, then back at me.

"She told you that?"

I nod.

They pause, then Jessica asks, "What else did she say to you?"

I tell them about our small talk, then how she got the phone call that made her get up and leave. I decide not to mention the business card, though I need to remember that I did tell Beckett about it and also that Ryan is supposed to have it. I'm going to need one of those detective notepads to keep my lies straight.

"What about yesterday after you arrived in Austin?" Jessica asks.

I tell them about Beckett showing up at the airport, how I got a tip to go to Heather Wilson's old house in Tarrytown, but I don't reveal the picture that Margaret stole from the premises depicting a still-alive Bernard Wilson or mention Kate's albino co-conspirator. I tell them about Beckett showing up after also being contacted, about Serrato's assassination, his final words, and skip the part about the albino fighting off the assassins. I also bring them up to speed on the situation at the morgue, the current resting place of the waitress from the bar in San Francisco. I even mention the photo of Heather and me in the foyer, and the third message from Kate.

"What do you make of Serrato's last words?"

I tell them about my project at MM&S and my recommendation to Preston Wilson to extend the improvement initiatives to New Orleans.

They listen without interruption.

"What did the victim at the morgue look like?" asks Butthead when I finish, his eyes glinting with an interest he is trying hard to suppress.

I have apparently touched another sensitive spot with the mention of the New Orleans connection, but there is no sense in asking him why, so I just answer his question. "She was blonde, attractive, narrow face, sunken blue eyes, late forties to early fifties, but probably more wrinkles than her age called for. Cops claimed she had a record of prostitution in California and Louisiana."

Jessica stares at Butthead, who reaches in his coat, produces an iPhone, and rummages through mug shots of women by running a finger across the top of each image, tilting it in my direction a moment later when reaching someone that he apparently believes matches my description. "Is this her?" he says.

I stare at the digital image of a woman younger and prettier than the waitress, and I shake my head.

He goes back to his private viewing, before finding another image that apparently meets my description. He shows it to me, and again, it's not her.

"Look, guys, it would really be easier if you just went to APD," I offer. "I've already told them what I just told you, and they have the body of—"

"We must keep this covert and clear of local cops to avoid a leak, understand?" Jessica interrupts before pointing back at Butthead, who has another image ready for me.

After about five minutes and a dozen images, he produces one that is awfully close to the waitress.

"That's her," I say.

"Sure?"

"Pretty sure," I reply, staring at the face of the woman I saw alive in San Francisco waiting tables and dead last night in Austin, though in this picture she is much younger. The lines on her forehead and around her eyes are finer. Her cheeks are not sagging as much. Her neck is smoother. Her eyes are clearer. Her lips are fuller. It's almost as if the woman I saw two nights ago is a shrunken, hollowed-out version of this person.

"Pretty sure or really sure?" presses Jessica.

"What do you think, Ryan?" I ask.

Butthead tilts the screen in Ryan's direction, who looks at it a moment, and also says, "Yep. Looks like her. Just younger."

"I agree," I say, then turn to Butthead and ask, "I'm surprised you didn't see her at the bar the other night. She was all over the place serving drinks."

He ignores me, looking at Jessica and saying, "She's the first to escape and make it back."

"Make it back from where?" I ask.

Butthead frowns, wishing he could take the comment back and puts away the smart phone. Jessica shoots him a disappointed look.

"Escape from where? What are you talking about?" I press.

"I'm afraid we can't tell you that," says Jessica.

"Just as you can't tell me the woman's real name, her connection to all this, or why I'm being targeted?"

She puts on her poker face.

Bastards. They're all the same, cops or feds. Give nothing; take everything.

"In that case," Ryan says, reading my mind, "we have a lot of work to do. Please visit us again when you have information you are either allowed or willing to share with my client and me. Until then…"

***

Five minutes later Ryan and I are alone in his office.

"How do you think it went?" he asks, reaching for his inbox pile and snagging the manila folder on top.

He leans back in his chair, crosses his legs, opens the case study of one of our new members, and starts leafing through it.

"Well, unless they were lying—which is entirely possible—I'm at risk of going from dumb to dumber."

He grins. "They were just on a fishing trip by using the age-old fear tactic to get you to talk. You gave them plenty as it is."

I tilt my head and roll my eyes. "Don't know about that."

He looks up from his work. "Don't know about what? The fishing trip or that you gave them enough info?"

"The former."

"Why do you say that?"

"For one thing, the bullet that killed Serrato buzzed by my ear too damned close. Fortunately the shooter didn't get the chance to fire again thanks to that albino guy who I now also suspect came to my rescue at the hotel, and who probably gave Caporini that nasty cut. Then the waitress gets killed after delivering the message at the shelter for the woman I still only know as Kate Larson. Then last night I found my place in shambles."

"What do you mean?"

"Someone had a field day with my place. That has a way of adding credibility to their claim that I'm a target."

"What the fuck?" he says, placing the file on his desk and dropping his forearms loudly on the dark veneer surface.

"It's torn up pretty badly," I add, "but I was just too tired to care last night."

"Did you call the cops?"

"Why? So Beckett and his pretty little female hound can ask me more questions I can't answer?"

"No, dummy, so there is a police record of it just in case."

"In case of what?"

"I have no idea, but I do know that you have the FBI on one side running some special investigation, there's this mystery woman dropping you notes, plus there's people getting killed all around you. That tells me something very big is taking place, and you seem to be somehow stuck in the middle of it."

"I still don't get what I gain by reporting the break-in. It's just going to lead to more questions I have no answers to."

"Again, just in case," he says, beginning to lose his patience with me.

"Dammit, Ryan, in case of what?"

"You never know until you do. But I do know that if someone is really pulling your strings, one form of defense is to have as much of what's happening on the table with the cops. The more they know the less they'll suspect you."

"Suspect me of what?"

"Who knows, but the way things have gone lately, just about anything can happen, so it's best to be as proactive as possible. Last time things went ape shit you ended up on trial. I'm trying to be a little more cautious up front this time around."

All I can do is nod.

"Is something missing?" he asks.

"Missing?"

"You know…as in not there anymore?"

"I'm not sure."

"What do you mean you're not sure?" he asks, his eyes wide in visible exasperation. "Shit's either there or not."

"If you saw the place you'd understand. Besides, I crashed last night just to be woken up by Dana, who dragged my butt over here for this lovely reunion."

"My point is," Ryan says in his older-brother tone, "if something *is* missing, it might give us a clue."

My legal counsel, the king of thinking things through, has a valid point, as always. "All right. I'll grab some lunch and go back to my place and see if something is missing. And yes, I'll call Beckett right away and report it as soon as I get out of here. Okay?"

"Thank you. Now, do you have any idea when that happened?"

"When what happened?"

He frowns and says, "When did someone break into your place? Are you feeling all right?"

I close my tired and aching eyes and shake my head. The caffeine and the Vicodin have not yet kicked in this lovely afternoon. "I've been gone all week, man. Last night was my first time back in the place."

"David," Ryan starts, blue eyes narrowing, his face hardening, becoming as stolid as when he counseled me during the darkest days of my trial. "The FBI may have a point. Maybe you have indeed become a target."

"No shit, amigo. But the question is, a target of whom? And, just as importantly, why? What do I have to do with any FBI investigation, Ryan? Why are people getting killed around me? Why is this albino superman apparently out there protecting me? Why is it that people shy away when I ask about what happened seven years ago? What is the damned connection? I just don't fucking get it. Besides, what else could I have possibly told the cops or the feds aside from passing them the notes from Kate, telling them about the albino man, and also showing them the picture of Bernard and Gus—which I don't actually have because you gave it to your guy to analyze?"

Ryan leans back and folds his arms firmly also in obvious frustration.

I reach into my pocket and pull out Kate's notes, holding one in each hand, looking at the handwritings again. Then I turn the business card over and stare at the AFA logo, at their address and phone numbers on the bottom left. One is a toll-free number. The other looks like a direct line preceded by the letters MOB, for mobile.

I raise my gaze and open my mouth but say nothing.

Ryan squints at me and asks, "What?"

I read the business card again; stare at the telephone numbers.

It couldn't possibly be this easy.

Before I know it, I'm reaching for my phone and dialing the mobile number on the card.

Two rings later a woman picks up and says, "Hello?"

It sounds like her, and my heart starts to do somersaults. I feel the buzzing in my ears returning as my pressure soars.

"Hello? Who is this?" she asks.

My mind is racing to find the right words, the right thing to say.

Finally, I settle for the truth.

"This is David Wallace."

She pauses, then asks, "What did I drink?"

I frown at the question but quickly realize she's just making sure it's really me. "A cosmopolitan."

"What was so special about it?"

I look away for a moment, then remember. "Cointreau instead of triple sec."

"How hot is it in Texas?"

I grin, my heart lurching inside my chest. "So hot that you see trees whistling at passing dogs."

Another pause while Ryan leans forward and mouths, *what the fuck?*

"Hello, David. What took you so fucking long?"

CHAPTER 15

Insisting for the time being she be called Kate, the mystery lady warns me that I will likely be followed anywhere I go, and I don't find that surprising. So, in order to meet, we will have to come up with something more creative, and it is me who actually thinks of a way.

"Are you sure it's going to work?" Ryan asks as I hang up the phone.

"It's a lot better than me going out to meet her with half the FBI and APD in tow," I reply.

"Got a point there," he observes with a touch of resignation since it's pretty obvious that despite his best attempts to dissuade me from pursuing this, I plan to see it all the way through.

His phone rings.

He answers it, listens for a moment, and says, "Are you sure?" He listens some more, then, "Thanks, man. I owe you one."

Hanging up, he looks over at me and says, "Picture is not only real but based on the height of the trees and the angle of the sun, my guy estimates is was taken about a year ago."

"I wonder if Preston knows," I comment, thinking of Bernard's son, who took full control of the company after his father was presumed dead. And a year later, after the courts declared the missing Bernard Wilson legally dead, Preston, the sole heir, inherited everything.

Ryan is now staring at me with a different face. The creases in his forehead tell me he is now transitioning from frustration to concern.

"Why don't you just ask him?" he finally says to my surprise.

"Before or after he knocks my teeth out?"

He makes a face.

"I thought you wanted me to forget about all this, Ryan."

"Well, that was before you went and poked your nose into the Wilson's former residence and stole the damned photograph and decided to visit Serrato, forever blowing your chance to walk away from whatever the hell this is. Now it looks like you're being encouraged, hunted, *and* protected. And for the record I'll remind you that I did try to stop you but you wouldn't listen."

"Yes, Counselor."

"Don't get smart," he replies, before adding, "Now, as evidenced by what happened at your place, by the killings, and by the warning from the FBI, you may have to see this through. I just worry about your stamina to go all the way."

"So, what you're saying is that since you couldn't stop me might as well join me?"

"What I'm saying is that you should continue to shake the trees, but do it more intelligently. Maybe take a lesson from this mystery Kate person and her pallid associate," he replies. "She's getting you to do the dangerous stuff. Maybe you should do the same."

"And contacting Preston might be a way to shake the trees?"

"That's one way, if done properly. I mean, if he doesn't know Bernard is dead, then he'll most certainly be motivated to find out. And if he is in cahoots with Bernard, then you would have—"

A knock on the door interrupts us.

"Come in," Ryan says.

Margaret steps inside, though for a moment I fail to recognize her. The Goth look is gone today. No red and black eye shadow. No black lips. Her hair is even light brown.

We both stare at her.

"What?" she asks, crossing her arms.

"Ah, nothing," says Ryan. "What's up?"

"Your three o'clock is here," she says.

"We need to continue this later," Ryan tells me.

"Ah…that's all right," I say, unable to take my eyes off her face. "I'm going to grab a sandwich and head back to my place and do a little clean up before shaking some trees."

As I walk out, a bruised woman I've never seen before steps in. Her right wrist is in a cast and she's limping.

She has tears in her eyes as she kisses Margaret on the cheek before going to shake Ryan's hand.

Margaret and I leave them to their attorney-client privacy. I stand in the hallway after closing the door and just stare at my very transformed assistant. She's dressed in jeans, a plain white T-shirt, and no bra, which in her case should be illegal. I try not to stare since I already got caught yesterday. Her pale face is clean today, giving her a much softer look. Her lips are a very light shade of pink. I can't remember the last time they were not dark or her eyes encased in thick black and red eye shadow.

"What's wrong with you?" she asks.

"Ah…nothing. How are you?"

"Fine. You?"

I point to my left temple. "Headache." Then I start walking towards the lobby.

"Hey," she says after me. "Need some help?"

"Help with what?" I ask, even though I do need her help to execute the plan I had just laid out to Kate.

"Don't get smart. Dana told me about your place."

"Dana has a big mouth."

"We all have our faults," she says. "Besides, I'm starving. Buy me lunch and I'm yours for the afternoon."

I laugh, welcoming the humor after the way my day has gone so far. "I thought you said I couldn't handle you."

"Oh, that was before," she says, her fine eyebrows rising three times over hazel eyes glinting with mischief.

Here we go with the befores again.

"Before what?"

"Before word got out about your shower scene this morning."

"Great," I say, also remembering that she saw the very revealing picture the police had of Heather and me. "Add that to my growing repertoire of privacy violations."

"I'm the last person on Earth you should have to worry about, David," she says.

I'm not sure what she means by that, so I let it go as we step onto a bright sidewalk under a steaming mid-afternoon sun.

She puts on her shades, which, combined with her porcelain skin and long hair makes her look like a movie star. My sunglasses, on the other hand, are lost somewhere in my bedroom, so I have to squint and suffer.

"How is Adelia holding out?" I ask.

"As good as can be expected. She's got plastic surgery scheduled in a week. The surgeon is optimistic."

In addition to general practitioners, gynecologists, and psychiatrists, we also get the pro bono services of two local plastic surgeons.

We reach a local sandwich shop at the corner that's typically well patronized from the many area businesses, but at four in the afternoon we get to walk up to the counter right away. Garth Brooks' *Friends in Low Places* streams out of unseen speakers, and today that seems quite appropriate.

I get a club on rye and Margaret, who is into not poisoning her body with fatty substances such as ham and bacon, gets a tuna wrap. My chips are the old-fashion kettle kind while hers are baked. I grab a soda and she takes a bottle of green tea.

I smile inwardly at the irony of her meal selection. A lot of good all of that health food is going to do her given that she smokes a pack a day. But I know better than to comment.

We find ourselves a table in the corner and dig in, eating in silence for a few minutes. That's something I like about being with Margaret. I don't feel the need to speak when I'm in her company, and neither does she unless one of us has something meaningful to say.

"Oh, I almost forgot," I say, grabbing my phone and dialing Beckett Mar's number.

"Who are you calling?"

"Ryan told me to call Beckett and report the break-in."

"Good advice."

"Yeah, he's certainly full of that," I say, frowning when the call goes to voicemail. I leave a short message that someone broke into my place and to please call me back.

"What did the FBI want?" she asks when I hang up.

"Same thing that the cops wanted, except Beckett at least shared some info. Ryan and I couldn't get one ounce of intel out of the Feds. Also, one of them is the bastard who gave me this bruise in San Francisco."

She puts down the wrap. "What?"

I tell her about Butthead.

"You've got to be kidding me!" she explodes. "And all the piece-of-shit could offer is that half-assed apology?"

People at nearby tables look in our direction.

"Easy, there."

She drops her voice to a whisper and says, "Don't *easy* me. That *motherfucker* nearly killed you and all he did was try to shake your hand before going on to fish for more information?"

"It's okay."

"The hell it is. What else did you learn?"

"That I'm now a target."

"A target of whom? And why?"

"That's precisely what I asked, and they basically told me to go to hell. It was pretty much a one-way conversation. They were fishing for anything I would tell them without having to go through the trouble of making it an official visit."

"That's probably because they don't have crap and are resorting to going after you so you can tell them the information they're too stupid to get for themselves."

That's one thing I really love about Margaret. She helps me add perspective.

"What did you tell them?"

"Same thing I told the cops, also holding back on the picture of Gus and Bernard, and the actual notes. They seemed quite interested in the first message from Kate about what happened seven years ago, and also about Serrato's last words. By the way, that photo of Gus and Bernard is legit. Ryan's guy called right before you showed up."

"So Bernard is still alive, and your old boss is in bed with him?"

"Pretty much, which adds more credibility to Kate's notes, and that's part of what I want to talk to you about."

"Fucking bastards. All of them," she fumes, anger glinting in her hazel eyes as she shakes her head and takes a bite of her wrap.

And at this instant, without the heavy make-up, the skull tattoo out of sight, sitting across from me dressed plainly, her fingernails painted in a soft pink instead of black, I'm wondering if our therapist is right. Is she emerging from her period of mourning? I remember the shrink elaborating that such change is typically associated with the abused entering a new and healthy relationship.

Has Margaret developed feelings for—

"Why do you keep looking at me like that?" she asks, her eyes narrowing. "Starting to get creepy."

"Like what?" I ask, hating myself for getting caught looking again.

"Like someone who...forget it."

"I think I need a break from all of this."

She shrugs. "Get in line. Now, what is it you wanted to tell me?"

I look around the place, not that I would know surveillance if it bit me in the ass, before dropping my voice to a whisper and leaning forward. She does the same.

"I made contact with Kate Larson, the live one, of course."

"No way," she hisses, sudden interest glinting in her stare, her face inches away as she leans forward. She places a hand over mind and squeezes gently. "How?"

I enjoy the physical contact as I tell her, and she briefly closes her eyes, releases my hand, and touches her forehead. "Of course. The best course of action is typically the one staring you in the face."

"That's right," I reply, taking a few minutes to explain my plan.

Margaret listens intently, finishing her wrap and chips, washing it down with green tea.

"What do you think?" I ask.

"I think it's, well...*brilliant*," she says, then adding, "I'll make all of the preparations. What are you going to do about Preston in the meantime?"

I tell her, and her already prominent eyes grow as large as saucers.

"Are you serious?"

I nod.

"When?"

"Tonight. Late. Right now I promised Ryan to get my place back in shape and see if anything is missing."

"So let's go tackle it," she says, getting up.

***

Five minutes later we're in my apartment. I take on the living room while she dives for the kitchen.

I lift the dark-wood shelves that surrounded the flat screen anchored to the wall, where I keep my old vinyl collection, a few dozen classic DVDs, and a handful of awards given to Hill Country Haven over the course of the last six and a half years by a variety of organizations, public and private. The majority of the awards we get are proudly displayed in our lobby, but I keep the few that were more personal, like the gold key the former mayor of Austin gave me last year. I find it beneath throw pillows and place it back on one of the shelves. I continue to make my way through the mess, straightening the sofas, picking up, stacking, and throwing away a few broken items, like my vintage turntable, which is busted up beyond repair.

Bastards.

But what really gets me is the two framed pictures of my son I find under a sofa. The glass is broken and the frames are bent, but I carefully slip the photos out. One is when David was a year old and the other was taken probably weeks before his death.

"How are you doing in there?" Margaret shouts from the kitchen even though she is less than a dozen feet from me.

"Okay," I reply, staring at David in his blue overalls. I remember the day Evelyn and I took him to the studio to get this portrait taken. We had a bad fight the day before and barely said a word to each other that weekend. A month later I had sex with Heather Wilson. "Nothing missing so far. You?"

"You're going to need new wine glasses. All but two are broken."

I groan while setting the pictures aside, thinking of how much of the taxpayer's money the City of Austin blew at Williams-Sonoma last Christmas to get me that gift as a token of appreciation for our services. I was going to sell them on eBay and donate the proceeds to the shelter but they came laser-monogrammed with my initials.

Thirty minutes later, while Margaret continues to clang her way through the kitchen, I sit on my couch contemplating my living room with everything back in its rightful place trying to assess if something is missing.

I don't have a lot of stuff, but what I do have I really like, including my vinyl collection and my classic movies. Call me sentimental, but most of my DVDs are flicks shot before color, including my all-time favorite, *It's a Wonderful Life*, which I like to watch whenever I'm having a bout with little-David depression. It actually works better and faster than a batch of Mexican martinis and without the bitter morning-after side effects.

And speaking of alcohol, Margaret emerges from the kitchen with my prized bottle of Silver Oak cabernet sauvignon and what I guess are my last two surviving Riedel Vinum glasses monogrammed with DW. Of all the bottles on the wine rack, she accidentally picks not only the most expensive, but the one Evelyn and I bought way back during a trip to Napa when we were still in love and planned to open it on our tenth-year anniversary.

"Payment," she says, sitting next to me and setting the glasses on the table before proceeding to butcher the cork of a $150 bottle of wine.

Although my feelings for Evelyn ceased long before her untimely death, something churns inside at the thought of uncorking it, but I just don't have the heart to say anything.

"I thought that's what lunch was," I say to hide my sudden state of depression.

"That's before I knew I had broken-glass detail. This is hazard pay, buddy. Besides, I never drink wine, so I want to find out what all the noise is about. Is this one pretty good?"

"It's reasonable," I reply.

And just like that, my prized bottle, which I've been reserving for reasons I can't explain for some special occasion that's never come, is mangled open at four o'clock in the afternoon on a Thursday by someone who couldn't tell Silver Oak from Yellow Tail.

She pours without waiting for the wine to breathe.

We toast and drink.

"Not bad," she says.

No shit.

"You sure you know what you're doing?" she asks, holding her glass with both hands, not by the stem, and that's when I notice that the color of her toenails match her fingernails.

"Enjoying the view?"

Crap.

"Just noticing the changes," I reply, amazed at how she can so very quickly steer my mind away from my painful past.

She raises her right brow. "Like?"

"Definitely," I reply as my heartbeat pounds my chest a little harder.

"Good," she says, smiling ever so slightly while dropping her gaze to her glass of wine, an index finger running back and forth over my engraved initials in a way that draws me in a dangerous direction.

Is what's happening what I think is happening?

Has Margaret exited a three-year period of mourning pulled by the hope of a relationship with me? Were those sexual innuendos more than just passing jokes?

You never really know with Margaret, but I do know that I don't have the best track record for lasting relationships, and I'm not sure if I can ever forgive myself if I hurt her—if my actions, however unintentional, push her back into the shadows.

So in spite of what I believe may be mutual feelings for her, I decide to play it safe and say, "I'm not so sure I know what I'm doing, Marge, but what choice do I have? According to the FBI I'm already a target, so might as well roll with it."

"That's pretty crappy of them to drop that bomb on you but not give you any info."

"Actually," I say, swirling the wine in my glass, "I did learn a couple of things from the Feds today."

"Such as?"

I tell her about Butthead's iPhone images and about what he said when I identified a younger version of the waitress.

"Escape from where?" she asked. "Prison? Are they tracking down escapees?"

"Don't know."

She crosses her legs almost as if she is practicing yoga and shifts sideways to me on the sofa. Her knees touch the side of my left thigh. "You said he had pictures of many women in his phone, right?"

"Yes."

"And he just showed you the ones that best matched the description you gave them?"

"Yes"

"And the cops said that the waitress was a prostitute, right?"

"Yes…where are you going with this?"

She finishes her wine while looking into the distance. I can see the wheels turning behind those eyes before she says, "I heard a story from a homeless man on Thirtieth and Guadalupe the other night about three runaway teen-age girls being forced into a van and driven away."

"Forced?"

She nods while pouring herself a second glass of wine. She is drinking Silver Oak like a soda. "According to the old panhandler a group of men who looked Hispanic pulled up with this van, talked to them for a while, then strong-armed them into the vehicle. And that's not the first time it's happened. Rumor on the street is that young girls are being abducted and forced into prostitution."

"That's terrible, but it's also nothing new," I tell her. "You saw what happened last night during rounds. Pimps wait for them at bus stations, in alleys, and especially around campus to catch one in need of quick cash. UT has seventy thousand kids and over half of them are women, and twenty-five percent of them are freshmen. That makes it what, around nine thousand female freshmen? And statistics show that the dropout rate for the first year at UT is over twenty percent. So around two thousand girls ages eighteen or nineteen drop out every year, some too embarrassed to go back home, or maybe they don't have a home to go back to, or maybe they were on some scholarship they lost as a result of bad grades, or they are burdened with school loans they can't pay back. Pick your reason. When you couple that with Austin being packed with affluent politicians and businessmen from many major industries, you get your supply and demand."

"I know," she replies, sipping her wine. "But this is different."

"How?"

"I heard they're being snagged from the streets, but they're not going back to work for the local pimps to suck Austin dicks."

Another vivid image from Margaret. "Then?" I ask.

"Word I got is that they're being shipped to Mexico."

"Mexico?"

She shrugs. "What I heard." She drinks more wine.

Damn, when you think about it, why not? Those pretty American girls are serious assets south of the border, and who will miss them? Who has time to follow up on abducted runaways, on college drop-outs? They basically fall off the system's radar. And unless the parents have means—and most don't—they are forgotten, presumed dead, just like the Drag Rats.

"Are you talking about a ring of sexual slaves? Of abducted American girls being smuggled south of the border?" As I say the word 'smuggle' I can't help but think of Sebastian Serrato.

"Like I said, that's the rumor," she says.

"And you're thinking maybe something has transpired that got the Feds' attention?"

She raises her narrow shoulders again. "That's one theory to explain the comment the agents made today, especially when you combine the fact that the waitress was a prostitute, and that according to them she was the first woman to escape and make it back here. Didn't you say the agent who hit you, what's his name?"

"Caporini."

"Yes, you said that in San Francisco he was dressed like a pimp and was in the company of what looked like an Asian prostitute?"

I nod.

"Those observations also fit the sexual slave smuggling theory," she says, draining her second glass, adding, "And wasn't that one of Serrato's final words?"

"Yes," I say, wondering if her attempt to connect the loose pieces of this puzzle make sense.

"Damn," she says, staring at her glass of wine. "I don't know my wines, but this is *very* good."

"It is," I reply, still nursing my first glass, trying desperately to enjoy it after all these years.

She puts her glass down, inspects my glass, decides I'm not going to drink any more, and proceeds to push the remains of the cork back into the bottle. "Maybe we can finish it later," she adds.

"Maybe," I say, my mind going in a direction I don't want it to go. But it doesn't travel far, suddenly halted by the flashing image of David, of Evelyn and Heather, of the pain I caused, of the lives I deprived them. I often wonder if Heather would be alive had I not fucked her. It is quite conceivable that Bernard, who apparently had hidden cameras all over the house, knew about us and probably either killed her or had her killed, and then framed me for it. Evelyn and little David would still be alive had I exerted a few ounces of self-control and walked away the moment Heather opened her front door. The way our marriage was going, Evelyn and I might have separated, but she would still be alive today, and I still would have my son, who would have been twelve this year.

But I had stepped in that foyer, had accepted Heather's offer for a nightcap, and ultimately had failed to keep my zipper zipped.

And sitting here in my apartment alone with Margaret drinking wine is beginning to feel like another disaster in the making. She may look normal. Her eyes might be clear.

Her face might be devoid of darkness. Her fingernails may be pink. Her tattoo may be out of sight. She may have become one of our best 'rescuers' of abused women during rounds while also turning out to be a great assistant. But beneath the veneer she is still damaged, still abused, still gang-raped, still one small step away from shattering again, from returning to the dark and cold place from where she is just now emerging.

There is a very thin membrane separating purity from the worst form of depravity.

Ryan's words resonate with this developing situation. The layer separating daylight from shadows is indeed quite thin for Margaret Black, and I just could be the guy to send her back into the darkness if I'm not careful.

She was right when she told me I couldn't handle someone like her. I would probably hurt Margaret just as my actions had led to the destruction of Heather and Evelyn.

But she is staring at me with eyes that awake feelings I fear I may not be able to control.

She is staring at me while grinning, while placing a hand on my thigh, while pressing the side of her face against mine, while kissing my cheek, then the corner of my mouth, before—

A triple knock pulls me out of the trance, jerking me away from the edge of an abyss I was not strong enough to avoid on my own.

She backs away slowly and whispers, "You'd better get that."

I welcome the intrusion, not caring who it might be, just glad that a higher force intervened in my moment of utter lack of control and prevented me from doing yet something else I may end up regretting for years to come.

"Just a moment!" I shout, standing with difficulty while Margaret takes the half-empty bottle and glasses back to the kitchen.

Someone starts knocking again, and I yank the door open halfway through the second knock.

I stare at my most unexpected visitors, and although I was right about the higher authority intervention, I wasn't quite thinking about the Austin Police Department.

Detectives Beckett Mar and Claudia Brand stand in the doorway, the latter with her hand in a fist about to knock again.

"Hey," I say. "I just called you and left a message that--"

"David Wallace," Claudia starts while Beckett looks on with the same stare he had the day of my arrest that dark Sunday morning a lifetime ago. "You are under arrest for the murder of Kate Larson. You have the right to remain silent. Anything you say can and will be used against you in a court of law. You have the right to have an attorney present during questioning. If you cannot afford an attorney, one will be appointed for you."

As Beckett and I continue to lock eyes, as I feel the room falling away, Claudia produces a pair of handcuffs.

"He was with me the whole time, you idiots!" Margaret explodes, rushing to my side when she realizes what is happening.

"Please step away, Miss Black," warns Beckett.

They are on official business now and will go by the letter of the law. I was charged, read my Miranda, and now I will be cuffed and taken downtown. His stare tells me they are not going to mishandle this case like he did the last one.

Margaret is about to intercede anyway but I gently put my hand on her arm and say, "It's all right, Marge. Get Ryan. That's how you can help me. Get him down to the station right away."

She nods, plants a surprising kiss on my lips, then whispers in my ear, "We will be at the station in no time. You hang in there. Be not afraid."

As I watch her slim figure race down the hallway, as Claudia snaps the cuffs tight around my wrists, as Beckett drops his gaze at me before glancing in Margaret's direction, I realize that unlike that dreadful day seven years ago, this time around I am indeed not afraid.

CHAPTER 16

I decide to keep my mouth shut the entire trip in the back of the cruiser even as they start another good cop bad cop routine, which is perfectly legal for them to do after reading me my rights.

When I get to the station, they take me straight to a holding cell with gray walls and a one-way mirror under glaring fluorescents, where I continue to maintain my vow of silence until my attorney gets here.

"This time there will be no technicalities saving you," says Beckett, pacing about me as I sit cuffed to a metal table bolted to the concrete floor.

"This time the people behind that window are going to make an example out of you, so if you think you're innocent, you better start talking. The longer you wait the guiltier you look."

Nice one there, Beckett. Straight out of the book.

"You think I'm kidding you? You think we don't know that you were on the same flight as Kate Larson from San Francisco?"

He gets me to look up on that one.

Slowly, he pulls out a pack of cigarettes and lights one up, drawing on it slowly, before blowing the smoke in my face.

My chemically-hungry body twitches in reaction to the addictive haze enveloping my head, and unfortunately there isn't a single thing I can do about it.

"Want one?"

I say nothing, trying to hold my breath for as long as I can, but the bastard keeps exhaling smoke in my direction. I finally inhale, driving it deep into my deprived lungs, which I feel coming alive.

He smiles and says, "We have video from airport security of you and her walking almost side by side from the gate. What happened? Did she proposition you, then you went to a hotel room, and then she tried to blackmail you with those old pictures of you and Heather Wilson?"

I almost tell him to get lost but hold my tongue.

"Yeah," he says. "That's what I thought. She tried to squeeze you, right? So you squeezed her right back, just like Heather Wilson. Isn't that true?"

I stick to my guns while wondering where the hell Ryan is. Assuming it took Margaret a couple of minutes to cross the street and get him, they should have been right behind us.

Beckett looks at me, slaps the table, which does have the desired effect of making me jerk back, and then walks away, leaving me for about a minute, before the door swings open and Claudia Brand storms in.

"You think it makes you a man to abuse women, Mr. Wallace?"

I stare back, certainly not expecting that one. After all, the mayor of the city of Austin, their boss' boss, gave me an award for my work rescuing abused women.

"You think you can go around strangling women, Mr. Wallace? Or when you don't have time to strangle them, just slice their throats like you did in San Francisco?"

Easy, David. They're just doing their jobs, feeding you stuff to get you to react, to force you to say anything they could use against you later. My hands itch to rub my nicotine patches, but in my current cuffed state all I can do is breathe in the remaining smoke in the room to appease my system.

"We know about your father, Mr. Wallace. We know how he beat your mother to death while you stood by watching. What kind of man are you that allowed his own mother to be beaten to death right in front of him? How can you live with yourself?"

Something is dangerously close from snapping deep inside of me; something I can't control. It starts deep in my gut, like some long-buried demon.

She continues, her narrow face just inches from mine as she adds, "You're just as guilty of your mother's murder as that bastard you call a father. And the fruit apparently hasn't fallen far from the tree. You killed Heather Wilson, Mr. Wallace. We don't care what sort of strings your attorney pulled. Your semen was in her. Your fingerprints were all over the place. You strangled her and then killed her husband when he got home and tried to intervene. And then your actions also caused your wife and son to die."

She pauses for effect, then adds, "That's right. You killed them, sir. Their blood's on your hands."

The demons are replaced by the face of little David, by his large brown eyes looking up at me.

Hold me, Daddy. Hold me tight.

"You were smart enough to hide his body and the murder weapon and got off on a technicality, but life is indeed funny, Mr. Wallace. Seven years later you did it again, first in San Francisco and the next day right here in Austin. I don't know what sort of fucked up investigation the SFPD is running over there, but we got you on video following Kate Larson at the airport. Heck, we show you trying to catch up to her. We have your fingerprints all over her hotel room. We even have two of your damned wine glasses with your fingerprints and even your initials engraved on them. This time around you're going to—"

"Enough!" shouts Ryan, storming into the room.

I stare at Claudia, who continues to be in my face.

"Step away from my client, Detective! If you have questions for him, you direct them to me!"

Claudia grins and calmly walks out of the room while saying, "No questions at this time. I was just cuddling with Mr. Wallace."

"I want a private room with my client," Ryan demands.

"This is private," Claudia replies, waving a hand around her.

"With that one-way mirror there? Tell you what, you deny my request for privacy with my client, and that's the first technicality I'm going to throw at the judge in the morning."

Just like that, two uniformed officers magically appear and five minutes later we are in a small conference room, where Margaret, who was not allowed to come into the interrogation room, joins us and sits by me.

"We'll give you a moment to catch up before we come back in to start asking real questions," says Claudia.

"Wrong, Detective," Ryan says. "Texas law allows me to confer with my client in private for as long as I, as his attorney, see fit. Unless, of course, you want to give me a second technicality to throw at you."

"Just call when you're finished," she says and walks out.

Ryan sits across from me and rolls his eyes.

We've been here before, he and I, though my state of mind back then was miles away from today.

"Did they hurt you?"

"No. They just annoyed me and blew cigarette smoke in my face."

"Did they read you your rights?"

I nod.

"I was with him the entire time, Ryan!" Margaret protests. "They had no right to—"

"We had a deal, remember?" Ryan interrupts her. "You could come, but I get to do all the talking. Okay?"

She twists her full lips into a scowl, crosses her arms, and sinks in her chair.

"They claim to have found a couple of your wine glasses with your fingerprints in the hotel room. Any idea how they got there?"

"Yeah," I reply, "the bastards who tore into my apartment must have taken them. I guess that answers why they did it. In hindsight, I should have reported the incident to the cops last night instead of calling Beckett after I left your office."

"So, you did call him?"

"Yeah, and left him a message."

"Good," Ryan says. "And you also told me, and you have witnesses, including Margaret and Dana."

"What about the strangulation marks?" I ask, remembering how that got me off the hook last time since they didn't match my hands.

Ryan shakes his head. "Don't know yet, but as soon as I'm through here I'm going to have a word with Beckett. Now, let's take this from the moment you arrived in Austin, and do it as close to chronological order as possible."

Over the course of the next hour, Ryan does his lawyer thing, helping me go through everything, step by step, from the time I landed at Bergstrom until the cops showed up at my apartment. We review his draft of my official statement a few times, until we get the closest version of the truth. From this point on he gets to decide what gets communicated to whom, when, why, and how. My butt is on the line for the second time in my life for a crime I didn't commit, and my best course of action is to relinquish all control to the one person on this planet that has protected me for as long as I can remember.

"Now," he says, "let's go over *exactly* what took place from the moment they took you into their custody."

That takes another fifteen minutes, time when Margaret objected twice about how they treated me, about the questions they dared ask me. Ryan had to remind her of their deal twice, and twice she sat back down fuming.

I give her a sideways glance and wink. She looks like a cornered cat ready to lash out with her pretty pink nails.

"So," I say. "What are my chances of getting out?"

"Actually, better than average," he says, surprising me.

"What do you mean?" Margaret and I ask in unison while leaning forward.

He slowly shakes his head while leafing through three pages of notes. "There isn't much here to get through a grand jury. The wine glasses are an obvious plant, especially given that your apartment was broken into. So unless they're withholding evidence—and I intend to find out in a moment—I'm guessing this is their way to step up the squeezing game because they feel you're holding back on them. Since they apparently couldn't do it by just asking you questions, they're resorting to this, hoping to scare you into talking."

"Makes sense," says Margaret, winking at me. "Like the old saying goes: grab a man by the balls, and his heart and mind will follow."

Ryan grins at that.

I don't think it's funny.

"And I don't believe this is their last round of squeezing," says Ryan.

I turn to Margaret. "Speaking of shaking trees, are you ready to do your thing?"

Ryan frowns. "Do you think it's a good idea to follow through tonight given what's just happened?"

"More than ever," I reply. "I need to know what in the world is going on and it doesn't look like any of the branches of our law enforcement establishment either know what's going on or are willing to tell me. Shit's happening to me, Ryan. People are dying all around me, and I need to start getting some answers. And by the way, so far Marge's theory fits. We worked it out this afternoon."

Ryan nods while frowning. "Yes, she told me on the way here. Quite the couple of conspiracy theory cowboys, aren't you? Tell me, guys, did you come up with that before or after drinking that bottle of wine?"

Margaret and I don't reply.

"Yes," Ryan says, getting up. "That's what I thought. Tell me, David, how far are you willing to go to find out what really happened seven years ago?"

I stare into the blue eyes of my best friend and confidant and say, "You have no idea what it's like to lie in bed all night long while the guilt chews you up from the inside. I just have to know."

He slowly shakes his head at my answer. "How do you know you didn't kill that waitress indirectly by how you reacted after getting that note in San Francisco? And do you think Serrato would still be alive if you had not visited him? And what about the Asian woman in San Francisco, who as far as I can tell was associated with Caporini, which makes it a Federal Agent or an informant. Would she still be alive had you not gotten involved?"

Before I can reply, he adds, "How do you know you won't end up hurting other people because of your obstinate behavior? Because of your obsession to—"

"Wait a second," I say. "You told me earlier that you were going to help me get to the bottom of—"

"I don't need to be reminded of what I said. I'm an attorney. And right now my primary concern is to get you out of this place. I'm going to have a word with Beckett. While I'm gone, I want you to think critically about what I just said. Is getting to the truth of what happened seven years ago worth the sacrifice you will most certainly have to make, and not just for yourself, but perhaps for those around you?"

With that, Ryan makes his exit.

I stare at the cuffs on my wrists, their cold steel pressed against my skin bringing me back to days I have tried so hard to forget.

These shiny shackles have a sobering effect on me, making the reality of my situation sink in, in some strange way even making me wish I had not stuck my nose into the past. Perhaps Ryan is right and I should try to walk away, let whatever powers that be simply be, and just return to the way things were.

But do I really have a choice in the matter? Is it really up to me to walk away, to escape the rapids and swim to shore? I didn't ask for any of this to happen. I didn't ask for that woman to approach me in San Francisco. I didn't ask for that waitress to follow me here. I didn't ask to get involved, but I also didn't ignore it. No one forced me to go to Heather's former home in Tarrytown. No one forced me to hold back information from the police or the FBI. No one forced me to go to Serrato's house. And certainly no one forced me to contact Kate Larson, or whatever her name is, and arrange a secret meeting.

"David?" Margaret says, taking my hand. "I'm scared for you."

I look into her eyes and I see fear glinting in them, the same fear gripping my intestines at the thought of being in way over my head.

But again, what choice do I have? And what can they possibly take away from me that I haven't already lost?

And at that moment, for the first time in many years, as I stare not at my bound wrists but at her hands holding mine, I suddenly realize that I do have something to lose again. I have built something more than just a non-profit organization at HCH. I have built a new family, brought together because of the evil in this world. Through my own guilt for what I did to my family I've created the promise of hope for so many who, like me, believed they had no hope left, and in the process I attempted to mend my tortured soul.

I do have something to lose.

They do have something they can take away from me.

Maybe I should back off.

Maybe I should listen to Ryan.

Maybe I should just come completely clean with APD, SFPD, and the FBI and give them everything I have.

I clasp Margaret's hands as hard as I've ever clasped anything, and it is her that brings clarity to my moment of self-doubt with her simple, yet honest, thought process.

"You've got a big problem," she starts.

"Really?"

"Shut up and listen," she snaps, tugging the stainless-steel chain of my handcuffs. "The way I read your situation, you are in the shit, stuck between the good guys—at least the guys who are supposed to be the good guys—and the bad guys they are trying to catch. You have two choices. First, you can take the easy way out and just roll over and let them bulldoze you; let them intimidate you with this arrest tactic crap and send you back to the world you have created since your family died. You can look the other way and simply accept whatever truth they may want you to believe. But beware that you will forever wonder what really happened seven years ago; you'll always wonder if you indeed were as responsible for what happened as you think you are; you'll forever feel that you must solely shoulder the burden of what happened."

"Or?" I ask as she pauses.

She looks straight at me, tears welling in her eyes as she says, "You can fight back. You can choose to tell those who are trying to force you into a corner that you will not cave, that nothing will stop you from doing the right thing. They may try to kick you into submission, but you will not yield. You can choose to be not afraid."

I stare at her, at the single tear rolling down her cheek.

Before I can think of anything to say, she continues, "Isn't that what you preach when we come to HCH? Isn't that what you try to make us believe when we arrive beaten, with broken spirits, wearing the scars of abuse on our bodies and in our souls?"

I take a deep breath and slowly nod.

"You tell us to believe in ourselves. You tell us to not be afraid. You inspire us to crawl out of the darkest of holes

and show those bastards who tried to pound us into submission that we can rise high above their cruelty."

"Marge," I say, "it isn't that easy…I'm not sure I can
fight the—"

She slaps me.

I tense and jerk back, but the cuffs hold me down.

"What the fuck?" I bark, angry not just that she struck
me but that I'm also defenseless.

"You listen to me, David Wallace!" she interrupts, my
right cheek on fire as she cups my face and pulls it inches
from hers. "I'm reading back to you the exact same speech
you gave me three long years ago, right after that bastard of
a boyfriend and his fucking friends raped me."

I freeze.

"He shot me up with heroin and beat me up before
sharing me with his friends, who also kicked me when I
tried to resist."

I'm shocked. "But…Marge, Dear Lord, I thought you
didn't remember—"

"I remember every fucking second of that fucking
night, David. I told the cops I didn't remember because
I was afraid, because I thought it would go away if I just
didn't talk about it. But that horrible memory is burned in
my mind, and the nightmares continue to haunt me. I was
a complete mess when I came to HCH. But I listened to
you. I *believed* in you. You showed me how to turn the evil
in our life to good, the fear to courage. You never judged
me. You just listened with empathy, with compassion, and
in the process you earned my trust and the trust of the rest
of the women who pass through this little piece of paradise
at the end of our dark alleys. And now you must trust me
when I tell you that you can't let those bastards bring you
down. You fight, David. You fight until your last breath

and you do not yield. Don't you dare be afraid of them. Don't you dare fail to live up to the words that form the very foundation of our shelter."

She stops, wipes her tears, gives me a kiss on the lips, and simply rests her head on my shoulder.

We stay like that for some time until Ryan returns holding a wad of papers. He stops and looks at us.

"What's up with you guys? You're drinking in your apartment in the afternoon and now you're hugging? Are you two a couple now?"

"What's it to you if we are?" Margaret retorts before I can reply.

"What happens now?" I ask.

"Now, we leave," he says. "You're free to go."

"What?"

Beckett walks in with Claudia in tow and says to me, "Next time someone breaks into your apartment, please be sure to call us *immediately*, Mister Wallace."

"But I did call. Left you a message."

"In my book, Mister Wallace, *immediately* isn't the afternoon of the *following* day," Beckett retorts.

"And what would you have done had I called you *immediately*? Ask me more questions I can't answer."

Beckett looks at Ryan, who raises an open palm at him to ward off what looks like a verbal attack.

"No," Ryan says, "so they can try to scrub the place for clues that may have helped with their investigation, especially given the strange messages you have been getting."

"As it stands, Mr. Wallace," says Claudia, "the way Mr. Horowitz explained it, you and your little girlfriend there contaminated the crime scene by picking up the place."

"They're going to send a couple of guys to check it anyway," says Ryan.

"You agreed to send cops to my place without consulting with me first?" I ask.

"That's part of the deal for letting you walk now," Ryan replies. "Their main evidence against you is the wine glasses, and our claim is that they were taken from your apartment following a break-in. We're going to keep the video from the airport on the side for now since it clearly shows that you never spoke to her and that you lost her in the crowd after someone bumped into you and made you spill your coffee. That was right before you were accosted by Detective Mar." Ryan looks at Beckett, who just sighs.

"All clear now, Mister Wallace?" Claudia asks. "Or do you want to spend the night in our very crowded holding cell and go from being her boyfriend to being someone's girlfriend?"

I sink back in my chair.

Ryan adds, "Good. Besides, they think they have a stronger suspect than you."

"Who?" I ask while Beckett, who pulls out a key and releases me, exchanges a glance with Ryan.

"That's not our concern," Ryan replies. "Now these officers have a lot of work to do. Let's get out of their way."

"We should be through dusting your place by nine tonight, Mr. Wallace," says Claudia. "Unless you hear from us, assume it's safe to go home by then."

"And keep your nose clean," warns Beckett. "You got lucky again."

And just like that—just as it happened seven years ago—charges for murder are suddenly dropped. And this time it even happens expeditiously. No courtroom, no jury of my peers, no press, no mourning relatives.

I sigh.

THINGS WERE NOT AS THEY
SEEMED 7 YEARS AGO.

Someone wanted that case closed, and fast, David. So they did.

And it now becomes quite apparent that someone wanted to prevent this case from ever surfacing beyond these walls, which also tells me there is probably no stronger suspect in custody, just as the killer of Heather Wilson was never found.

THINGS WERE NOT AS THEY
SEEMED 7 YEARS AGO.

The phrase fills my mind while Claudia escorts us out of the conference room and towards the elevators to head down to the lobby.

She leads the way followed by Margaret and Ryan. I'm behind them with Beckett, who stops by an adjacent conference room, opens the door, and goes in.

But in doing so, he intentionally holds the door open just long enough for me to get a glimpse of FBI Special Agents Jessica Herrera and Max Butthead Caporini engaged in what looks like a heated debate with the APD chief of police. And next to them stands none other than SFPD Detective Marley Quinn.

They don't notice me, but I sure as hell see them.

As he closes the door, Beckett Mar winks at me.

Before I know it I'm reaching in my pocket for a Vicodin.

CHAPTER 17

"What the hell just happened in there?" I ask as we get in the van and head back to HCH, my flaring headache chiseling deep into whatever is left of my sanity.

"They let you go. That's what happened," Margaret replies as she starts the van.

My hyper-stimulated brain can't stop churning as I sit sideways to her in front so I can also see Ryan, who gets the middle row to himself.

"They were just fishing, trying to get you to talk, which you didn't," he replies as Margaret backs out of our parking spot. "They had your release papers ready all along."

We pull out of the police department and head for IH-35. Ryan and Margaret light up cigarettes almost in synchronization. Smoke swirls around me.

"I *meant* about the FBI and SFPD talking to the APD chief of police in that conference room on our way out."

"What?"

"Don't fuck with me, Ryan."

"I…I'm *not*. What are you talking about?" He takes a long drag and exhales through his nostrils while rubbing his chin.

I stare at him a while and realize he actually isn't kidding around. So I tell him what Beckett allowed me to see.

Cigarette hanging from her lips, Margaret nearly swerves out of her lane.

Ryan leans back and pinches the bridge of his nose while closing his eyes.

This is bad. Really bad.

"Ryan? What's going on?"

It takes him another moment while Margaret shoots me a nervous sideways glance. "Are you sure it was the FBI *and* SFPD?"

"As sure as I have been of anything in my life. Caporini, Jessica, and Detective Marley Quinn. Clear as day. The Feds were engaged in some sort of argument with the chief and too busy to notice me staring right at them."

"Are you sure it wasn't an accident that you saw them? I mean, are you sure that Beckett *wanted* you to see them?" Ryan asks, blinking while massaging his right temple with an index finger.

"Absolutely. Beckett could have gone in after I passed or after we got in the elevators. He did it on purpose so I could see who was in that conference room but without alerting them. The bastard winked at me before closing the door."

Ryan nods, an index finger tapping his scarred chin.

"So, I take it you never saw them while you were getting me out?"

He slowly shakes his head, takes a drag of his cigarette, and says, "Don't ask me that again. I told you I didn't. My conversation with them after I left you was in the hallway."

"What do you think they were doing?"

"I'm not sure, but I'm *pretty sure* of what they were *not* doing."

"And what's that?" I ask.

"Forming any sort of task force with APD or SFPD," Ryan says.

"I'm not following," I say.

"Neither am I," pipes in Margaret while turning onto the service road leading to the highway entrance.

As the city of Austin passes by and the late afternoon sun beams burnt-orange into the van, Ryan leans forward so we both can hear him. He looks tired, with bloodshot eyes and a five o'clock shadow.

"All right, guys," he starts, "here's what typically happens: the FBI can take over a case if they believe that a federal crime has been committed or if the crime has crossed state lines. In addition, it has to be in one or more of the following categories: terrorism, cybercrime, public corruption, civil rights violations, organized crime, white collar crime, or weapons of mass destruction. In those cases, the FBI would contact the relevant mayor and the chief of police to inform them of the situation and request that the investigative officers—in this case Detectives Beckett Mar and Claudia Brand for APD and Detective Quinn for the SFPD—turn over responsibility and all information on the case to the attending Feds, who in this case are Jessica Herrera and Max Caporini. In some cases, the FBI could also form what's called a task force, where it joins forces with local law enforcement for a limited period of time. My guess is that APD and SFPD got their respective murder cases swiped away by the Feds and Beckett pulled that little number to screw with the FBI for pissing in his pond."

"If that's your theory," I say, "then how do you explain the fact that APD is going to be dusting my place this evening?"

He shrugs. "Maybe the Feds agreed to let them do that and turn over any findings to them."

Again, more guesses but no answers.

"In any case," Ryan adds, "we're going to drop this case."

"Who's we?"

"Not funny."

"Who's laughing?"

He exhales heavily and leans back, adding, "By continuing to pursue this, you're letting yourself get manipulated, and in the process, you're playing with your life and the lives of those around you. Look at what happened to Serrato, Kate Larson, and the Asian woman in San Francisco. It could happen to me, or Margaret, or anyone else you try to drag into this."

As always, Ryan makes a strong point. Unfortunately, I have to know what happened back then.

"Did you tell them about the picture?" I ask.

He shakes his head. "Just as I didn't give them any info on your pretend-astrologer friend who calls herself Kate Larson."

"What do you think about Margaret's theory of an illegal prostitution ring in Mexico supplied by kidnapped American college girls? That sort of trafficking certainly falls into multiple categories of interest to the Feds, including organized crime and civil rights violations."

"I think Margaret had too much vino with you this afternoon."

"Now who's being funny?" she says. "Tell me one fact so far that doesn't fit the theory, Ryan, including Serrato's final words about Preston being involved in some sort of smuggling operation?"

The great litigator doesn't reply, and that tells me her theory fits the facts quite well.

"Who do you think is running it?" I ask.

"Running what?" Ryan replies.

"This sex ring."

He closes his eyes, shakes his head, and says, "I suggest you go back to whatever it was you were doing in that apartment over wine before the cops showed up. However inappropriate, it will probably be more productive *and* enjoyable than continuing with this Mickey Mouse conversation. As for me, I have restraining orders to file and divorce papers to process."

We drift into uncomfortable silence for the remainder of the drive.

It's dusk by the time we pull up to the single loading dock behind HCH. Ryan goes straight to his office while I go straight to mine. Margaret heads for the kitchen to set up the meals for rounds this evening. Two vans have already driven away from the loading dock headed for other areas of the city. Ours will be ready to roll in another hour, and I'll be joining as part of the deal I worked out with the live Kate Larson.

Settling behind my computer, I decide to do a little Internet browsing while also pulling up old files from my final days at Mercer, Martinez & Salazar.

Everyone else around me seems to be fishing. Might as well join them and see what I can catch.

I start with my own files, refreshing my recollection of the current-state analysis and recommendations we made to Preston that Friday morning, before the celebration that changed my world. I review the transportation schemes I had mapped for them to create a supply chain rhythm between the Austin and Monterrey campuses, showing how shipments to and from both locations arrived at irregular times of the week, sometimes via air transport and other times via trucks, but there was no consistency.

I spend ten minutes reviewing the design I had created to replace the irregular shipments with two daily round trips between the cities, one in the morning and another in the evening and only by truck, and then synchronized the shipping and receiving operations and timetables to match the trucks departure and arrival dates. Doing so removed the need for excessive inventory at the receiving and shipping locations at both sites as everyone now knew when to expect shipments, and those shipments would always be of the same quantity. No more half-filled trucks, or the famous "one-offs" where a handful of items would be shipped in emergency status by air.

I sit back, enjoying the simplicity of my design, remembering how well it worked even though I was no longer with the firm when Premier Imports implemented it. But I did get word that shipping costs alone amounted to roughly half of the actual savings because Premier transitioned to using only two trucks each day on round trips, allowing them to negotiate better deals with a trucking company. Predictability always leads to savings.

During my analysis, I had also come across irregular shipments between Mexico and New Orleans, and also between Costa Rica and Houston, so there was also an opportunity to reduce transportation costs there, which I had included in my report. Finally, I review the last section of the proposal that dealt with transaction traffic between the International Bank of Texas, a wholly-owned subsidiary of the Premier family, and the New Orleans casinos.

Nothing I read triggered an alarm, so I go through it again, browsing document after document. In a way I'm almost going down memory lane, remembering how great I was at this line of work, recalling the analysis, the presentations, the lively discussions, and challenges. I recall how I was always able to break through the skepticism that companies have of consulting firms by providing them with great value while also collecting our expensive fees. And in the process, I continued to line the pockets of Gustavo Salazar while he dangled the carrot of partnership as soon as I finished paying my dues.

I finally decide there is nothing valuable in these documents—at least as far as I can tell. So I Google Premier Imports, which results in over fifteen thousand hits.

I narrow down my search to news from eight, seven, and six years ago, figuring I hit the year of my downfall plus and minus one year.

That brings me down to just over two thousand hits, so I pull up the first ten and stare at the headlines.

Terrific. Over half of them have to do with my scandal and trial. I read through the articles and they all basically say the same thing: I'm accused. I go to trial. I'm set free. Nothing new. I continue to the next ten hits and find more of the same.

Frowning, I decide to skip ahead a few pages, and look at the articles.

The theme revolves around the investments made by Premier in the State of Louisiana in late 2005 and through 2006, as New Orleans was trying to recover from Katrina. There are pictures of Bernard Wilson accompanied by Preston walking with then Mayor Ray Nagin through sections of downtown New Orleans amidst bulldozers, dump trucks, cranes, and National Guard Humvees.

The title of the article reads: *TEXAS INVESTORS FORM ALLIANCE WITH CITY OFFICIALS AND*

LOCAL BUSINESSMEN TO REBUILD CASINO INDUSTRY IN THE BIG EASY.

I pull up other related articles, showing yet more photos of Bernard and Preston accompanied by Nagin and other local and state leaders and business executives. I notice a recurring theme in many of them: Lisa Ang, an Asian businesswoman in her fifties with salt-and-pepper hair framing her disk-like pale face. According to several articles, Lisa Ang is the brains and the power behind the casino business not just in Louisiana but also in Mississippi.

What is also interesting is that Ang is accompanied in one picture by a man named Joe Castaneda, who the article indicates was the head of her security, and who looks awfully close to Kate's elusive borderline-albino friend.

I frown, wondering if my mind is playing tricks on me or if that is indeed the same person. After all, I've only gotten quick glances of the guy.

I check my watch and decide it's time to check up on Margaret. As I walk out of my office, I notice Ryan also leaving his with a pack of cigarettes in hand.

"Where are you going?" I ask.

"Smoke and a walk," he replies. "Got to clear my head. Want to join me?"

"Nah. You go ahead. I'm going to The Drag with Margaret and Dana."

Pausing, he regards me with narrowed eyes. "Are you going to do what I think you're going to do?"

"It's all set up," I say. "We just need to follow our scheduled stops like we always do. Our mysterious Kate Larson will show up if she feels safe and come back here as a homeless."

He closes his eyes, shakes his head, and leaves.

I head for the kitchen to check on Margaret and see if the van is ready to go. Once we get Kate to HCH no one will know who she is, what she has done, and most importantly, she could stay here for as long as she pleases without the police or the FBI knowing. And while we're picking her up, either Smith or Wesson will drive by Preston's home on a bike and drop off something guaranteed to stir the pot.

And that's the extent of my brilliant plan.

By the time I reach the kitchen, Dana and Margaret have already loaded the van parked just beyond the doors connecting the loading dock to the rear of the kitchen.

"Are you sure you're up to it?" I ask Margaret as she stands next to the van while Dana Knox handles paperwork in the dispatch office. Dana will accompany us at my request for added protection given everything that's been happening lately. Margaret, of course, plays the key role of recruiting the homeless, which this evening will include Kate Larson. Although she has done this hundreds of times, tonight I can't help but be worried, and for a moment wonder if Ryan is right about my obsessions placing those around me in danger.

Margaret tilts her head and smiles. "Yes, I am. Why would you ask?"

I get closer and add, "I worry that something may happen to you and—"

She takes my hand, and says, "The feeling is mutual, David. Maybe we can finish that bottle of wine when we come back?"

"I'd like that very much."

Before I know it, she leans forward and gives me a small kiss on the lips. I react by gently placing a hand behind her head and holding her close to me, running my fingers through her hair and gently pressing my forehead against hers. She cups my face and gives me a longer kiss before smiling, her hazel eyes now completely stripped of defenses. The rough and tough Margaret Black has completely opened herself to me, just like that.

"I want you to know I'll never hurt you," I whisper. "You will be safe with me. I'll take care of you."

"I know," she replies.

"You two need a room," booms Big Dana as she walks up to the van.

I kiss Margaret on the forehead and let her go.

She slips behind the wheel as Dana goes around and takes the front passenger seat while winking at me and giving me a thumbs up.

I guess the secret is out about Margaret and me.

I ignore the former wrestling champion and crawl in the rear seat, behind the boxes of food, out of sight in case anyone from my fan club is considering following me.

As Margaret and Dana engage in a lively discussion about self-defense, health food, and other uninteresting topics, I peer at the early-evening traffic behind us through the dark tinted rear windows, trying to spot anyone following us.

I see no one, though I have no idea how to spot surveillance in the first place. I turn my gaze to Margaret beyond cardboard boxes packed with goodies, enjoying just watching the back of her head and a partial profile as she converses with Dana while smoking.

But as I try to relax, as I try to reassure myself that I have taken all of the necessary precautions to bring Kate Larson in, Ryan's voice echoes in my head like an everlasting warning.

You're playing with your life and the lives of those around you.

CHAPTER 18

Night on The Drag.

Neon lights hiss overhead as a flow of students depart the UT campus and head home for the evening, many with a quick stopover at one of the many eateries lining the west side of Guadalupe.

An eclectic infusion of smells invades the van through the open windows by Margaret and Dana as we drive past dozens of ethnic restaurants. Margaret steers past hordes of students towards the back alleys west of this bustling corridor, where we settle into our routine: stop in the shadows of filthy alleys, wait for the homeless to emerge, and deliver the goods while Margaret tries to work her recruiting magic, with the added twist that Kate Larson could be joining us at some point on our route.

Our stops don't last more than fifteen or twenty minutes, and by the time we reach our fourth location at almost 9pm, our goods are already down to a third and still no sign of Kate Larson.

Wondering if she had a change of heart—or perhaps she is making sure I was not followed—I fill my lungs with the cool night air and briefly glance at the stars towering above the fire escape ladders lining the rear of buildings looking down on us.

As expected, shadows shift in the darkness as homeless denizens stir out of their hideouts in dark recesses, behind dumpsters and mounds of stacked garbage bags, slowly forming a single line.

Dana and I start to hand out the supplies while Margaret toils around the front of the van surveying the group, searching for a target. So far, the evening has yielded no recruits, but we still have two more stops after this one, so there is the possibility of finding someone willing to take a chance with us.

And I'm rubbing my nicotine patches while desperately hoping one of the shadows belongs to the elusive faux Kate Larson.

At the front of the line is a classic meth addict female of unknown age. Her teeth are gone and the gaunt face and bloodshot eyes staring back at us convey a life of regrets. She narrows her gaze at Dana's size before accepting a sandwich and a soda from her and a tube of lotion from me.

Next is a man in his fifties wearing a large overcoat and holding a small canister in his right hand that resembles a deodorizer spray. I can't tell for sure but it really doesn't matter. I glance at Margaret resting against the hood of the van with her arms crossed before I offer the homeless a tube of lotion.

As he takes it, I glance past him down the line of people to see if I recognize—

A hissing noise precedes a horrifying pain shooting into my eyeballs like acid, bringing me down to my knees before I realize the homeless is emptying the contents of the canister into my face before shifting to Dana.

I fall to my side screaming, the pain so intense it feels as if my entire face, mouth, and nostrils are on fire.

Through the maddening cloud blinding me, I hear Dana scream as she too collapses, as footsteps click hastily on the pavement. The line of homeless disperses while they scream and cry, rushing away from us.

"David!"

I try to get up, to—

An impossibly hard object strikes me on the side, sending me rolling against a dumpster. The back of my head hits something hard, and I come to a stop while I hear what sounds like a fist fight. It's Dana, grunting, apparently fighting back. But I can't help her. I can't even help myself as the pain in my eyes overwhelms my senses.

I hear the former wrestler groan, then hear others cry in pain. But then it's Dana who screams in obvious agony. She is hurt and--

A gunshot cracks in the night, and I hear her scream a final time before dropping to the wet concrete right next to me.

No! Oh, Dear God! This can't be—

"David!"

Margaret!

I try again to get up, but my body will not respond, paralyzed by the pepper spray, by the—

"David! Please help me!"

I hear a vehicle accelerating towards us, screeching to a halt. I hear men shouting but I can't understand them.

Spanish!

They're speaking in—

"David! No! DAVID!"

Oh, Sweet Jesus! No!

I finally get to my knees as Margaret continues to yell, as I hear her kicking and screaming, shouting at people to let go of her. The doors to the vehicle slam shut, and I can no longer hear her. Tires spin, squeal. The vehicle accelerates away.

And Ryan's words crash down on me like the fist from the devil.

You're playing with your life and the lives of those around you.

CHAPTER 19

I am cursed.

Every last cell of my miserable body is cursed.

There is nothing I can do that would redeem what I have done to those who got close to me. Evelyn. Little David. Heather. Dana.

Margaret.

Each of them trusted me.

And each of them is now dead, hurt, or missing.

There is no salvation for someone like me, a gutless bastard who placed a woman who obviously loved him in harm's way.

There is no denying I came up with the idea to pull in Kate Larson and then convinced her to do it. And Margaret, having fallen for me, did it just because I asked, because the one person whom she had latched on to with the hope of starting a new life asked a favor.

It didn't take me long to screw up this new relationship.

I stare at the damned green brew of the Mexican martini in my hands while rubbing my double nicotine patches as I sit alone at some nameless bar on Sixth Street. I had to get away from all of them, especially from Ryan, the one person who'd tried to talk some sense into me.

But his words fell on my deaf ears.

On my cursed ears.

I just couldn't let it go. I couldn't simply walk away, heed the warning shots being fired all around me, and move on with this life I had made for myself. I had to probe, had to push, had to pretend to be the detective I'm not, and in the process gamble with other people's lives.

And speaking of other people, Ryan is at the hospital along with half of the HCH staff praying in vigil for Dana. While me, the instigator, the one who came up with the brilliant plan that sent her to the operating table, just couldn't stay there. I simply couldn't face any of them until I got my head screwed-on straight again.

So, the moment the ER doctor finished washing my eyes, I took one of the vans and drove myself to Sixth Street to get a drink. But I can't bring myself to drink it while Ryan texts me to keep me up to speed on Dana's situation. The mere fact that she is still alive amounts to a miracle as she was stabbed six times and shot once in the head. But apparently the same thick skull that saved her from the beating she had taken five years ago managed to deflect the bullet.

I shake my head at the irony. Dana was back in the same emergency room of the same hospital where I found her a lifetime ago—and where my irresponsible desire to seek the truth sent her hours ago.

The good news was that she made it through a four-hour surgical procedure to repair the damage inflicted on her by the same bastards who took my Margaret.

Ryan's last text thirty minutes ago indicated that Dana had lost her spleen, a kidney, had broken ribs and a broken leg, and a massive concussion. But she had managed to survive.

And there was still no word on Margaret. Although APD had been at the scene and later at the hospital taking our statements, Ryan had been unable to reach Beckett Mar or my FBI pals.

Funny how the bastards have a way of making themselves scarce at the precise moment when you need them most.

The bartender, a scantily-dressed woman in her late twenties wearing a bikini top, low-cut jeans, with a midriff as flat as this counter, swings by to eye the level of my alcoholic beverage. She's got very short, hot-pink hair and matching eye shadow, lips, and fingernails.

I just continue to stare at the Mexican martini, and I think that's starting to annoy her.

But I need a clear head. Margaret needs me to think, to pull myself together. I need to organize the loose pieces of information into a cohesive story.

And rescue her.

I can't afford to fall apart now. She needs me more than ever, and I must do everything within my power to figure a way to find her.

So I may be cursed indeed, but I am also desperate, with nothing left to lose after they took her away from me.

But she is still alive. I can feel it with every breath of recycled air I breathe in this crowded bar.

As I clutch the martini glass with both hands, slowly swirling the potion I have used so many times to help me forget, I force my mind to think of a way to get her back.

But where do I start?

I already tried calling this woman who insists upon going by Kate Larson to no avail. The number was disconnected, which is unfortunate because I get the strong sense she could have explained what in the hell happened at The Drag and how I can get Margaret back.

I certainly don't lack observations and questions, but I have no answers. The only working theory was Margaret's, and even considering it makes my head explode. The thought of her being forced into a life of—

"What are you drinking?"

I turn around and stare at APD Detective Beckett Mar's massive head. He is dressed in blue jeans, sneakers, and a white button-down shirt not tucked in, sleeves rolled up to his elbows. Behind him I recognize none other than Detective Marley Quinn, also dressed casually, jeans and a T-shirt. She gives me her best version of a smile, which her stoic face displays as a half scowl.

"Hey, look," I start as they occupy the two empty stools on the right side of me. Marley sits closest to me and leans back a bit while Beckett settles in the next stool, resting bronze forearms on the counter while inspecting me with beady eyes. "The officers at the scene of the crime already took my statement and again at the emergency—"

"We're off duty," Marley replies while flagging Miss Pink, and ordering an imported Mexican beer called *Negra Modelo*. Beckett gets a scotch, neat.

"We live in a fucked up world, David," Beckett says, interlocking the fingers of his hands.

"I would actually drink to that," I reply. "Unfortunately tonight I need to steer clear of alcohol so I can think."

Marley points at my Mexican martini.

"That's just so I can sit here alone, where no one could find me. I guess that didn't work."

"We're cops," Beckett decides to point out. "We find people."

"How about finding Margaret Black?"

The comment makes Marley and Beckett exchange a glance while Miss Pink delivers their orders and once more checks the state of my drink, which I surround with both hands, protecting it from her in an act of defiance that sends her away shaking her head.

"What about cutting us a little slack?" Marley replies, taking a swig directly from the bottle.

Beckett tastes his scotch before setting it back on the counter and exhaling with eyes closed. "Much better," he adds.

I stare at them in disbelief for a moment before I blurt, "*Me* cutting *you* slack? Are you fucking kidding me? I told you everything I know and you have told me dick. How about *you* cutting *me* some slack and help me find Marge—and in the process perhaps explain what the hell is going on?"

"I think I speak for both of us," says Beckett, "when I say that you didn't quite tell us everything."

They regard me with a serenity I find quite disturbing given my altered state.

"For starters," Marley says, "you didn't tell me about the note this woman who goes by Kate Larson gave you in San Francisco. You also didn't tell Beckett about Gustavo Salazar purchasing the Wilson home. You didn't call *immediately* about the break-in at your apartment. You didn't tell him about spotting the waitress at the airport or about bumping into her associate and spilling your coffee. You certainly didn't tell him about the picture Margaret stole from Gustavo Salazar's house the other day. And you also forgot to mention the albino mystery man who keeps popping up in different places."

Beckett, drink in hand, adds, "And I still haven't really gotten the full picture behind what you were trying to pull on The Drag this evening that resulted in that attack. Criminals usually don't go after charity organizations unless they have a good reason."

"So, you see, David," says Marley in her best soothing voice while patting my forearm, "trust works both ways."

Crap.

They are, of course, not only spot on but also quite in sync with one another. These two have apparently shared notes, while I, on the other hand, have not played it straight with them *or* with the FBI for that matter. Perhaps the time has finally arrived to come clean, for Margaret's sake.

So I do.

Sitting at this bar, swallowing my pride instead of my martini, I confess to the last individuals on this planet I ever expected to trust. I tell them everything, starting at the bar in San Francisco, including my close encounter with Caporini, through discovering the picture of Gus and Bernard with the scribbled note to show the photo to Serrato. I tell them about making contact with the other Kate Larson and about the pick-up I had staged to bring her into HCH. I tell them about the FBI meeting with Ryan and me this morning. And lastly, I pull out the two notes I received from the elusive Kate Larson and hand them to Marley.

"There you have it," I say as she inspects them and passes them to Beckett. "No more secrets at this end."

Beckett nods, puts the notes on the counter, and pulls out a smart phone, fingering the screen for several seconds before tilting it so Marley and I can see the streaming video.

I recognize the images of the Wilson's former residence, and I assume it's from one of the same security cameras that resulted in my acquittal seven years ago. It is a video of the albino Joe Castaneda—Lisa Ang's head of security—breaking in, positioning the picture on the foyer table, and then taking off. The clock on the bottom advances ten minutes and then there's Margaret and me stumbling into the same spot. I keep watching the little screen and frown when seeing Margaret snatch the picture frame, which she slides under her bra strap in one swift and fluid motion.

Beckett says, "We're still inspecting the video from the other cameras, but so far the foyer is the only one with any worthwhile evidence, and you just saw it."

I nod while inhaling deeply, trying to get a grip. "What was the FBI doing at your place?" I ask.

He takes a sip and replies, "Taking my case away from me."

"And mine," adds Marley before taking another swig of her beer.

So Ryan was right, as always. It was a federal jurisdiction takeover.

"But I don't mind it so much," continues Marley. "I have enough homicides to keep me busy."

"Speak for yourself," Beckett replies. "I endured seven years of people second-guessing me about how I handled the evidence, and when there's finally a new lead in the case, they come and take away my one chance at redemption."

Marley tilts her beer in his direction. "I feel your pain and frustration, pal," she says.

Beckett touches the rim of his glass against the bottom of her bottle. "Thanks."

"Have you come up with leads on who killed Sebastian?" I ask.

Beckett and Marley exchange another glance, before he replies, "No, but you're not going to believe what we *did* find. Turns out the IRS was apparently after him for tax evasion. I didn't get the full story because the FBI shut us out, but apparently he had some accounts in Houston which amounted to far more than his college professor salary would justify, so we were about to sit down with IRS agents when the FBI got in the way."

"On what grounds?"

Marley gives me her version of a cop shrug, barely raising her shoulders and replying, "That's the thing about the FBI—or the IRS for that matter. They don't need to provide us with an explanation other than--" She throws up air quotes before saying, "--*national security*."

"So you guys are off the case?"

"Officially," they reply in unison before grinning and clinking their drinks again.

I tilt my head and frown.

"But unofficially," Beckett adds, surprising me while also staring at me long and hard with his beady eyes. "There's something you may not be ready to see. But...if you're really, really interested in understanding what happened seven years ago..."

"And also finding Margaret Black..." adds Marley.

"I'm in," I reply without hesitation, not certain where they are headed but willing to do anything to find her. "A hundred percent."

"How bad you want her back?" Beckett asks.

"As bad as I have wanted anything in my life."

"Are you certain?" presses Marley, doing a wonderful tag-team on me. "The reason I ask is that once we show you what we need to show you, your life will never be the same again. Are you sure you're ready to cross that line?"

The events seven years ago resulted in the knockout punch of my life. I've been trying to get off the canvas since, and I need something more than HCH to fill the void left behind when I lost all of the people that meant something to me. And Margaret…if she's still alive, she could be the one I rebuild my life around. She could be the one to give me a real chance to make amends.

BE NOT AFRAID.
HAVE THE COURAGE TO BE GOOD AGAIN.

"I must get her back," I say.

Beckett pulls out a folded five by seven photo from his shirt pocket, and before handing it to me, he says, "Last chance, David. There is no going back after you see this."

I take the photo and immediately recognize Gustavo Salazar and Bernard Wilson dressed up in tuxedos along with Heather wearing a gorgeous ball gown. They are walking towards one of those Hummer stretch limousines from what looks like a casino accompanied by the Asian woman from my Internet search, Lisa Ang, as well as her bodyguard, Joe Castaneda. There are three more people with them in this photograph, and I suddenly realize that the pain in my chest comes from having stopped breathing.

"This was taken about seven and a half years ago by an undercover cop in New Orleans at the opening of a large casino. Six months before your arrest. I just got it an hour ago. The Feds haven't even seen it yet."

I first stare at the well-dressed Asian lady behind Lisa Ang. She is the mystery Asian killed at the hotel in San Francisco.

But the surprise of seeing her pales in comparison to the utter shock gripping me as my eyes lock on the couple holding hands next to Gus, Bernard, Heather, Lisa, the mystery dead Asian, and Joe.

It is the Kate Larson I met in San Francisco. The hair is longer, and she is certainly younger, but it's definitely her. I notice that Heather is standing to one side of Kate with her arm around her and smiling, almost cheek-to-cheek, in a way only best friends do.

My eyes, however, can't believe who is standing on the other side of Kate holding her hand in a way that conveys intimacy.

My vision tunnels.

Beckett was right. There is no turning back now. Life as I know it can never be the same again as I stare at the face of the last person on this planet I would have expected to see in their company, and much less holding hands with the woman I know as Kate Larson.

As I clutch the picture while staring at the face of Ryan Horowitz, a deafening explosion rocks the bar.

CHAPTER 20

The smell of smoke and the water spraying my face awakens me.

I blink through the thickening haze as I try to sit up but fall back on my side.

What the hell is happening?

Water.

I see water—lots and lots of water spraying from the ceiling—as the ringing mixes with moans, with cries from patrons I can't see in the surrounding debris.

I try again to sit up and succeed in getting an elbow under me, propping up just enough to notice many figures sprawled across the bar's floor amidst broken furniture and smoking plasterboard under the incessant water streaming from the building's sprinkler sys—

I recognize the person next to me, the young bartender with pink hair, her eyes wide with fear as she trembles.

I put a hand on her shoulder and try to console her as flickering flames draw my eyes away from her. They're pulsating on the other side of the bar, tongues of crimson and yellow-gold defying the fire-extinguishing system.

Then I see three figures standing, walking, using flashlights to check the stunned patrons.

Are those firefighters? Emergency crews?

But the faceless men don't bother assisting any wounded reaching up to them. It looks like they are looking for someone.

For someone?

Shit!

As two of them converge on me while I'm still trying to sit up, I realize they are wearing hoods.

"Here is one of the *pendejos!*" the tallest says to his companion in heavily accented English as they push the bartender aside.

"No! We can't kill this one! Only the cops!" warns his shorter but stockier companion as he grabs my right arm just beneath the shoulder and pulls me up to within inches of his hooded face.

"Listen, *Pendejo.* If you want to see your bitch alive again you better get your life insurance ready for a trade. We will contact you. Get it?"

What insurance? What's he talking about?

I want to ask but my voice fails me. The explosion has knocked the wind out of me.

Before I can muster a word, he tosses me aside with incredible ease.

The floor and the ceiling swap places again as I roll away before hitting something hard, bouncing off, and landing on my back.

White spots floating about me, signaling that my mind is about to go. I glance in their direction and watch them through the haze move towards a man trying to sit up on the floor. I recognize his massive head.

Beckett.

The short one kicks Beckett on the side of the head while the tall hooded assassin swings his gun around.

Oh, my God! He is going to—

A shot reverberates across the bar. Followed by another. People scream, shout. I hear the bartender somewhere in my vicinity howling at the top of her lungs.

I freeze at the thought of the bastards killing Beckett in cold blood just a dozen feet from me, but instead their hooded silhouettes remain immobile for another second, before falling to the side, as if pushed by an invisible force.

It takes my confused mind another second to realize that someone else is—

The leg of a table next to me explodes an instant after I hear a deafening report from the front of the bar. A loud cry behind me in Spanish signals that the shooter's bullet has found another hooded assassin.

I take a chance and peer towards the street just in time to spot the face of Joe Castaneda, as clear as day, with his gun pointed in my direction as people moan, scream, cry, as the smell of cordite assaults my nostrils, as water continues to spray the locale.

"Get down!" someone shouts while an invisible force grabs me by the collar of my shirt and drags me behind a pile of tables and barstools.

I blink and recognize the silhouette of Beckett Mar, weapon drawn and trained towards the spot where Castaneda had been an instant ago, but he has vanished.

I squint to get a better look, wondering what the hell is happening.

I duck as more gunfire reverberates inside the bar, the muzzle flashes casting bursts of light, allowing me to see the side of Beckett's head. He is bleeding and his shirt is torn on the side, exposing his torso.

"Beckett, what the—"

"Everybody down!" he shouts before firing once, twice, the reports, amplified by the enclosed structure, assaulting my eardrums, making me wince.

I hear a scream across the bar, then a loud noise, as if someone tripped and fell.

Did Beckett just nail some—

Multiple shots originating behind me rattle me, but I notice Beckett doesn't turn around. He continues to train his weapon on the—

"I'm out!" screams a woman behind me above the noise and the increasing ringing in my ears.

Beckett reaches into a side pocket and tosses something over his right shoulder, which I follow as it flies over me and lands in the hand of Marley Quinn, who reloads her weapon. Clutching it with both hands, the SFPD detective sweeps the muzzle back and forth apparently searching for a target.

"What the hell is—"

"See anyone else?" hisses Beckett over his right shoulder.

"None from this angle!" Marley replies as the detectives instinctively divided the front of the bar into two sections and each continues to scan it with fingers on their weapons' triggers.

"Everyone stay down!" he shouts. "This is the Austin Police Department. No one moves!"

All motion ceases, but the cries and pleas continue to hover in the murky bar.

"What is happening?" I finally ask.

"They came for us, David," Marley explains without taking her eyes from her area of responsibility.

From my angle laying on the floor she looks tall, almost omnipotent, water soaking her as she rests her left knee on the ground while maintaining laser-like focus on the potential threat.

Beckett does the same for another minute, until I hear sirens, and he gets on his cell phone, dials 911, identifies himself to the emergency operator, and provides her with some numbered cop code.

As Beckett stands with caution and pulls out his badge while Marley does the same, I look at my hands and notice, to my surprise, that through it all I never let go of the picture.

CHAPTER 21

"But I know what I heard," I insist while sitting outside the bar in the back of an ambulance amidst a dozen emergency vehicles and police cruisers. Their red, yellow, and blue lights flash against the surrounding buildings, casting a stroboscopic glare on everything, including the mob behind the yellow police tape. "The bastards said they were after you two, not me."

"But they weren't counting on Castaneda showing up," says Beckett, holding a bandage against the side of his head.

"What I don't get is why they bombed the place if they weren't supposed to harm me," I ask, trying to settle down my frayed nerves, my system screaming for the comfort of a cigarette. I mean, what's the point of putting myself through the agony of quitting smoking if someone is trying to kill me?

Beckett smiles at the same time as Marley.

"What's so funny?" I ask, rubbing one of my nicotine patches.

"That was a flash banger—a concussion grenade—not a real bomb," explains Beckett, pointing at the patrons sitting nearby on the sidewalk. "There were no casualties from the blast."

"What about the flames?"

"That's the risk of a flash banger in a bar," Beckett replies. "Alcohol is flammable."

I look over at the ambulance parked next to us and spot Miss Pink sitting in the rear. She glances my way and gives me an appreciative nod and half smile.

I return the smile.

"It's meant to stun, not kill," adds Marley. "Whoever's after you wanted to knock people out to give them enough time to kill us without harming you. They just didn't count on Castaneda coming to our rescue, giving Beckett and me enough time to recover and fight back."

I close my eyes and remember the assassin's voice before saying, "One of them said something about trading my life insurance for Marge. What does that mean?"

After exchanging a glance, Beckett puts a hand on my shoulder and says, "Somehow someone high up must think that you have damaging evidence, and moreover, they must think there is also a process in place such that if something happens to you, this evidence will automatically reach the right hands. That's what we call a life insurance policy."

"I have to agree," says Marley. "It fits the events, including why they kidnapped Margaret."

The cacophony of sounds from alarms, sirens, engines, and people fade away as I stare at them, then say tentatively, "Let me get this clear. You guys are saying I have something on them, even though I don't know what it could be, and I don't even know who they are, and that Margaret was kidnapped so I can turn whatever it is over to them?"

Beckett pulls out a pack of cigarettes and frowns when water drips from it. Tossing it aside and flagging a nearby cop, he says, "Something like that."

"Do you realize how crazy that sounds to me?" I ask.

"Apparently not to them," Marley replies while a uniformed cop brings Beckett a half-smoked pack of Marlboros and a lighter.

Beckett tilts the pack in my direction.

"Jesus," I mumble, shaking my head, resisting the impulse while realizing just how deep down in this hole I am, and how much deeper Margaret is because I have no such documents. "Why would they think I have something on them?"

"My guess," says Beckett, "is that somebody back then sent them part of the proof, maybe even made it look as if it came from you, along with a warning that it would all be released should you be harmed."

"For what possible reason would someone do this on my behalf?"

Beckett pulls a cigarette out of the pack with his lips, lights up, takes a long drag, and says, "Probably to protect you from whatever happened seven years ago," before exhaling through his nostrils.

"Protect me from what?"

"David, it's obvious that a lot of strange stuff happened seven years ago, so in addition to getting you off the hook, someone also tried to protect you by sending those behind the scenes a message to leave you alone, to let you be. You had already suffered enough, and whatever it was they wanted buried was buried. Whatever secret they wanted to keep from surfacing was kept underwater. So you were also left alone to piece your life back together. And you did. But now this mystery woman who goes by

Kate Larson is using you to do the dangerous job because she knows you have plenty of motivation to uncover what really happened back then."

Sighing in exasperation, my eyes drop back to the picture in my hands. "Who is she?" I hiss before breathing deeply, trying to wrap my head around what my eyes are seeing.

Marley says, "The dead Asian's name is Tonya Ang. She's the daughter of Lisa Ang, the casino chief from—"

"Screw her," I reply. "She's dead. Who's *she*?" I stab the face of the woman holding hands with Ryan.

"That's Sheila Castaneda," replies Beckett.

Sheila.

Ryan's Sheila.

Jesus Almighty.

"She's Joe's Castaneda's sister, and from the looks of it she was also Ryan's girlfriend."

I stare at her while taking another lungful of air stained with smoke.

Sheila.

Ryan's dead girlfriend, the one he never talked about after she supposedly died.

"Guys…this is the woman who approached me in San Francisco at the bar."

They stare at me as if I'm from Mars.

"Come again?" says Marley.

"She's the one who goes by Kate Larson," I reply with a serenity that surprises me. "The one who keeps passing me notes."

The cops exchange another glance, before Beckett mumbles back to me, "That's…impossible."

"Yeah. Welcome to my hell of impossible shit."

Marley says, "Sheila Castaneda was killed in an auto accident the weekend before your arrest."

"Obviously, she didn't die," I offer.

Beckett adds, "Her accident was on the Bonne Carré Spillway Bridge. She drove her car through the guardrail and into an alligator-infested bayou. Authorities recovered the vehicle but her body was never found. She was presumed to have become gator food."

"A car accident..." I say more to myself.

THINGS WERE NOT AS THEY SEEMED 7 YEARS AGO.

I stare at my two favorite police officers in the midst of all this chaos and say, "You don't think that Sheila's car crash and my wife's crash are in any way—"

"I wouldn't jump that far just yet," says Beckett, "but it's an interesting observation. By the way, according to the NOPD, Sheila Castaneda and Heather Wilson were sorority sisters and roommates at Tulane University in New Orleans, as you can pretty much tell from this picture."

WE MUST AVENGE HER, DAVID. HELP ME AVENGE MY FRIEND.

I roll my eyes and half laugh at the irony. For the past three days I had complained about not getting answers, and now the damned answers are coming in hot and overwhelming my tired mind.

Sheila and Heather sorority sisters?

Could that explain the strange similarity in mannerisms I noticed at the bar three nights ago?

I close my eyes and try to connect the dots for Margaret's sake. What do they say about missing persons? That if they can't be found in the first forty-eight hours the chances of ever finding them drop off significa—

"Do you think Ryan knows Sheila is alive?" asks Beckett.

I have not thought about that yet. After a moment I say, "Ryan's an attorney, which means he's a vault when it comes to information. So you never really know what he knows or doesn't know. But he did tell me way back that Sheila had died unexpectedly. That was shortly before I got arrested and he left Gardner & Gardner to defend me. He never mentioned Sheila again."

"Like you said," Beckett mumbles, drawing on the cigarette and exhaling toward the sky before adding, "a vault."

"And what about Tonya Ang?" Marley asks. "While Ryan was negotiating for your release this afternoon Beckett showed him the digitized image I sent him, and Ryan claimed he didn't know her. Obviously this picture contradicts that."

Before I can formulate a response, Beckett takes over. "Could Ryan have known Sheila is alive and perhaps is trying to protect her? What about her brother, Joe? Could Ryan be protecting him as well?"

"Why would Ryan protect Joe Castaneda?" I ask. "Based on the past few days, Joe doesn't look like he requires protection. He just saved your bacon."

Beckett looks away and says, "Fair enough, but just ask Ryan about Joe. We've checked with the Pentagon without the FBI knowing about it, and it looks like Ryan and Joe served together in Iraq."

"What?"

He nods. "I think they're war buddies, and I'm guessing that's how he met Sheila."

I briefly close my eyes. After all of these revelations, I still don't feel I'm getting any closer to finding Margaret than when Beckett and Marley showed up.

Margaret.

For a moment I forget about theories, about revelations, about connecting dots, and I just think about her, about the bottle of Silver Oak we shared, about her child-like ignorance that made me fall for her—about the taste of her on my lips when we kissed.

I feel lost and alone. And cursed.

"What now?" I finally ask.

"Now I'm going to bed. The Feds are in charge, and I'm beat," says Beckett, crushing the cigarette with the toe of his shoe.

"And I have an early morning flight," adds Marley. "A pile of open cases back home."

"C'mon, guys. Don't fuck around. What do I do now?"

Marley grins and puts a hand on my shoulder in an almost motherly way while Beckett looks on. "Now you need to get your answer fast, before they contact you."

"Contact me?"

"If our theory is correct, those who snatched Margaret are very likely going to make contact soon. And when they do, you'd better be ready to trade."

They start to walk away. I instinctively grab Marley's forearm. "Wait."

She stops, frowns, and looks down at my feeble attempt to hold her back.

I slowly let go. "Look...even if I get this so called evidence, how do I trade without getting Margaret and me killed in the process? I mean, how do I give them what they need and still manage to walk away?"

They smile again, and Beckett says, "When you get this evidence that has kept you alive all these years, call me. I'll help you."

I look away, not sure how to proceed.

"Look," Marley adds, apparently feeling sorry for me. "You're going to have to hang tough if you want her back. And that means you're going to have to get through a few difficult situations, and I'm not talking about fistfights. I'm talking about really hard-to-do things, like confronting people with evidence to get reactions, to shake trees."

That reminds me of what Ryan told me.

"Where do I start shaking?" I ask, even though the acid churning in my stomach is already broadcasting the answer through my entire digestive system.

"The very first tree that needs shaking has been right under your nose all these years," says Beckett. "His name is Ryan Horowitz."

CHAPTER 22

Hospitals, and in particular Seton Medical Center in downtown Austin, evoke mixed feelings for me.

I guess most people probably don't care much to be in one as it usually means a friend or loved one—or even themselves—is undergoing some procedure or treatment.

On the one hand, I hate hospitals because they bring me back to some of the most painful moments of my life, physically and mentally.

I remember the dozens of times I had to accompany my mother here to get stitched up after my father's beatings—not to mention the occasions when I landed here after trying to shield her from the bastard. Over the course of a decade my father managed to break six of my ribs, my left wrist, my nose twice, and three times dislocated by shoulders. And the irony of it all was that the social workers kept sending me home with the motherfucker.

But on the other hand, the times my mother and I spent alone in this hospital's recovery rooms—in some cases up to a week—were some of the most peaceful of my otherwise violent childhood. We cried, laughed, and simply enjoyed the quiet pleasure of each other's company without the fear of my drunken father crashing through the door with his belt in hand.

And I also remember how my mother, every time I swore to exact revenge against my father, would place her hands over mine, look me straight in the eye, and recite an old quote from Lord Francis Bacon.

A man that studies revenge keeps his own wounds green.

Sorry, mom, I'm nowhere there yet.

As I watch the automatic doors swing open and I step into a sterile lobby leading to those sparkling-white corridors, the smell of disinfectant strikes me like a moist breeze. It reels me right back to those bittersweet days forever burned in my mind.

I didn't want to come here, to these hygienic hallways where the lights always seemed too bright, perhaps to compensate for the depressing reality that either you or a loved one is in dire need of healing, or in some cases, of a miracle.

But I had to check in on Dana. According to the last text message I got from Ryan as the detectives and I parted ways, she was still in ICU.

I approach the information desk and ask for Dana Knox while showing them my HCH credentials. They point me in the direction of the large waiting area, where I spot Patricia Norton, another one of our gate keepers at HCH, nursing a cup of coffee amidst a dozen sleeping volunteers. For a moment I panic about who is guarding the shelter, but I relax when I don't see Smith & Wesson among them.

I also don't see Ryan Horowitz, which is strange because I just got an update from him less than thirty minutes ago.

I approach Patricia.

"How's she doing?"

Patricia's large disposition includes a pair of what some people refer to as "man hands," which she uses to completely cover the plastic cup. Most women would see that as a form of disfiguration, but not her. The massive hands are valuable assets in her line of work. You do not wish to be at the receiving end of one of those fists. When you first meet the Amazon-like Patricia, your initial thought is that, like Dana, she had crossed over, but you soon learn she is an original, though she does leave you wondering if her gene pool got a little mixed at conception.

"As good as can be expected," she replies, her rough voice matching her physique. She rubs a hand over the U.S. Army Ranger tattoo on the side of her upper left arm.

Her face, however, seems a bit out of place. Patricia has beautiful skin and attractive features, including large brown eyes, which today are bloodshot. "I would love to get my hands on the bastards who did this to her," she adds.

And in my current state of mind, I would love to see her get those hands on those assholes indeed.

"Ryan told me she lost a kidney and her spleen, plus she has some broken ribs, a broken leg, and a concussion."

Patricia nods. "The concussion is from a shot to the head that just nicked her cranium at a shallow angle and bounced off. She also lost a great deal of blood, but she pulled through and should make a complete recovery."

"Thank God," I mumble, sitting next to her while trying to block the screams and cries of those agonizing moments in that alley. "How are you doing?"

She lifts her broad shoulders and frowns. "I'll be better once I can talk to her. Any word on Margaret?"

I slowly shake my head.

Patricia does something she has never done before, she holds my hand, which basically disappears in hers. "We're going to find her, David. Don't lose hope, all right?"

I try to be brave but my insides are a mess. Fighting like hell not to break down in front of her, I ask about Ryan while slowly retrieving my hand from under hers.

"Just missed him," she replies. "Went out to smoke by the ER entrance."

I yawn and slowly bob my head while getting up. Even though I certainly got plenty of sleep this morning, it's been a long and stressful day, and I feel the adrenaline rush departing my bloodstream.

I leave the waiting area and work my way across the hospital to the north end, where the ER is located.

There are twelve or so people sitting about with various illnesses not deemed life-threatening by the staff. I frown when my eyes land on a woman of about thirty with a young boy by her side. She has an ice pack pressed against the side of her swelling head, and her little boy is sobbing. Her forearms are also bruised, and her lower lip is busted. A female cop is kneeling by them taking her statement.

I briefly close my eyes and move on, reaching the exit and stepping out into the cool night.

Beyond the circular driveway is the helipad, which I never had the pleasure of using. My mother and I always arrived here via ambulance or taxi.

A lone figure stands against the silver moonlight by the steps leading up to the helipad. A thin trail of smoke coils skyward above his husky build, which looks steady, like a rock, hands on the railing.

I contemplate what Beckett and Marley told me, about Heather and Sheila, about her brother Joe, about the events that preceded my downfall. I think about the evidence I'm supposed to possess, and the possibility of having to trade it for Margaret's life. I'm not sure where to start.

I approach him quietly, my mind in turmoil about losing Margaret, about so much information I'm not sure how to process, and for a moment I wish Ryan made it all go away. I wish he could simply wave his magic legal wand and make my Margaret reappear and all of my problems disappear.

"Hey," he says, turning around, cigarette in hand. "You all right?"

"I wish," I say. "Heard anything?"

"Dana's going to pull through. The doctors—"

"I know about her," I interrupt. "I spoke with Pat. I was asking about Margaret."

Ryan turns away from me, cigarette wedged between the index and middle fingers of his right hand as he brings it up to his face and draws on it hard, ashes glowing red. "I tried to warn you. Damn it, I *really* tried." Then he exhales. "These characters don't screw around."

"I guess you should know," I reply.

He spins around. "What?"

"I said, I guess you should know that these characters," I say, making air quotes with my fingers, "don't screw around."

He drops the cigarette, steps on it, and asks, "What the fuck does that mean?"

"That you have first-hand experience on how dangerous these bastards are."

"And how, precisely, is that, David?"

Here it is. I am about to really shake my first real tree. Unfortunately, it happens to be my dearest friend, the one person on this planet I consider my family, my older brother, my protector, and for a moment my heart sinks at the thought of hurting him.

BE NOT AFRAID.
HAVE THE COURAGE TO BE GOOD AGAIN.

"It's about Sheila Castaneda," I say.

Ryan pauses in a way I have never seen before. He just stares at me, fists tight, the veins on his thick forehead throbbing, the scar on his chin trembling as he clenches his jaw. For a moment I think he is going to punch me. But instead he slowly turns back to the helipad, hands clutching the railing, his knuckles turning white.

"What about her?" he asks.

"For one thing, she's alive."

Ryan remains still. After a long pause he says, "Go away, David. You have no idea what you're talking about."

"I can't," I reply, swallowing the lump that has formed in my throat. "Sheila's alive, man. She didn't die seven—"

It happens very fast. One moment his back is to me, and the next his hands are clutching my lapels, his face inches from mine as he stares me in the eye. "What are you talking about?"

"She's alive, Ryan!"

He shakes his head, his wide-eyed stare piercing into my soul. "That's...*impossible.*"

"It's not! She is alive, dammit!" I insist, adding, "Now let go of me!"

"She died!" he hisses, tears welling in his eyes. "Seven years ago!"

Slowly, he releases me and brings both hands to his face. He is sobbing.

Dear God.

My powerful protector, the guy who rescued me so many times, is breaking down right in front of me. And unless he is the finest actor in the world, I realize at this moment he simply doesn't know.

Ryan Horowitz, the savviest guy I have ever met, the great litigator, the king of the loopholes, doesn't know his fiancée survived the car accident; doesn't know she has been alive and well all these years.

"The body was never recovered," I add as he turns away from me once more and latches onto the railing, and for an instant I think he's going to yank it out of its foundation. "But somehow she swam to shore, she survived. She is alive."

"How…how do you know this?"

"Ryan, Sheila is the woman who approached me at the bar in San Francisco and pretended to be Kate Larson. She's the person who fed me those notes."

And once again, Ryan faces me, but this time he is ashen. "How…how do you know what she looks like?" he asks. "You never met her. You never saw a picture of her. All I told you was her first name."

I'm impressed. Despite the shock, he is thinking, analyzing, challenging.

Slowly, I reach into my side pocket, produce the folded photograph, and hand it to him. "This was given to me tonight by someone who is trying to help me find Margaret."

"Jesus," he whispers, taking the picture with trembling hands, staring at the image for a long time.

"You didn't know?" I ask.

Ryan doesn't reply.

"Did you know she was alive?"

"I…always hoped," he says, eyes on the picture. "When the body wasn't recovered. But she never made contact. She never…then Heather was killed and you needed my help." He looks into the distance, and I get the sudden feeling there is more to this than he is telling me.

"What were you doing partying with these guys?" I ask.

He squints at my question. "My project in New Orleans with Gardner & Gardner…I provided all of the legal services for the International Bank of Texas, a wholly-owned subsidiary of Premier Imports. They were financing the casinos. And you already know Bernard and Gustavo were close friends. That's how I met Sheila. She was one of the CPAs running the casino books."

"And she was Joe Castaneda's sister," I say.

Ryan sighs and drops his eyebrows at me.

At his silence, I add, "Joe was posing as a security guard at the hotel in San Francisco, and he killed Tonya Ang, who was torturing Sheila along with Max Caporini. Joe bumped into me at the airport when I spotted the real Kate Larson by our arrival gate. Beckett showed you Tonya's picture earlier today and you denied knowing her. Do you mind telling me why you did that?"

He opens his mouth but doesn't say anything. It's obvious I have shocked him, and I hope the shock softens him up so he shares what he knows, and I really hope it's enough to find Margaret.

"What happened, Ryan? What did Joe and Sheila do in New Orleans that led to their falling out? And how is Heather's death connected? And how do I fit in the picture?"

He takes a deep breath and says, "Joe was a bit of a paranoid nutcase. Some, including me, felt he was on the psychotic end of the spectrum. He talked, acted, and even looked like someone operating on the edge, like he didn't care who he pissed off. And he did so on a regular basis, making plenty of enemies in a very unforgiving industry. Face it, casinos are typically associated with the netherworld, and good old Joe didn't have many fans there. But he had a knack for security, and his specialty was personal security, and man, he was amazing at it, and that got him very close to this woman, Lisa Ang, who in turn protected Joe. Until…"

I wait.

"Until he got caught skimming—or at least got accused of skimming—from one of Lisa's casinos, and the charge also involved his sister, Sheila, who being on the finance team was accused of providing Joe access to the system to facilitate the theft. Tonya Ang, who also worked security under Joe, and who was trained by Joe, was the one who brought up the charges to her mother. You have to understand that someone like Lisa Ang wouldn't be in business long without having spies everywhere, including security. She had her daughter trained by Joe with the goal of policing her own police. Although Joe and Sheila claimed to have been set up, the evidence against them was quite overwhelming: Bank accounts in the Caymans Islands and the Bahamas, a flat in New York, houses in Cape Cod and Santa Monica. Anyway, they swore they didn't own any of that, but everything looked quite legit. I reviewed the paperwork myself. If someone did set them up, it was a masterpiece. Their reputation went south overnight and a day later Sheila died in a car crash. Joe goes nuts, blaming Lisa for his sister's death, threatening Tonya for fabricating evidence and double-crossing him. He even went as far as hinting at going to the FBI and the IRS with charges of laundering drug money through Lisa's casinos and IBT. And just like that, he also disappears. That's when I decided it was probably best to pack it up and return to Austin. I haven't been back since."

"Did you and Joe serve together in Iraq?"

Ryan stares at me. "How do you know that?"

"Did you?"

"We did, during my last tour in-country, and saw some pretty bad stuff. Joe was always pushing things, taking unnecessary risks. I think four years under the Iraqi sun must have boiled some brain cells. Some of us in the unit believed he had a bit of a death wish, almost as if he didn't want to come back home. But again, David, how did you learn this?"

"That's not important. What is relevant is that Sheila is alive," I say. "It was definitely her at that bar in San Francisco."

"Damn," Ryan says, breathing in and out through his mouth, shifting his gaze from the picture to the star-filled sky. "After all these years."

"What do you think she's trying to accomplish with all these games? Why go through me and not contact you directly? Like you said, I'd never even met her or seen her picture."

"Heck if I know," he replies to my disappointment because I just know he's holding back, though I restrain from showing it externally.

"Take a guess," I say. "Try to put it together."

Rubbing his chin, Ryan rolls his eyes. "Well, Joe did make an interesting claim about Lisa Ang and the casinos, and if it's true, then IBT and its parent company, Premier, were likely accomplices in a money-laundering scheme."

"Is it true?"

"Not as far as I could tell. I mean, I audited the books at the insistence of your old boss, Gustavo, as well as my superiors at Gardner & Gardner since our combined reputation was on the line as IBT's legal consultants. But we found no sign of wrongdoing—except for the stuff Joe and Sheila were accused of, which again, looked quite real to me. Still, remembering the Enron-Arthur Anderson scandal way back, we probed even deeper, and still came up empty handed. In the end we decided to ignore Joe's claims, especially after his disappearance. Things just died down on their own, and everyone returned to business as usual."

"So, what do you think your old girlfriend is up to with all the messages, and why now, after seven years?"

He folds his muscular arms and gives me another exasperated glare. "I'm afraid you're going to have to ask her the next time you see her because I don't have a fucking clue. And while you're at it, ask her why she never contacted me. Ask her why she made me mourn her all these years. I would have tried to help her. I loved her."

"Could it be because you were on the team that reviewed the evidence against them and claimed it was legit? Is it possible she thinks you betrayed her?"

The tears filming his eyes give me my answer. But I also believe there are things he is not telling me. Ryan is an attorney, trained to be a tomb. His livelihood relies on the proper control and release of information.

But I'm growing very disappointed here. Somehow I had expected to get far more out of the revelation than Ryan is giving me. So, I decide to throw my last ace at him.

"How did you manage to keep me—and you—alive all these years?"

C'mon, Ryan, tell me something I don't know. Help me find Margaret.

"Huh?" he says, looking up.

"Why am I still alive?"

He shrugs. "Genes? A good diet and exercise? How should I know? I'm your attorney not your fucking doctor."

"Funny," I reply. "That's not what I—"

"I know what you meant, dumbass, and I also don't have an answer."

"Can't answer? Or won't answer?"

"What do you think?"

"That's why I'm asking the question, Ryan," I retort. "People are dying all around me for reasons I can't explain. Heck, even your old courtroom adversary Sebastian Serrato got whacked right in front of me, but I walked away without a scratch. Why?"

He just looks away.

"See, it doesn't make any sense," I press, feeling a weakness in his shield, looking for a way in, trying to get him to look at me again, which he finally does. "I feel caught between the bad guys, the FBI, the APD, the SFPD, dead people, hurt people, missing people, and ghosts like Sheila and Joe who are trying to make me do their investigative job while they watch from a safe distance. I'm in the middle of this deadly circus, and I don't have a clue why I'm still alive. The people the FBI are trying to put away don't like loose ends, and based on everything I know, I'm the king of loose ends. But I'm still here. Why keep me alive? It seems to me that if I were to die in a car crash, or if my apartment caught fire, or if someone mugged me and killed me for my wallet, or if I died of a Vicodin overdose—which isn't too farfetched given the way I've been popping them lately—a lot of stuff would simply die away just as it did seven years ago when Sheila and Joe vanished and the powers that be returned to their version of normalcy."

Ryan hesitates a moment, and then says, "I hear what you're saying, but I still don't know what sort of document or proof you are—"

"Dammit, Ryan!" I interrupt. "Isn't it obvious I'm being protected? And my educated guess is that someone way back made sure those who could kill me knew the dire consequences of doing so in order to make sure I was never touched. And this stupid bruise doesn't count because an undercover FBI agent gave it to me. So, my questions are: Who is protecting me? Why am I being protected? And, how am I being protected?"

"And why do you think I've got the answers?"

"Well, you have been protecting me all of my life, and I don't know of anyone else out there, especially seven years ago, who gave a shit about me except for you. So it's quite logical for me to believe you're behind this protection scheme which has kept me breathing all these years."

"Why is knowing this so important to you?" he asks.

"Because I also believe that those who kidnapped Margaret will be soon asking me for said information in return for her life."

"Come again?"

"What I have learned so far tells me that whoever kidnapped her are the same lowlifes who whacked Sebastian and who would also like to take me out, but they can't. So they went after my girl."

"Your girl? Are you and Margaret—"

"Yes, yes. We are. And that's also part of the issue. Very few people knew, which means that in order for them to go after her to get to me, they had to have someone on the inside very close to me. And when I put two and two together, meaning someone who would protect me and also someone who is close to me…that leads me to you, Ryan."

"Are you suggesting I had something to do with Margaret's kidnapping?"

"Be real, Ryan," I reply. "I love you like a brother, and you would never hurt me like that. But I am begging you, if you have any inkling—any whatsoever—of who has managed to keep me alive when those around me are either dead, pretending to be dead, hurt, or kidnapped, now would be a very good time to tell me."

Ryan closes his eyes, confirming my suspicion. He knows more than he is letting on.

"Look," he says, handing the picture back to me. "I'm not sure how else to tell you I can't help you."

"C'mon, man! Level with me. What the hell is going on?"

"I truly don't know!" he hisses. "Why do you keep insisting I know something when I've already told you I have no idea? Just like I had no clue Sheila is still alive. Why won't you believe me?"

I realize my frontal approach has gotten me as far as I'm going to get. I need to switch tactics, go around the sides.

"Did you know Tonya Ang?"

He pauses, then says while dropping his gaze to the picture in my hands, "Obviously."

"Then why did you tell Beckett you didn't?"

"So it was Beckett who gave you—"

"Never mind him. Answer the question."

He just stares back, and I say, "Ryan, this is precisely why I have such a difficult time believing you, not only because every logical explanation tells me you should know, but also because your actions strongly suggest you know more. But fine. If you claim you don't know, then in spite of the conflicting findings, I will respect that. But do know this, Ryan: I feel deep in my gut you're holding out on me, and while you may have your reasons, at the moment Margaret's life is on the line. If something happens to her and you could have prevented it by leveling with me...well, that's one I may not be able to forget."

He still doesn't reply, but I can see the anger filming his eyes.

I turn to walk away.

"Where are you going?" he asks.

"Where do you think? I'm going to scorch the fucking Earth until I find her, and I will do it with or without your help."

"Damn you," he hisses before turning away from me. "You simply couldn't leave it alone. Damn you."

I leave him standing there while I start planning my next move. My mind is cranking in overdrive with options, trying to decide which tree I'm going to shake next, trying to prioritize not only which one but also how I'll do it, and how the information I extract may allow me to come back and shake Ryan some more.

But what if Ryan was telling me the truth?

He *has* to be the one who has managed to protect me all these years. Who else could it be? And why deny this obvious fact?

For reasons I can't explain, I decide not to go back into the hospital and face HCH people in my current state of mind. So, I continue down the front of the hospital facing 38th street and reach the dark parking lot near IH-35 a few minutes later.

I try to gather my thoughts while walking to the HCH van parked way in the back of the—

"Hello, David," says a familiar male voice. "It's been a very long time."

CHAPTER 23

I slowly turn around to face Preston Wilson dressed in a sharp business suit flanked by two massive Hispanic men also dressed in suits holding guns pointed at my chest.

The years have treated the only child of the missing Bernard Wilson quite well. He looks just as manicured as he did the Friday afternoon when I made my finest and last presentation to him.

His eyes, as dark as his well-groomed hair, regard me with a mix of surprise and something else that borders on disdain while standing in front of a black Mercedes sedan. He's holding the manila envelope I had delivered to his home earlier this evening—and which I had completely forgotten about.

"Where is Margaret Black?" I ask, surprising myself.

"David, David, David," Preston replies in a soft and controlled voice. "I remember you were a much better negotiator than this."

"I'm not in the mood, Preston. Where is she?"

"This is very impressive indeed," he says, waving the color copy of the photo of Gus and Bernard, his father.

"But then again, you were always full of surprises. How in the world did you get this?"

"You're not the only one with contacts south of the border," I reply, though I can barely hear myself talk as my heartbeat is pounding my temples like the hammers from hell. "I will only ask you one more time, where is Margaret Black?"

The sole heir of Bernard Wilson's massive empire regards me with indifference before saying, "The insurance policy Ryan took out on your behalf seven years ago only protects you, not your whore or anyone else in that dump you run in north Austin."

My vision is tunneling, and in the center of my narrowing field of view is the face of one of the bastards I now know to be behind it all. "If something happens to her—"

"You're going to do what exactly?" he asks, leering, revealing gleaming white teeth.

I stare at his perfectly tanned features, at his elegant pose, at the fine tailored suit, at an impeccable blue silk tie hanging from a perfect knot and can't articulate the words of hatred boiling in my gut.

At my silence, he adds, "That's what I thought. Your lack of resources to venture beyond empty threats is what made you such an attractive fall guy seven years ago."

And just like that, in one simple sentence, Preston Wilson answered most of the questions that have haunted me for the past two days.

"But I'll tell you what. I was ready to make a clean trade with you. The insurance for the girl. But since you tried to get smart with me, I'll add a little twist to my offer." He looks at his muscular companions.

I try to back away as they nod in unison at their boss and charge towards me, but I don't get far.

They catch me almost in choreographed synchronization, lift me by my shoulders, and force my back onto the hood of a car, knocking the wind out of me as I crash hard against sheet metal before they drive their fists into my solar plexus.

My headache flaring, my vision blurring, my lungs screaming for the air my collapsed diaphragm can't deliver, Preston's face looms above me blocking the night sky.

"I happen to know that Ryan's insurance only covers death," he says while producing a glistening knife. "It doesn't pay off for losing an eye, or your balls."

Tension stabbing me in between my shoulder blades, my mouth wide open trying to breathe in, I struggle against the vise-like grip of Preston's hit men. One of them plants a massive hand on my neck and pins my head against the hood.

"It's useless to resist," Preston says as he positions the tip of the knife an inch from my right eyeball.

I try to scream as the blade glows in the night, as I try in vain to break free, to break the—

"You're losing one today, David," says Preston, "but look at the bright side. You have a spare one, plus you're already at a hospit—"

A gun cracks in the night and suddenly the pressure vanishes. The hands holding me down disappear, and I hear footsteps clicking over asphalts.

What in the world is—

Another gunshot whips across the parking lot, punching a hole into the side of the Mercedes as I slide off the hood and land on my butt, finally getting some air into my lungs while blurry figures rush away from me.

Doors slam shut and the Mercedes' engine roars to life. Wheels spin furiously, the sedan fishtailing, disappearing from view an instant later.

I sit with my back against the car looking about me, making sure I still have two eyes while painfully inhaling and exhaling, my torso on fire, my back stinging, my temples—

"Hey, Sport."

FBI Special Agent Max Caporini quickly approaches, gun in hand, muzzle pointed at the ground. He stops in front of me, looking larger than life.

I stare up in dumb surprise and manage a slight nod.

"Was that who I think it was?" he asks, squinting towards the front of the lot as the engine noise blends with the surroundings and my own throbbing heartbeat.

I nod again, my hands shaking, my nerve wracked system screaming for a cigarette. But before my over-stimulated mind can form words to muster appreciation for his impeccable timing, the FBI agent takes a knee while holstering his weapon.

Grinning, he asks, "Interested in finding Margaret Black?"

CHAPTER 24

The drive south of Austin takes almost thirty minutes, time I spend settling down while gazing out the window with renewed appreciation for my sight as well as for the Federal Bureau of Investigation. However, Caporini would not tell me what's going on, insisting everything would be explained when we get to wherever it is we are going.

We exit the highway in the city of San Marcos and follow the signs to the municipal airport

"Going somewhere?" I ask.

Caporini simply drives past the airfield's main entrance and continues down a road that curves around the rear of a large clearing. From a distance, we can see the small terminal building in front of the main ramp, where small airplanes are tied down under glaring yellow floodlights. Beyond that stand dozens of hangars, grey metal structures of varying height.

He stops by a wooded area just out of sight from the hangars bordering the west end of the runway, where an orange windsock points in our direction guided by the same breeze cooling the perspiration filming my face.

It's almost two in the morning, and I'm operating entirely on adrenaline, which I fear is going to run out soon. My body is one aching mess and I really, really want to smoke.

"You don't happen to have a cigarette, do you?" I ask in desperation.

He shakes his head. "Stuff will kill you."

I almost laugh at that.

"Follow me," he says, reaching in the rear seat, producing two pairs of binoculars, and handing one over. "Almost show time."

"What do you mean?"

He doesn't reply as he gets out of the vehicle and starts towards the woods leading to the edge of the field.

A pine-resin fragrance tickles my nostrils as I follow him, binoculars in hand, threading through knee-high bushes beneath a canopy of trees, the distant lights from the ramp casting a dim glow on this narrow strip of forest.

He takes a knee at the edge of the tree line, sinking his wide body in the shrubbery, and I do the same.

"What are we looking for?"

He stretches an index finger, touches the tip to his lips, and then uses it to point to the end of the runway closest to us before checking his watch.

Although I'm growing weary that he has not asked me a single question, especially since he saw me being bruised by Preston and his hired guns, I give him a resigned nod and settle in the dew-filmed vegetation. The moisture brushing onto my exposed arms slowly soaks through the fabric of my T-shirt, soothing my very sore back.

The windsock continues its dance in the light breeze under a star-filled sky. Insects click nearby, their sound mixing with my breathing, with my beating heart, with the throbbing behind my eyes.

I reach for my bottle of Vicodin and pop one under the curious glare of my new best friend, who raises both eyebrows and shifts his gaze back to the field. I try not to think he's the reason I'm rapidly getting addicted to this stuff.

We wait for almost an hour, as the cool and humid air seeps deep into my bones. But the night is spectacular, in a way almost magical as the sky pulsates with bright stars.

Then, in the distance, I hear engine noises above and behind us.

"Here we go," he mumbles, glancing at his watch before adding, "right on schedule."

The engine rumble increases, and I see lights looming beyond the trees, piercing through the night air as a twin-engine propeller plane crosses right over our heads, glides several feet above the runway threshold, and drops gently onto the pavement's centerline, touching down on its mains before the nose gear slowly drops as it decelerates.

The plane looks large enough to carry at least a dozen passengers and reminds me of the island commuters Evelyn and I took during our Caribbean honeymoon a lifetime ago.

"Who's that?"

"Not who, but what," he replies, pressing his binoculars against his eyes.

Still not sure what is happening, I also bring the binoculars to my eyes and start to track the airplane stopping halfway down the runway, turning around, and back-taxiing to the threshold, very close to where we are hiding.

"What's it carrying?"

"Shhh."

I frown and continue observing just as a large windowless van appears from somewhere and starts making its way down the main airport road. Being just a small municipal field, security is nonexistent at this hour.

The van steers away from the ramp and proceeds down a taxiway which leads to this end of the runway as the plane also reaches the touchdown spot and points its nose back into the light breeze before idling the engines.

The van pulls up next to it just as the plane's side door swings down and serves as a short stepladder.

Two Hispanic-looking men dressed in jeans, T-shirts, and sandals exit almost immediately, hauling large square containers, which they take directly to the waiting van.

Before they get there, two other Hispanics step out of the van clutching rifles, which make my skin crawl.

I lower my binoculars and look at Caporini, but he is intently observing the scene. When I look again, I see the men lowering their rifles and reaching inside the van for limp figures, which they hoist over their shoulders and carry to the plane. Their wrists are bound behind their backs and they are either unconscious or dead; it's hard to tell from here.

But they are clearly women.

I tense, tightening the grip on the binoculars as I watch them go back and forth for a few minutes, struggling to see if Margaret is among the women being transferred to the twin-engine.

Holding my breath, I shift from one to the next, but none of them is wearing a margarita-green T-shirt like the one she wore for rounds, and I don't recognize her face.

Slowly exhaling, I watch as the last man to board the plane pulls up the door and locks it as the engines rev up. In another minute everyone is gone.

In the increased silence as the engine noise fades in the night sky, I ask, "Were those women dead?"

"They were very much alive but drugged."

"What did I just see?" I ask as he stands and heads back into the woods. I follow him.

"A trade, Sport."

"A trade?"

Caporini makes a face and cocks his head at me. "You'll have to be smarter than that if you're going to see this through. A trade of drugs for fresh college drop-outs to be used for sex south of the border." He continues into the woods.

Margaret had suspected something like this.

"Why are they unconscious?"

"Easier to transport."

"Why didn't the FBI intercede? Why did you let the those bastards take those girls to—"

"Listen, Sport," he says as he stops in the middle of the woods, the lights from the field casting a dim glow around us. "The FBI is going after the big fish. This was just one of dozens of trades that take place each night."

"One of dozens?"

"That's part of the problem. Their operation is so distributed that stopping one shipment will not even put a dent in their business, but it will telegraph our presence. What you saw tonight takes place at dozens of remote airfields such as this one, from Texas and Arizona to California, and the fields and the hours are never the same. Bastards fly in under the radar and the cover of darkness, and slip in and out before the sun comes up. It's quite the business. We estimate that each girl is traded for around twenty to thirty grand worth of dope, depending on looks and age, and they produce about ten times that in business over the course of their first year alone, though they typically don't last more than two. They literally get fucked to death in straight prostitution, live porn acts, and extreme videos on anything from real rape scenes to bestiality. Pretty sick stuff, but you wouldn't believe how much people will pay for it, especially rich bastards from Europe, Asia, and even the U.S. looking for the kind of sex action that's illegal everywhere else, especially here. But just about everything goes in Mexico."

In the half light of these narrow woods I think of Margaret and cringe as I stare at him.

"So, Sport," he says, "I had a feeling you were holding out on us yesterday. How about coming clean given what you just witnessed and also your little chat with Preston Wilson? It could help us stop this madness and find Margaret."

My heartbeat is on the rise, and I have difficulty standing as the implications of what I've seen and what that means for Margaret sink in. I grab a nearby branch to steady myself.

"Sorry, Sport," he says, giving me a gentle pat on the shoulder. "You had to experience Preston and his guns back in the parking lot so you believe me when I tell you that you're in grave danger, and you also had to see this trade with your own eyes so you can understand that this is a huge and very complex case. It involves over seventy agents like me across four states, and I've been at it for five years, but this scheme has been in place for at least a decade."

A decade? Jesus.

"How can that be? How did the system allow that to happen? I mean, how many girls have disappeared in the past—"

"Thousands," he says. "But over ten years that's just a drop in the bucket of missing persons, especially runaway kids. Last year alone the reported number of missing kids reached eight hundred thousand in the United States. Eight hundred thousand, Sport. And that's kids under the age of eighteen. The figure goes up to a million when you include everyone up to twenty years old. Who's going to miss a few thousand over the course of ten years?"

I'm having a hard time visualizing this, but there is no denying that if what he is saying is true—and based on what I've just witnessed it looks pretty damn real to me—then I must come completely clean with the FBI, just as I did with Beckett and Marley.

"What do you wish to know?"

He grins. "That's more like it. Why don't you start with the woman who introduced herself to you as Kate Larson?"

"That's not her real name."

He just stares at me.

"Her name is Sheila Castaneda," I reply, taking the next ten minutes to explain everything I have learned in the past two days, and in particular in the past few hours from Beckett, Marley, and Ryan. I even mention the insurance thing the Hispanic assassins at the bar and later Preston were after.

The Fed listens without interruption, apparently soaking it all up. But unlike Beckett and Marley, he offers no information in return. He just stares at me with the same indifference he displayed in San Francisco, which makes the hairs on the back of my neck stand straighter than a Marine drill sergeant. There's something wrong with this guy, but I can't put my finger on it.

"Do you know where Sheila is now?" he asks.

"She was supposed to connect with us at The Drag," I reply.

"But then you guys were attacked," he says.

I nod and add, "Where is Margaret?"

"Do you know how to contact this Sheila?" he asks, ignoring my question.

I stare at him for a moment before saying, "I have a number but it's no longer in service." I pull it out of my pocket and show it to him. "She claimed to be part of that AFA convention at the hotel, but the SFPD verified she wasn't."

He stares at the business card. "But she answered this mobile number the first time you called?"

I nod.

Caporini looks away for a moment, eyes narrowing, peering into the darkness around us.

"What's wrong?"

Slowly, he shakes his head. "Thought I heard something." He then turns to me. "Is there anything else you may have forgotten."

"I think that was it."

"You think or you know?"

I don't like his tone, and I especially don't appreciate his unwillingness to share information, even if he saved me from becoming One-Eyed Jack. And the fact he is keeping me in the middle of these cold woods instead of getting back in the car and driving me home just adds to my renewed dislike for this man.

"It depends," I reply, something telling me it may be wise to push a little.

He drops his bushy brows at me. "Come again?"

"I said, it depends."

"On what?"

"On what you're also willing to share with me. So far this conversation has been a one-way street."

"So, you're calling the fact that I saved your ass back at the hospital and then brought you here to witness an exchange of drugs for female sex slaves a one-way street?"

He does have a point there, but having done all of that isn't getting me one step closer to finding Margaret. If anything, I'm now beginning to wonder if I'll ever see her again, and if I do, what kind of shape she'll be in.

"Where is Margaret Black?"

"That depends," he replies, winking.

"On what?"

"On what you're willing to share with me."

"I already told you what I know!" I hiss. "You asked me outside of the hospital if I was interested in finding her. Well?"

"Well what? I didn't say I would help you find her. I just wanted to know if you were interested in finding her."

"You're an asshole," I say, immediately downgrading him back to Butthead.

He grins. "That's because you're still holding out on me. Keep stalling, Sport. It isn't my girlfriend who's going to get fucked by a Mexican *burro*."

I tighten my fists but somehow muster enough control to remain calm in front of this abomination of a man. And as my fury rockets, as anger, desperation, and pure despair collide in the center of my drug-tainted and very tired mind, a thought emerges. I'm not really sure how or why it came to me at this precise moment, but it suddenly presents me with a way to trick this annoying son of a bitch into telling me what I suspect he knows—Margaret's location.

"I told you everything," I say, deciding to shake this tree, "unless…"

"Unless?" he leans closer.

"Well…there's this document from seven years ago, the one Ryan set up to make sure nothing happened to me or him after Sheila and Joe Castaneda mysteriously vanished."

His eyes flash a surge of interest he fails to contain as he asks, "The insurance Preston Wilson asked about?"

I nod, certainly seeing why the FBI would salivate for such a document as it would very likely provide them with the evidence they need to crack this case. And this is precisely the leverage I need to get her back.

"Keep going," he says.

"What do you mean keep going?" I ask, somehow finding the courage to screw with him.

"Where is this document you're talking about?"

"In a safe place." Again, I can't believe I'm replying like this to an FBI agent, but a strange rush of confidence sweeps through me.

"Don't screw around, Sport. This is the FBI you're talking to."

"And this is *my* life insurance I'm taking about," I reply with a serenity that even impresses me. "Unless the FBI is willing to not only get Margaret back but also guarantee our protection, this is all Ryan and I possess to keep us alive."

"I see," he says. "How about if I put you away for obstruction of justice?"

"That just tells me you don't really know where she is," I say.

He closes his eyes, and for a moment I think he is going to head-butt me again, but instead he just turns away and starts towards the car.

I'm about to follow him when he spins around clutching a weapon, which he points at the center of my chest.

"Sorry, Sport, but you need to tell me everything you know. What's the evidence and where is it?"

Although this is the first time I'm staring at the barrel of a gun, my wired mind continues to spin. He obviously can't kill me because he is an FBI agent, and last time I checked federal agents don't go around shooting innocent civilians. However, who would ever know if he whacked me out here in the woods? No one saw me leave with him. But what would he stand to gain by killing me? Certainly not the evidence he seeks.

And then it hits me.

If Butthead takes me out right here, and if he indeed believes I do have such insurance policy, then by killing me this incriminating evidence would be released, which in essence does his job for him.

On the other hand, I always had a bad feeling about this guy, and the fact he has pulled a gun on me suggests he may be corrupt, working for those who kidnapped Margaret, and he is trying to intimidate me into releasing the only leverage I have. Is it possible that the whole Preston thing was staged so he could come to my rescue in an effort to get me to release this insurance to him?

Of course, this is just all theoretical crap my tired mind is conjuring because I have no idea if such document even exists.

"Time to come clean, Sport."

"I don't react well to threats," is all I can think to say while I struggle to figure a way out of this predicament, my mind trying to play the odds. Given everything I know and everything I sense, I decide he is no good. And that means he can't afford to kill me because he doesn't get the information his superiors—probably Preston Wilson—have probably ordered him to deliver: the insurance policy that someone took out on my behalf, and which for them is a perpetual dark cloud.

Whether this document actually exists at the moment is really irrelevant. Butthead obviously thinks it exists, and that perception is enough to give me an edge.

He grins again. "Do you really want to test me?"

I give him my best cop shrug imitation.

His wrist flicks in the night, and before I know it I'm on all fours and my right cheek is burning as if he poured acid on it. The bastard just bitch slapped me with his gun, and I nearly pissed my pants again.

Things start to spin, and I close my eyes while trying to hold it together, while the headache behind my eyes skyrockets, pounding against my temples, against my throbbing cheek.

"Want another one, Sport?"

I open my eyes and notice the blood dripping onto leaves and pine needles littering the ground, clearly visible as my eyes have fully adjusted to the half-light of these woods. In my moment of agony, I become profoundly aware of everything around me: mosquitoes buzzing by my ears; the light wind rustling the branches overhead; my heavy breathing.

"Well, Sport," Butthead insists. "Would you like me to even you out? This is your last chance. Tell me where those documents are or you die tonight, right here, right now."

As incredible clarity descends on me through the turbulence of pain, I also realize there is nothing this bastard can do to me that Margaret isn't going to experience a hundred-fold if I fail to get her back. Sticking to my guns, and realizing he's very likely going to stick it to me with his gun, I reply, "Go fuck yourself, you son of a—"

The blow to my left cheek sends me crashing against the trunk of a towering pine as a thick veil of tears swallows my world.

I lay there on my back scourged, whipped, beaten, my head about to explode. Immense pressure builds suddenly on my chest with crushing force.

I tense, try to cry out, but an invisible claw is gripping my throat, choking me, and as I clear my sight, I realize he is on top of me, strangling me.

I try to fight him, try to kick, jerk, but he is sitting on my chest, knees pinning my elbows, his hands compressing my larynx.

"Hey, Sport!" he hisses in my ear as my mind starts to go dark from lack of oxygen, as my wide-open mouth fails to draw any air—as I start to lose sensation from my arms and legs. "It's almost poetic the same hands that squeezed the life out of Heather Wilson and Kate Larson—the same hands that drove the car that forced Sheila Castaneda off that bridge, and your fucking family off that cliff—are now going to choke you to death."

In spite of the raw pain consuming me, of the surreal force against my throat, my chest, and my arms, my mind processes the unexpected words, the shocking revelation that the monster who took everything away from me has been standing in front of me all this time.

But I can't move.

I can't scream.

I can't cry out the injustice being done to me just as Evelyn, Little David, Heather, and Kate were not able to protest, their lives extinguished by this disgrace of a human being.

I see his leer above me, like the devil himself in this final twilight eve of my life. I see his eyes gleam with dark anticipation during my final struggling moments, as my mind fades away under his deadly clasp, as the world around me starts to vanish.

But another image floats in front of me, blocking the monster. It's my little boy, the son I'd always thought I killed. He is looking down at me with tears in his eyes as he stretches his arms at me.

Hold me, Daddy. Hold me tight.

I try to reach out to him but he slowly turns around and walks away.

Wait!

Don't go!

I'm sorry! I'm so sorry! Oh, Dear God! Please forgive me! I have tried to make amends!

But David is gone as an overarching darkness cloaks everything around me, as I no longer feel my body, no longer hear sounds, no longer feel any pain.

A profound sense of isolation envelopes me. And it is in this deep state of loneliness that I see her face, her smile—feel her powerful embrace.

Margaret.

A damaged soul who was just emerging from the shadows of her past.

Margaret.

And those bastards took her away from—

I hear a scream, but it's not her.

A man is shrieking in agony, in pain, screaming at the top of his lungs before silence suddenly returns.

Slowly, somewhere in the darkness of my world a speckle of light flickers, like a distant star, slowly expanding as sound returns, as the insects clicking and buzzing around me tell me I'm still alive, that I've somehow survived.

I fill my lungs with air, cough, and breathe again through my aching throat, feeling my limbs come alive, stretching them, flexing my fingers. But along with life comes the throbbing pain from my face, from the blows the bastard inflicted on me.

My vision starts to clear, like an image slowly coming into focus.

Someone is standing over me.

Did he take me to the brink of death and then pull me back? Did he do this just to torture and get me to confess to information I really don't have?

I blink, desperately trying to see, to remove the veil filming my tired eyes. My head is killing me as much as my neck. My cheeks are on fire. I desperately need a Vicodin. But suddenly I feel my strength leaving me again. My body is demanding rest.

I struggle to hang on, to remain awake, slowly resolving the image, until I finally see clearly. But as has been the case for the past two days, I don't believe what I see.

My mind doesn't register the face of the murderer, of the monster.

Instead, I see the face of Sheila Castaneda.

CHAPTER 25

I was happy once.

I just didn't know it.

I had a family. I had friends. I had a good job.

And one day it all ended.

There are defining moments in people's lives; times forever etched in our minds. Some are good. Others not so.

For me, there was no worse time than receiving the news of my family's death while confined to a jail cell on murder charges.

For me the sun never shone quite as bright again. The sky has never been as blue. The rain stopped tasting sweet.

You could say a part of me died inside that cell that Sunday afternoon; the consequences of my actions raking my insides like a sizzling claw.

For me there would be no turning back.

There would be no amends.

No forgiveness.

No redemption.

My actions had caused my family to die.

By fire.

At least that's what I was led to believe.

I thought I caused much suffering, and I survived to live with the pain of having survived, to be consumed with the guilt of what I did. And in my attempt to achieve salvation through Hill Country Haven, I witnessed even more suffering, more abuse.

And one strange side effect of having caused, experienced, and witnessed so much affliction, is that over time I became somewhat desensitized to it. In particular, when that suffering happened to people who had it coming, like the abusive husbands or boyfriends we put behind bars for violating restraining orders, or the lowlifes we ordered beaten by some of Ryan's unsavory clients on parole.

Or the bastard who killed my family, Heather, and Kate, and almost choked me to death had it not been for Sheila and her brother coming to my rescue in my time of guttural need.

The demons of guilt still grip me for having cheated on Evelyn, causing her and little David to be at the wrong place at the wrong time. But I also feel a small amount of redemption at the knowledge that she didn't run off the road as I was led to believe.

I sit on a stool by the countertop separating the living room from the kitchen, staring at the half-drunk bottle of Silver Oak while Joe Castaneda works on Max Caporini in the bathroom. The Ranger-turned-bodyguard has gone to work on Butthead with a stainless-steel cocktail shaker, a blow torch, duct tape, and a pair of gerbils, which he stole from a pet shop on our way here.

Exactly what Joe is doing with that stuff behind that door—something he claimed to have learned in Iraq—I don't really want to know. But whatever it is, I sure hope it hurts like a motherfucker.

It was Agent Max Caporini who killed Heather and then framed me for the murder.

It was Agent Max Caporini who killed my family hours later in a car crash similar to the one Sheila Castaneda nearly died in the week before.

It was Agent Max Caporini who also strangled Kate Larson while she was helping Sheila feed Beckett and me more clues to their wrongdoing.

It is because of Agent Max Caporini that my throat is on fire and it's hard to swallow even water.

And I know deep in my gut it is because of this bastard Margaret was abducted.

But Joe smiled a chilling smile as he assured me that before the sun came up he would know everything the corrupt federal agent knows.

Everything.

And I believe him.

Ryan was right. There is something scary about the borderline-albino Joe Castaneda which instantly commands the kind of respect you give the playground bully. He projects himself as someone who carries a death wish; almost as if he really doesn't care what happens to him. You can even argue that his ghostly appearance makes him look like death itself. And that makes him dangerous, but in my case, that also makes him a key asset in my quest to find Margaret. At the moment, I'm in desperate need of someone in my corner who doesn't know how to play by the rules.

And as Joe disappeared into the bathroom to go *cuddle* with Caporini—as he soberly put it—I realized perhaps I did have a coveted dark angel watching over me tonight.

There will be no Miranda Rights for Agent Max Caporini.

He gets no lawyer and no phone call.

The bastard gets the blow torch on his balls and the gerbils up his ass or wherever it is his bloodcurdling torturer will shove them.

As they helped me back to the car at the perimeter of the municipal airport, I remember Butthead hissing to Joe to just get it over with and put a bullet in his head. Joe had leered back at him for a long time. Then, still smiling, said, "Sorry, Sport, but today just ain't your lucky day."

I called Ryan on the way back from San Marcos and urged him to meet me at my apartment immediately. Although I didn't tell him why, I insisted it was an emergency and also asked him to bring Patricia Norton along, though I didn't tell him it would be so she could assist Joe. On the way in, I asked Patricia to swing by the shelter and grab a medical kit from the nurse's station—and not just to stitch me up, but also for Joe, who apparently intends to keep Butthead alive so he can continue to Guantanamo Bay him.

Ryan arrived thirty minutes ago to the surprise of his life. He indeed had no earthly idea that his former fiancée as well as his former brother-in-arms were alive, and the shock nearly brought him to his knees.

Sheila and he had quite the emotional reunion, though it was a bit hard to tell if it was because of joy, anger, regret, or all of the above. In any case, they are catching up outside, in the privacy of his car while Joe works his CIA black site magic assisted by Patricia, and while I continue to stand in my kitchen, staring at this most special bottle of wine.

I close my eyes at the thought of Margaret selecting the one bottle I had been saving for a special occasion. Life, it seems, isn't without a sense of irony because as it turned out that half hour drinking with her had certainly been the most intimate since I began to piece my life together.

I just didn't know it at the time.

But now, as I close my eyes in hope that Joe's skills are still as sharp as Ryan claimed they had been back in the old days, I am counting the hours since her kidnapping. It's almost five in the morning and we were attacked at nine last night, so I'm hoping she is still in the country, still somewhere easily reachable as soon as Joe extracts what we need.

I stare at the Ibuprofen I started taking an hour ago to reduce the swelling from my aching neck and cheeks, which are turning purple and starting to pull on the stitches Patricia applied when she arrived with the medical kit.

She is now assisting Joe in his *cuddling* duties, and for a moment I actually feel sorry for Butthead. I wouldn't want to be on the receiving end of the type of persuasion those two have honorary degrees in; although they've never met before, their military backgrounds made them click almost instantly.

Sheila and Ryan come back into the apartment, but they seem strangely distant, quite unlike two reunited lovebirds. I remember how angry Ryan had been that she never did contact him, though I have a feeling she may have had very good reasons for not doing so.

"Hey, handsome," Sheila says, her face reminding me of the few pleasant moments we shared in San Francisco.

"Yeah," I sigh. "Quite the prince charming."

"How are you holding up?" Ryan asks, putting a hand on my shoulder as Sheila takes the second bar stool to my right and Ryan stands between us. His eyes are a bit bloodshot, as if he's been crying. Sheila's are also red.

"Ask me after Joe and Pat finish up in there. How are you guys doing?"

They exchange a glance, and then she says, "We have a lot more to talk about."

"But first we need to finish this once and for all," Ryan adds. "No more hiding. No more running away. No more living in fear."

Sheila nods. "No more being afraid."

I stare at her, at her uneven features, imagining the physical and emotional suffering she has gone through, and the courage she is displaying by refusing to surrender.

I learned from this brave woman on the drive here that she had been forced off the bridge by Butthead and had suffered lacerations to her face, which explains the faintly unbalanced features that had captivated me the first time I met her. But she had survived, rescued by a nearby boat, and she had been able to contact Joe, who made the necessary arrangements for her disappearance—and his own—to shield themselves when his protection vanished. And it had broken her heart to keep Ryan in the dark all these years, but at the time Joe trusted no one, including Ryan, who was, after all, one of the Gardner & Gardner lawyers who reviewed the accusations against him and reported they were real. So Joe had used his resources to get her out of the country to undergo lengthy surgical procedures and even longer recovery periods out of harm's way. Meanwhile, a mourning Ryan Horowitz used his knowledge of the casino-banking operation to create an insurance policy for him and me.

"Where is this document?" I ask.

Ryan frowns. "That's the thing. The way I set it up prevents even me from finding it. Otherwise what keeps those bastards from just torturing me to get it? The document is out of my reach in the hands of the contacts of my contacts. If something ever happens to you or me, the document would automatically find its way to the media as well as to the local, state, and federal authorities."

"What's in it?"

"Casino books and bank accounts in the International Bank of Texas that the IRS doesn't know about. It's got tons of illegal transactions and transfers to overseas account that were never reported to Uncle Sam. And the irony of it all is that much of what I was able to document was related to the consulting work you were doing."

I slowly shake my head, still refusing to believe the current-state analysis I had reported to Preston Wilson that Friday, including my recommendations to perform efficiency improvements at their banking operations, had been the trigger that brought the monster to my family.

"So our insurance policy is basically the threat of exposing a money-laundering operation?" I ask.

He nods. "For the most part. Remember that to the lords of organized crime, it's really all about the money. You whisper that to them and they all start listening. So I set it up right after Sheila and Joe were reported dead and Heather was killed and you got blamed for it."

There are many questions taxing me. I blurt out the first one that comes to mind.

"Was this document what set me free? Was this what got the powers that be, those controlled by the likes of Bernard and Preston Wilson and Lisa Ang, to find new evidence and get me acquitted?"

"I'm sure it didn't hurt," he replies, "though I never used it directly. I just let them know I had it."

"So," I say, "all this time you've been lying about not knowing why evidence suddenly appeared and set me free seven years ago."

Another shrug. "I was afraid you'd end up dead like Sheila and Heather. Maybe the cops would find you hanging from your cell one night. At the time, suicide would have worked perfect. So I had to send them a message for your own protection. Afterwards, I just maintained the illusion—also for your protection. I needed you behaving normally because I also knew we were being watched."

Closing my eyes I gently massage the bridge of my nose, my cheeks throbbing, my head hurting, slowing my thought process. "I still can't believe this bastard killed everyone, from Heather to my family. Fucking monster."

Sheila takes my hand and smiles at me just as she did in San Francisco. "That's how they operate, David, which is why I had to be so careful."

"What you haven't explained yet," I say, as another question makes it past my veil of neurological pain, "is why contact me? Why not go directly to Ryan?"

They exchange a glance and then Sheila says, "They found me. We always knew that even with all of the precautions Joe took, including our decision not to contact Ryan, in part for fear of him being under their watch, we still ran the risk of being spotted. And a big part of the problem was Max Caporini. See, he was another one of Lisa Ang's bodyguards along with her daughter Tonya and also Joe. And you now know that Joe killed Tonya while trying to rescue me at the hotel."

"Did you know Caporini from way back?" I ask Ryan.

He nods. "But it wasn't until he showed up in my office yesterday with Special Agent Jessica Herrera that I realized he was an undercover FBI agent. I'm sorry I didn't share that with you, but both Caporini and his partner pulled the national security card on me," he says, rolling his eyes.

I look back at Sheila. "Why did they go after you and Joe back then."

"I was one of Lisa Ang's CPAs," Sheila says, "And I noticed irregularities in some of the bank transactions, in particular deposits from the casinos to the International Bank of Texas and then onto a number of bank accounts in the Cayman Islands that didn't exist in the books."

"You got too close," I say, "just like me at Premier with my efficiency consulting."

"Yeah. Then I made the mistake of reporting my findings to Tonya and Lisa, who told me to forget about those accounts. But I couldn't, you see. Lisa's casinos, like any other industry, get regularly audited, and not just by the IRS but also by the Louisiana Gaming Commission. And I didn't want to get in trouble and lose my CPA license."

"So, you became a liability to them, just like me."

"And that led to Tonya framing us for skimming profits. And that's when Caporini approached us and identified himself as an FBI agent and offered protection in exchange for our testimony. We didn't know at the time he was a rogue agent, but he obviously had the resources of the FBI behind him. Caporini arranged for separate meetings with his superiors to kick off the process, and I was driving to meet them when he ran me off the bridge. Joe went nuts, thinking that Lisa and her gang had gotten to me before the FBI could protect us. He also tried to play ball with Caporini and was about to head to his FBI meeting when I reached him and warned him about Caporini. That's when we realized we had to escape while we could. There was no way we could combat both the casino mafia and a corrupt FBI agent. But in order to vanish we needed resources of our own to remain below radar, so I helped Joe drain millions of dollars from those bank accounts that didn't exist. We escaped to Spain, where he used part of the funds to reconstruct my face, which was pretty smashed when Caporini drove me off the bridge."

I sit back and draw a deep breath.

Caporini.

The Butthead.

My throat clamps up each time I think of the misery this bastard has brought to my life.

Sheila adds, "We spent three years in Spain before relocating to northern California, where we got wind of the prostitution ring Bernard Wilson and Gustavo Salazar were running with the help of Lisa Ang, and in the process we were sort of forced back into this after our long sabbatical."

"How?"

"Kate Larson," she replies.

I blame my Vicodin haze and the throbbing pain for not having asked the question sooner. "I've been meaning to ask about her. Who is she?"

"Kate was the reason they found us. She was what you would refer to as the madam of the call-girl service at Lisa's casino in New Orleans. Apparently, someone decided it would be a lucrative business to take runaway teen girls and force them into prostitution in Mexico. Their logic was that those teens were going to die as crack addicts in the back alleys of America anyway, so might as well squeeze some profit out of them."

"Caporini told me as much," I say, adding what he said and also what I saw at that field.

"Well, that's what made us get back in and try to do something about it," Sheila says. "I couldn't bear the thought of our own youth being shipped off to become the object of sexual perverts. Kate was sent to Mexico by Lisa with the goal of starting up these high-class bordellos in industrial cities like Monterrey, where businessmen from around the world could enjoy some downtime engrossed in their sexual fantasies. What Kate didn't know until later was that the source of the female talent wasn't going to be local but mostly from America. But by then she was trapped in Monterrey and forced to become part of the entertainment. She used to be quite beautiful. But six years of abuse aged her to what you saw in San Francisco."

"How did she escape?" I ask, remembering what Caporini told Jessica in Ryan's office about Kate Larson being the first one to escape. "And how did she find you when the combined powers of the casino mafia and the FBI couldn't?"

Sheila smiles that crooked smile of hers while Ryan just stares at her with a mix of regret and admiration. I don't think I've ever seen him stare at anyone like that before. But he remains quiet, listening to Sheila answering my questions.

"Life is funny, David," she says. "Joe and I became very close friends with this surgeon in Barcelona by the name of Manuel Espinoza who reconstructed my face. Although he was a bit of a womanizer, he was also one of Europe's finest plastic surgeons, and we kept in touch even after Joe and I returned to America. Manuel happened to be at a plastic surgery convention in Monterrey and ended up at one of the high-class bordellos run by Lisa and her partners in Mexico. And it just so happened to be the place that Kate worked. Now, the way she explained this to me, they had close-circuit cameras in every room to monitor every movement made and every word the girls said. But

the girls knew this, and they also knew what would happened to them if they tried to alert their clients to their
predicament."

"What kind of punishment are we talking about?" I
ask even though I don't really want to know.

Sheila's voice drops a few decibels even though there
is no reason to whisper. "They had this masked guy who
would wear this contraption that resembled a penis but it
was made of rusty razor blades, and he would—"

I raise my right palm and shake my head. "Dear Lord."

"And he did it in front of the others."

"Like a public hanging?" I say.

She slowly nods. "According to Kate they didn't have
to do it very often. Something about watching one of your
colleagues be brutalized in that way before bleeding to
death keeps your lips from loosening up."

"But that didn't deter her," I mumble.

"She ended up in the same room with Manuel
Espinoza one night," Sheila continues. "And he commented
on her fine wrinkles and how easily they could be fixed.
Apparently, the whorehouse management decided it would
be good for business to have some of their more experienced but maybe a bit worn girls touched up, and Kate was
among them. It was during pre-surgery that she ended up
talking to Manuel about her ordeal, including her years at
Lisa Ang's casino, and that led to me. Manuel arranged to
make it appear as if Kate had died on the operating table
from an unexpected reaction to the anesthesia and had her
body cremated. He then helped her back to the United
States and to me. Once we heard what was going on, we
really had no choice."

"But Caporini spotted you."

Sheila nodded. "Apparently the people in Mexico didn't quite buy the Kate Larson story, tracked down Manuel in Barcelona, tortured him, and he obviously talked. Joe and I became suspicious something was wrong when I got word Manuel had died in a car crash two weeks after Kate knocked on my door."

"And to your credit you didn't run, but you also didn't go to the authorities because of Caporini."

"That would have been suicide," Sheila says. "Caporini had quite the sweet deal going. Being deep undercover gave him plenty of latitude to play things close to his chest. Joe is quite sure he's in possession of some pretty fat bank accounts in places beyond the reach of Uncle Sam."

"So you decided to make contact with me while I was out of town instead of Ryan because you figured they would not be following me to San Francisco."

"That's one reason," she says, exchanging a disappointing glance with Ryan. "But he tracked us down anyway."

"Who warned you on the phone when you were sitting at the bar with me?"

"Joe. He was hanging out by the front desk. He rushed to our rescue when you screamed, tried to get Caporini but Tonya got in the way and he killed her instead while the bastard got away."

I close my eyes and frown, my cheek muscles tugging at my stitches.

She adds, "Joe had spotted Caporini outside and told me to go straight to the rear of the hotel. But somehow Caporini made it inside and grabbed me before I could warn Joe. Had it not been for you..." She puts a hand just below by bruised cheek and gently pats the side of my face by my jaw line. "You are an amazing person, and I see why

Ryan did what he did to protect you. I'm sorry I brought so much pain to you."

I feel color coming to my face.

"You have no idea how much you've helped me," I say. "These bruises will heal. But by contacting me you have managed to help me heal a little. Now I need to get Marge back, and I know that bastard knows where she is."

"If anyone can extract it from him, it's Joe," says Ryan, speaking for the first time in a while.

My eyes gravitate to the bottle of Silver Oak, and for reasons I can't explain, another question makes it through the layers of chemicals and pulsating pain. "How did Caporini get to Kate?"

Tears fill Sheila's eyes. "The three of us, Kate, Joe, and I, were trying to figure out the best way to alert those who we believed were not corruptible, and that included Detective Beckett Mar. Joe delivered the picture frame to the foyer while she worked on delivering a message to your front door, and while I did the same to Beckett. The idea was precisely what happened, to get you guys together and show you that Bernard Wilson was alive and well. We think maybe she was followed from your shelter. We were all staying at the same hotel but in different rooms. Joe and I got there two hours later and saw the cops and heard about the murder."

Sheila then glances in the direction of the bathroom and adds, "Whatever Joe's doing in there, I hope it hurts like hell."

I stare at her, at her glistening eyes, at her slightly uneven frown, and say, "I still don't get why Heather was also murdered."

"Well, let's see what Joe finds out. But my educated guess is that her assassination was opportunistic," Sheila says.

"What do you mean?"

"Remember that she was my best friend, and after I supposedly died and Joe vanished, she went to New Orleans for my funeral and started asking questions, going to see people like Lisa and Tonya, demanding answers. Heather never bought the car accident story and smelled foul play from the beginning. Also remember that Bernard had many mistresses and that Heather was just a trophy wife, so he was infuriated with her for ruffling the feathers of his business associates, especially Lisa. When she returned to Austin, I'm guessing she was already on the hit list. Meanwhile, according to Ryan you were starting to poke your nose into the financials of IBT and Lisa's casinos, so when the two of you ended up in bed that Friday night, I think it became a huge opportunity to take you out."

"But I wasn't killed. Only Heather."

She lifts her narrow shoulders. "Again, let's see what Joe learns."

I'm getting some answers, but not enough of them fast enough. I stare at my watch again while trying to ignore the nasty spikes of pain pulsating from my cheeks as well as the strange air between Ryan and Sheila. Something's up with those two but at the moment I have bigger fish to fry. Time is running out for Margaret, and we're sitting here theorizing. What's taking Joe so damned long?

I force discipline into my sore mind and ask, "Do you have any idea what happened to Bernard Wilson? Where is he?"

She nods. "Kate told me he lives in a mansion in Monterrey. She did a few jobs there, which is where she stole that picture of him and your old boss, Gustavo Salazar."

I think about that for a moment, deciding it does make sense. "What about the photos of me and Heather she had with her when they found her dead in the hotel room?"

Sheila shakes her head. "I don't know anything about that. Maybe Caporini planted them after he killed her. Perhaps he was planning to use them to—"

We hear the door to the bathroom open and close. A moment later Patricia emerges from my bedroom, her face filmed with sweat, her shirt peppered with red dots.

She goes straight for the kitchen sink and splashes water on her face before reaching for a paper towel under the counter, drying her face with her massive hands, which are also bloody.

"That man doesn't screw around," Patricia says. "I've never seen such shit, but damn, it really works. Do you have Ziploc bags. Quart size will do."

I narrow my eyes at her.

"Why?"

"You don't want to know. Do you have some?"

I point to the cabinet above the sink where I keep a box so I can carry my toiletries during business trips. She opens it, takes the whole box, and heads back to the bathroom.

"Wait a second. What did you learn?" Ryan asks.

Patricia stops in midstride. "We have a location where they hold them in this region before shipping them to Mexico."

"Where?" I ask, standing.

R.J. PINEIRO

"A ranch near New Braunfels. We'll be right out. Just need to clean up and sedate him," she says, disappearing in the bedroom, and we hear the bathroom door open and close. And in the few seconds in between a faint, muffled cry escapes into the kitchen.

I take a deep breath. Even though Butthead has brought complete misery to my life, at this one instant in time a trickle of sympathy worms its way through my ocean of abhorrence for this devil incarnate.

"Where is that?" asks Sheila, apparently not familiar with the area.

"We were almost there when you found me," I say. "It's about twenty minutes south of San Marcos on the highway. We don't have a lot of time," I add, searching for the keys to the van. "I saw their process. I saw how they transport them. We need to get down there right away."

"Hold on, Cowboy," Ryan says. "We need to think this through. Let's not just rush down there. I mean, what are you going to do when you get to this ranch? Stand in the middle of the road at high noon and draw your six-shooter?"

"She has to be there, Ryan."

"That's hardly an argument for rushing off without a plan. In fact, that's not an argument at all."

"Don't get all fucking lawyerly on me. What if Sheila was the one waiting to be shipped off into God knows what? How much of an argument would you need to rush after her, Counselor?"

Sheila shoots Ryan a sideways glance of pure contempt, and I think somehow, I must have struck an old nerve.

"All right, all right," Ryan says, ignoring her. "What I mean, is we need a plan. We can't just crash the place

280

without first planning how we're going to deal with people armed with machine guns, at least that's what I remember you saying they had when you watched them load up those women in that plane."

I'm about to reply when we hear the bathroom door open and close again. This time both Patricia and Joe emerge through the bedroom door. He is bloodier than she and holding a pair of Ziploc bags filled with what looks like flesh, blood, and dead gerbils.

Sheila covers her mouth. I feel my stomach contract and press a fist against my mouth. Ryan, who's been to Iraq with Joe, regards the bloody mess with detached indifference.

"It's dawn, guys," Joe says in a monotone voice that sounds almost like a hiss, like a viper. His eyes behind the small round rimless glasses are the lightest of hazels, which combined with his pale complexion and his ash-blond hair, gives him an eerily, ghost-like presence which sends disturbing chills up my spine. Add to that his shirt and hands splattered with blood, and your first instinct is to run for cover.

He calmly hands the gore to Patricia as if he's handling bags of potato chips, which she dumps in the garbage can next to the sink. None of us say a word. And that alone gives me a sense for how far off the edge my mind is at the moment. There's a federal agent—corrupt or not—bleeding in my bathtub, there's pieces of the bastard in my garbage can, and I'm perfectly fine with that.

"And according to my former associate," Joe adds in that whisper-like voice, "who is occupying your tub at the moment, they only move them at night. Since Margaret was kidnapped at around 9pm last night, and since Preston is interested in trading her for your insurance, it's a pretty safe bet that she will remain at the holding ranch in New Braunfels at least until tonight. We have time to plan properly."

"How heavily guarded is that ranch?" I ask.

"Very," Patricia replies, turning on the kitchen faucet and lathering her hands and forearms with dish soap.

"Eight armed men all the time, to be precise," Joe says.

I reach for my mobile phone but Ryan puts a hand on my forearm. "Who are you calling?"

"Beckett and Marley. We're going to need reinforcements."

Joe steps towards me, regards my facial bruises a moment, then looks over to Patricia. "Tight stitching. Good field job."

She shrugs. "Some things you just don't forget."

He then levels those sinister hazel eyes on me and says, "David Wallace, do you trust Detectives Beckett Mar and Marlene Quinn?"

I consider that for a moment, remembering my long discussion at the bar. "As much as I can possibly trust anyone today."

"What about FBI Special Agent Jessica Herrera?"

"I'm not sure, though I doubt she's corrupted like the bastard you have in there."

Joe's uncanny stare stays on me, and I feel it digging through the glasses, beyond the bruises, through my optical nerves, and right into brain. I try to look away, but he uses his index finger to bring my eyes back towards his. "Before we do bring the police and perhaps the FBI into this, there are a couple of things we need to acquire."

"Such as?"

"What's kept you alive all these years?"

I stare at him.

Joe looks over at Ryan before removing his glasses, breathing on them, and polishing them with a napkin as he adds, "We're going to need his insurance."

CHAPTER 26

I've never been much of a conspirator. In fact, every recent attempt to craft some sort of plan has backfired, and in some ways you could argue that I'm only alive because of people who actually know what they're doing, like Ryan, Joe, and Sheila.

Left to my own devices I would have gone the frontal approach, called Beckett and Marley, and foolishly tried to form a posse to head down to New Braunfels and heroically rescue Margaret.

Instead, in the pre-dawn hour of this third day since my life began to head in a completely different direction, as faint shafts of burnt orange stab the indigo sky, I'm standing in the middle of this alley holding a large manila envelope filled with blank sheets of paper.

But the eminent Preston Wilson doesn't know that.

I see the headlights of his Mercedes Benz sedan cut through the darkness enveloping this place of his choosing, where I'm certain he has posted plenty of back-up help, especially given the sudden disappearance of his alley cat, Max Caporini.

But Joe was right. The Mercedes comes to a stop a dozen feet from me, and I spot his Hispanic bodyguards exiting the front of the vehicle before one of them opens the rear door and Preston, casually dressed in a white polo shirt, light-green slacks, and loafers, emerges slowly. The lure of Ryan's insurance was enough to draw the big fish out from the safety of his lair and straight into Joe's elaborate trap.

I inhale deeply while foolishly hoping that Margaret would be accompanying him, but Joe had warned me that the likes of Preston Wilson do not operate that way.

"So we meet again," he says, hands in the pockets of his slacks while narrowing his gaze at my facial scars. "What the hell happened to you?"

"I'm having a really bad week."

"No shit," he replies while dropping his gaze to the folder in my hands.

"Where is she, Preston?"

Keeping his hands in his pockets, he lifts his shoulder while looking away. "Nearby. Safe."

I take a step back, playing my role just as Joe choreographed it. "The deal was an exchange of the documents for Marga—"

"I know how this works." He lifts his left hand and checks the time on the Rolex watch hugging his wrist. "My tee time is in an hour. Is that Ryan's document?"

"What...this?" I say, waving the manila folder. "It all depends on where you have Margaret," I insist, taking another step back.

Preston looks at his bodyguards and they start to move towards me.

As I'm about to take another step back, a pair of hands press against my shoulder blades. "Where do you think you're going, Amigo?"

Before I can turn around to look at the bastard who sneaked behind me, he palm-strikes by back.

The pain stabs my already sore back and propagates like sheet-lightning up my spine and deep into my brain while thrusting me towards the incoming dynamic duo.

In a blur, I watch them palm-strike me on the chest just as I'm about to collide with them.

Jesus!

The raw pain now shoots deep into my chest cavity as I find myself flying back towards the third guy in an agonizing game of ping-pong that ends with me tripping and falling on my butt.

As I try to get my bearings, as the pain on my back and chest somehow blends into a sizzling throb engulfing my upper body, they form a semicircle around me making room for Preston, who approaches me slowly, smiling.

"David, David, David. When are you going to learn to—"

A shadow detaches from the rear of the Mercedes. I watch it through the tears welling in my eyes. The world starts to slow down around me as once again my body is taxed beyond my endurance, as all three bodyguards drop to their knees and collapse on the wet alley floor.

In a blur, Preston takes a step back, but the shadow has converged on him.

My mind grows dizzy from the strain as this dark cyclone swirls about me, pulling me away from the agony of my bruises, of my physical punishment.

But not before I hear a hiss—the voice of Joe Castaneda.

"Time to pay for your sins, Old Friend."

CHAPTER 27

In my dream, I depart this world of smoke and mirrors, where nothing is as it has seemed for so many years. I leave behind the memories of countless nights lying awake in agonizing remorse for my transgressions. I rise above the shocking revelations, the seemingly endless series of completely disturbing surprises. In this dreamlike state, I see Evelyn and David walking in a park, hand in hand, dressed in black, the sky above them grey, cold, as they approach a gathering. I see a priest in front, watch him read from a small book in his hands but I can't hear him. The sky grows darker; the wind picks up, swirling Evelyn's hair, her black dress flapping in the breeze. She continues to clutch David's hand while toying with a single strand of white pearls with the other as she listens intently to the words spoken by the cleric while standing over a coffin as grey as the enraged cumulous twisting above them.

And then I see the other faces.

Joe and Sheila.

Ryan, Patricia, and Dana.

Beckett and Marley in full uniform.

And then I see Heather Wilson walking up to Evelyn and David, and hugging them both. Then together, the three of them approach the woman in black sobbing quietly by the coffin, just to the right of the priest, who continues his speech almost in slow motion. Lightning flashes and thunder rumbles. Heather and Evelyn flank Margaret Black as she throws a single red rose on top of the open coffin. I contemplate the velvety pedals landing on my chest, as my ghostly face, deformed by deep gashes on my cheeks, stares at the angered heavens.

Lightning gleams. The sky opens up and rain pelts my face, my dark suit. The priest issues his final blessing as Heather and Evelyn hug Margaret and slowly nudge her away from the coffin, as David's face fills my world.

Hold me, Daddy. Hold me ti—

Massive hands reach for the lid, and it drops over me, shutting everyone out with a clap of thunder.

I jump in my sleep, feeling motion. Sitting back up, bright sunlight pierces my eyes. I shield them with a hand.

Sheila gives me an amused smile before crossing her legs. Up in front Joe drives the van and Ryan sits next to him. The middle row is occupied by the towering Patricia and an obviously shocked Preston Wilson still dressed in his golfing outfit, his hair messy, his face darkened by a pair of bruises on his cheeks and left eye.

Half-asleep, I blink, making sure I'm awake, then say, "I guess you missed your tee time."

"David, you have no idea who you're fucking with," Preston starts. "I will have your—"

Patricia slaps him hard on the back of the head with one of her sailor hands, smashing him against the back of Ryan's seat, before grabbing him by his shirt's collar and shoving him back into his seat. She then looks at me and prompts me to be quiet.

And those were the last words I hear from him as we ride in silence down IH-35 to where I presume is the ranch where Margaret and probably many other captured women are being held before shipping off to a life of sexual slavery.

As I spot the sign on the highway announcing New Braunfels' city limits, Patricia rips a strip of duct tape and presses it over Preston's lips before bagging his head with a pillow case she took from my apartment.

Ten minutes later, as we approach the large parking lot of a water park by the name of *Schlitterbahn* adjacent to the Landa Park Golf Course, Joe abruptly pulls up on the side of the street.

Ryan looks back at me for a moment. His face tense, he glances at Sheila, who nods. And he's gone, rushing towards the woods bordering the golf course, vanishing a moment later.

Since I must have been out of commission when they worked out this part of the plan, I'm about to ask what that was all about when Sheila reads my mind and presses her index finger against my lips, before pointing to the pillow case on Preston's head.

I sigh.

According to the large billboard up front, the water park is not scheduled to open until ten in the morning, and it's barely eight, so there are just a few cars in the vast sea of asphalt connecting the access road to the entrance and the towering amusement rides beyond. And all of the vehicles are parked by the main entrance roughly a quarter of a mile away, which suggests they belong to the staff.

Joe stops by the outer perimeter of the parking lot backing into the woods leading to the golf course.

"Showtime," Patricia says.

Showtime for what?

She removes the bag from Preston's head but leaves the duct tape in place, opening the side door, and dragging Preston out. His smaller stature makes it quite easy for the former prison guard to manipulate him.

As she tugs him by his white polo shirt towards the woods, Preston peers in my direction, his eyes wide with either anger or fear. I can't tell which.

"Stay inside," Joe warns Sheila and me as he steps away from the SUV. But before he leaves he really stares at Sheila, who nods.

What was that all about?

Joe leaves the engine running, closes the door, and joins Patricia and their hostage on the other side. A moment later they vanish from sight beyond the towering pines.

"What the hell is going on?" I finally get the chance to ask. "What did I miss? Are we making the trade now?"

"Not exactly," she replies.

"What does that mean? I thought the whole idea of kidnapping him was so we could use him as a bargaining chip to get Marga—"

Once more she shuts me up with just her index finger, and for reasons that escape me I do put a clamp on it. There is something about her I find unable to resist.

"Do you trust me?"

"What's that supposed to mean?"

"I know you've suffered much, just as I have, but in order to put this behind us it's going to take much more than simply getting Margaret back, even though I know that's paramount to you at the moment."

"Of course I want Marge back, and I also realize that the only way to stop living in fear is to hit those bastards hard. Why are you telling me this right now?"

"Because you have to promise me something."

"What?"

She takes my hands in hers just as she did in San Francisco. I find Sheila's eyes on me. They regard me with the same softness as that evening at the bar.

Even after her accident and the surgery, even after life dealt her such physical and emotional blows, Sheila Castaneda is still a very intriguing and attractive woman. Her nose may be a dash too long and slightly curved. Her eyes might be a bit too close, and her lips a bit too full, but when thrown together into a triangular face framed by thick and wavy dark-brown hair, the effect is quite hypnotic.

"Trust Joe, David," she says, placing a hand on mine. "He's the only reason I'm still alive. You need to promise me that no matter who comes out of those woods you will remain in this vehicle."

I'm not sure how to reply to that, and just as it has been the case multiple times these past few days, I'm at a momentary loss for words. Finally, I say, "Stop playing games with me, Sheila. What in the hell is going—"

Two gun shots crack from the direction of the woods. They sound more like fireworks, but we're nowhere near the Fourth of July.

"It's begun," she says.

"What? What the hell is happening?"

"David," she says, cupping my face by the jaw line to avoid pressing on my stitches. "We could not wait until tonight. We had to pull in the timetable and risk an exchange in plain daylight, though we're hoping the woods will help."

"Why? What are you not telling—"

Two more shots whip across the parking lot. I see people coming out of the park's main entrance, but they're too far away to be of any immediate concern.

"Sheila, for the love of Christ! Would you tell me what's going—"

She points in the direction of the woods, where four figures are emerging from the shadows, wading their way through the bordering waist-high shrubs.

It's Joe Castaneda, his right hand clutching a pistol and left hand grabbing the back of a still gagged Preston Wilson. Next to them is Patricia Norton carrying in her arms a slim figure wearing a margarita-green T-shirt and faded jeans.

Margaret!

I'm about to jump to the middle row and open the door when Sheila pulls me back.

"Don't! Or you'll ruin everything! Trust me!"

"But they're—"

She grabs my forearm with a force stronger than her slim arms would suggest. "David! Stop! They'll be here in less than twenty seconds!"

Tension stabbing me in between my already sore shoulder blades, I watch them rush in our direction. Then two men emerge behind them clutching weapons.

"Oh, my God!" I shout, once again going for the door, and once again she holds me back in a way that doesn't make me want to fight her.

"Watch!" she says, pointing at the tree line.

Another figure emerges.

Ryan.

He has a pistol and shoots them in the back of the head before they get the chance to fire on the foursome almost by the SUV. Their faces exploding, the armed men drop to the asphalt already corpses, their weapons clanging away from them.

I'm in utter shock at what I've just seen. Ryan has killed two people without an ounce of hesitation.

Joe breaks my trance as he reaches the side of the SUV and yanks it open to help Patricia deposit an unconscious Margaret on my lap before shoving Preston into the middle seat.

Patricia hops in next to our hostage and shuts the door while Joe runs around the front, gets in, and starts to drive away.

"Wait!" I shout. "Ryan's back there!"

But when I look he's already gone.

"Where the hell is he? Did they get him? Is he hurt?"

The SUV accelerates across the parking lot.

"Dammit, Joe! We're not leaving without Ryan!"

"Let him go, David," Sheila says in the most soothing of voices. "Please, you need to let him go."

And yet once more, I'm not sure how to respond. I have questions, objections, complaints! But my mind is rapidly shifting to the person I'm suddenly and surreally clutching in my arms.

Margaret.

Dear God, I have her back!

She's back with me!

And for the first time I notice that although unconscious, she is shaking. She is also bruised. She has a black eye and a busted lip, there are bruises on her forearms, and her wrists are blackened from being bounded. Her T-shirt has multiple tears and so do her blue jeans. And she is barefoot and reeks of body odor, urine, and other smells I'd rather not think about.

But I hold her even tighter, whispering in her ear that I'm here with her, that I will take care of her, that I will never let her go again.

Joe keeps driving, reaching the highway, and heading back to Austin.

"What's wrong with her?" I ask, her face pressed against my chest as I embrace her like a mother would a baby.

"Drugged," says Patricia. "They drug them before transporting them."

"She's beaten up, Pat. Those bastards abused her! Those motherfuckers!" I protest, tensing again as I hold her, my jaw suddenly clenching as I force back tears of rage.

I want justice for this. And having seen Ryan blow up their skulls just doesn't feel like enough punishment.

I try to breathe, to get a grip. Margaret needs me to be calm, to regain my composure, to be strong for her.

"Bag him," Joe shouts from the front.

Patricia slips the pillow case over Preston's head, and I suddenly remember that this was supposed to be a trade. Preston for Margaret. Yet, Preston is still here.

"What happened in those woods?" I ask. "How come Preston is—"

Sheila, who surprises me by having tears in her eyes, presses an index against my lips once more, reminding me that Preston is back in the car. We need to be silent.

Then she leans over and whispers directly into my ear, "I will tell you everything later. I promise."

"What have they done to her?" I whisper.

"We came as fast as we could, David," Sheila replies. "I swear to you we came as fast as we fucking possibly could."

CHAPTER 28

I want blood.

I want somebody to pay, to scream in agonizing forever-medieval pain for what happened to Margaret.

I want to unleash the fucking Guns of Navarone.

I demand vengeance, and I desire it right now.

There are monsters out there, like Max Caporini, Preston and Bernard Wilson, Lisa and Tonya Ang, and even Gustavo Salazar—abominations who think the rules don't apply to them. They think they can hurt anyone anytime and get away with it. They think they are above the law.

But they're not above *my* law.

And it infuriates me to know that in this moment of intoxicating lust for blood, I find myself once again in a damned hospital.

I'm back at Seton. Back in a waiting area as a doctor and two nurses work on stabilizing Margaret, who went into convulsions shortly after I rushed into the emergency room clutching her in my arms almost six hours ago. It took two orderlies to force me to release her, for me to break my promise—once again—that I would never let her go.

Yet, here I am, pacing this antiseptic place barely hanging on to my sanity.

I stare at the double doors leading to the recovery room guarded by this powerhouse of a nurse who reminds me of that unsettling woman from the movie *One Flew Over the Cuckoo's Nest*.

What was her name?

Nurse Ratched? Retched?

Anyway, she stopped me dead in my tracks as I attempted to pursue the orderlies hauling Margaret away. And when I tried to force my way in, she threatened to neuter me with her stiletto fingernails.

"The only attitude that will get you *anywhere* here is an attitude of *gratitude*," she told me, before pointing me straight to this penalty box.

But the matronly nurse, whose first name, Mildred, jogs my memory of Nurse Mildred Ratched from that old movie, did apprise me of her situation thirty minutes ago. Margaret is stable but still unconscious and getting much needed rest.

And to her credit, the good nurse also spent fifteen minutes cleaning Patricia's stitch job with peroxide before dressing the wounds so I wouldn't walk around looking like I just stepped off the set of the AMC TV series *The Walking Dead*.

However, she won't tell me what happened to my angel.

No one will tell me what was done to her in the hours since her abduction. And a part of me isn't sure if I really want to know because anything, even the slightest notion of physical abuse, shoots my blood pressure straight to the moon.

I remember what Joe told me before dropping me off. I recall how he basically handed me a script of what I could and could not say, including not discussing anything that had taken place in the past twelve hours, especially Caporini's attempt on my life. It was vital for Joe's plan to work that I stuck to the story at all costs.

They dropped me off a block from the emergency room, claiming it would be best if I wasn't seen with them for the time being. They had a few housecleaning items to take care of before it would be over, and he indicated they would be back to check in on us in a few hours.

As well as to explain everything to me.

Well, that was almost six hours ago.

It's nearly four in the afternoon now, and I have called Ryan seven times on his mobile and Patricia four times. But all I accomplished was filling up their damn voice-mails. I swung by the waiting room on the opposite end of the hospital, where a half dozen HCH volunteers were still in vigil for Dana, who has apparently pulled through but remained in ICU.

And no one has heard from either Patricia or Ryan. I then called the shelter, and Smith & Wesson told me there was also no sign of them at that end. Finally, I called my own apartment, but I got the answering machine.

So, completely cut off from whatever plan Joe and his little gang is carrying out, I continue to pace, craving blood and answers. The disinfectant smell hovering in these colorless and impersonal hallways fills my lungs as I release another glance of forced gratitude toward Nurse Retched while wishing for better company.

And it is at this moment of complete anxiety that my prayers are technically answered: Right there, standing in the hallway, appearing seemingly out of nowhere, are Detectives Beckett Mar and Marley Quinn accompanied by FBI Special Agent Jessica Herrera.

Swell.

He's in a grey suit, no tie. Marley is wearing jeans and a white long-sleeve shirt. Jessica has one of her FBI-blue skirt and jacket combos, which partially conceals her shoulder-holstered sidearm over a white blouse.

"Not a good time, guys."

They exchange a glance before approaching me.

"What the hell happened to you now?" Marley asks.

Joe and I actually didn't discuss what I would say regarding my facial lacerations, so I fall back on poorly-timed humor. "You should see the other guy. What are you doing here?"

"David?" presses Beckett. "What happened to you?"

"Some bastard delivered Margaret to the shelter," I say, reciting the part of the script I knew. Then I improvise by adding, "As I tried to follow him, he beat me up and told me to just be grateful I had powerful friends."

"What did he look like?" asked Jessica.

"Dark, muscular, strong Hispanic accent. Never seen him before, and to tell you the truth, I hope I never see him again."

"How did you get here?" Marley asks, putting a hand on my shoulder, genuine concern in her brown eyes.

Good. They're buying it.

"Drove myself from the shelter." I still have the van parked outside from last night, and I also still have the keys in my pocket.

They nod and decide that's a good enough answer. Of course, they could check the surveillance video from the parking lot and realize the van has not moved in over twelve hours, but fuck them if they do.

"How's she doing?" asks Beckett while Jessica and Marley look on with a mask of compassion, which just adds to my confusion.

I take a deep breath, letting the disinfectant and any surviving airborne bacteria hovering in these premises reach deep into my core. Exhaling through my nostrils, I stare at his basketball head and his bulging nose spiked with dark capillaries. It's almost getting to be five in the afternoon and the effects of my powernap on the way to New Braunfels are now a distant memory. My eyelids are once again growing heavy.

Yawning, I raise my shoulders a trifle. "Stable, but that's all I know. Nurse Retched over there won't talk, and she threatened severe groin trauma if I tried to get past her."

Beckett looks in her direction. "Maybe I'll have a word with her in a minute."

"I will," Marley says. "They just can't refuse to tell you what's going on. You're the closest thing she has to family."

"All right, guys. Why are you here? And why are you together? I thought the FBI had taken over jurisdiction of the case from your respective police departments."

"I take it you haven't seen the news being reported by Laurie Fox from Channel Seven in the past hour?"

I glare back with narrowed eyes in my best attempt to convey that I have not had the fucking time to watch the fucking news.

"The headline," Jessica says, "is that Ryan Horowitz surrendered documents ten hours ago linking Premier Imports, IBT, Gardner & Gardner, MM&S, and the New

Orleans casinos to a decade-old illegal operation ranging from money laundering and drugs to human trafficking. And to make sure we didn't sit on the documents, he also released them to Laurie Fox two hours ago."

Ryan gave them the documents *ten hours* ago? That's before Joe kidnapped Preston.

"I think he cashed in your insurance policy," adds Beckett.

I'm only half listening. My mind once more circling the turmoil drain. Ryan assured me he could not reach such documents.

And since this little fact wasn't part of Joe's script, I don't know what to say.

I look away, amazed at the stuff happening around me that I can't control, which tells me how much I truly don't belong in this underworld of smoke and mirrors.

"There's more," says Marley. "Two hours ago we found the bodies of Max Caporini and Preston Wilson in a ditch outside the police station. They were executed. Because of these findings, we have now formed an investigative task force between the FBI, the APD, and my own SFPD to expedite the case. We also have a contingent from the IRS since it involves *a lot* of money. And we're, of course, working with Laurie Fox to control the release of information to the public in exchange for an exclusive."

I make a face, though it's in part an honest reaction at the thought of Joe, Ryan, and Patricia executing them. I guess you have to become worse than the monsters chasing you to win this.

Having thought that, I do find it very interesting that the knowledge of their death still doesn't make me feel any better. I guess there's nothing anyone can do to take back whatever was done to Margaret Black, to my family, to Heather Wilson, Kate, Dana, and even Sebastian.

And that brings back again one of my mother's favorite quotes from good old Lord Francis Bacon.

A man that studies revenge keeps his own wounds green.

Mom was right, of course. Because at the moment, all of my old wounds, piled up on top of Margaret's, are feeling pretty fucking green.

"You okay, pal?" asks Beckett.

I slowly bob my head, then mumble, "Preston? Caporini? Dead? And before that Serrato and Kate Larson. Christ. Who's next?"

"You'd better sit down," says Beckett.

"Why?"

"Because of what we're about to tell you."

I reluctantly comply, though I'm glad when I sink in the soft cushion and lean back.

The law-enforcement trio sit across from me in this waiting area, where we are alone for the moment, if you ignore Nurse Retched a couple hundred feet away at her station guarding the entrance to the forbidden kingdom.

"I owe you a huge apology, David," says Jessica, her dark-olive face tightening with concern, her brown eyes staring into the distance before focusing on me. Fine wrinkles form on a narrow forehead framed by very short dark hair. "All this time I thought that you were the one to blame for what happened to Evelyn and her family. That the stress from you cheating on her had caused her to crash her car."

"Excuse me?" I ask, though I know what she's going to tell me.

"It was Caporini who killed your family," Jessica states matter-of-factly.

I paint on my best attempt at an Oscar-performance puzzled face. "What…what are you talking about? They died in—"

"Caporini drove them off the road," adds Marley.

"We're really sorry, pal," Beckett says as he places a hand on my shoulder.

"I…why? Why would he kill an innocent woman and a child? Why?"

"David," Marley says, "Caporini was actually trying to kill you."

I stare at her with real confusion.

"You were supposed to be in the car with them," Beckett explains as my heartbeat is back on the rise. "But I arrested you before you could go with them, remember?"

"So…you're saying that…"

"You were supposed to die with Heather," Jessica says. "But you left early. So they pinned it on you and also planned to run you off the road. That way it would have been all very clean. Heather's killer dies in a car accident. It was all a complete set up."

"Our combined teams are pouring through the documents Ryan provided," says Jessica, "including folks from the DA's Office and plenty of IRS agents, but this is just the tenth hour since we received them. We still have a long way to go."

"Ryan gave us three boxes worth of files, DVDs, and data CDs. The works," says Beckett.

"But in general," says Marley, "these bastards just do these things to get to people…to break them down, just as they went after Margaret to get to you."

I pause, then say, "All this time…all these wasted years gripped by guilt. I mean, I did sleep with Heather. I did betray Evelyn…but we were on the verge of a divorce…I thought…"

"I know," says Marley. "It wasn't your fault."

"Caporini was tortured," says Jessica, switching gears too suddenly. "You wouldn't have any idea who did that to him?"

I stick to my script and slowly shake my head.

"And even if you did, you wouldn't tell us, right?" the Fed presses.

"That would be obstruction of justice," I reply in my most sincere and resigned voice, which at the moment isn't that hard to fake. "I would most certainly cooperate."

"Yes, he would," says Beckett. "He's been on the level with me since last night."

"I also believe him," adds Marley.

"What happened to Caporini?" I ask.

"Pretty barbaric stuff," Jessica says, crossing her arms. "He's got these burrowing holes in his abdomen. Something ate into him. The Medical Examiner is trying to determine what. Looks like mice. Corrupt agent or not, no one has the right to torture an American citizen. We'll catch whoever did that. We can't have people taking the law into their own hands."

Those are fine words, but the problem is that if it wasn't for Joe Castaneda and his simple but efficient methods, Margaret would probably be in Mexico by now. I would be dead. And Caporini, Preston, and the rest of their kind would be torturing a thousand times more American citizens through their sex slavery operation.

But I stick to the script and just ask, "Where's Ryan?"

"Don't know," says Beckett.

"What do you mean? I thought you said he gave you all this—"

"He did, but not in person. He had a Hill Country Haven volunteer named…" Beckett pulls out his little detective notepad. "Patricia Norton. She dropped it at the station. We already questioned her. She also doesn't know anything. Ryan used her as a courier. And no one knows who dropped a similar package at Channel Seven."

I'm having a hard time keeping track of how many times Ryan has lied to me in the past few days, and especially in the last twenty-four hours—not the mention the last seven years.

"But it's not surprising he didn't deliver it himself," says Jessica.

I look at her round brown eyes. "Why?"

"Because…the documents also incriminate him."

That's another surprise, and my blood pressure has shot past the moon, circled Mars, and it's cruising through the damn asteroid belt.

"Come again?"

"Gardner & Gardner handled the legalities of Premier Imports, which owns the International Bank of Texas, including a dozen secret accounts which were used to fund drug and human trafficking."

This is now happening too fast. Ryan involved in such corruption?

"Slow down a moment," I say. "You're saying that Ryan was forced into managing these illegal accounts."

"I'm afraid it's bigger than that," says Jessica. "If the information he provided is true—and we're still pouring through it—he wasn't only involved. Ryan Horowitz was the architect of their scheme."

As my vision starts to tunnel, Jessica adds, "He conceived it, piloted it, rolled it out, and polished it over time into a well-oiled machine."

"Which explains why you got set up," says Beckett. "Your consulting project was taking you in a direction Bernard and Preston Wilson—and even Ryan—didn't want you to go."

"So someone gave the order to take you out, but Ryan must have interceded on your behalf," says Jessica, adding, "and based on what we've learned so far we believe that in spite of Ryan's intervention they went after you. But then you survived both assassination attempts, giving Ryan time to react. Since he had access to everything because he pulled it all together for Premier, Ryan used that as a threat to get you off the hook. But in the process an arrangement was made where he was ousted from that operation in return for his life—and yours—and he must have taken some sort of oath never to look back. This also explains why he hooked up with you at HCH."

"And the Mafia wasn't being kind," says Beckett. "They knew that if Ryan tried to incriminate them by releasing the documents, he would be incriminating himself as well, so the arrangement had built-in poison pills for both parties. If they killed him or you, the documents go out and everyone loses. If Ryan decided one day to release them, as he did, also both sides lose because Ryan is now a fugitive."

"What about Heather? Who killed her?" I ask to test just how much they're willing to share with me.

They exchange a glance and Jessica says, "I'm afraid we can't share that at the moment. Rest assure we have complete proof that you were innocent."

Of course she would say that. Corrupt or not, Caporini is one of her people, so on top of everything that's happening the Bureau has to protect the Bureau. But since I'm in the mood, I decide to ask for shits and grins, "Who killed Kate Larson?"

"Sorry, pal," says Beckett. "We already told you more than we should, but I convinced Jessica that you deserve this much given what you have gone through. But know this, if you tell another soul what you've just heard from us, I'm personally throwing the book at you. Clear?"

"Crystal."

"Good," Jessica says. "We need to do this one by the numbers to make sure we can prosecute everyone."

"Prosecute whom?" I ask. "Preston's dead and who knows where Bernard Wilson is."

"We just began working with Mexican authorities to extradite him."

"Oh, so in Mexico. Good luck with that. What about all the girls down south? Are you going after them."

Jessica nods. "That's one of the first things we did. We're raiding hundreds of establishments and private estates real time in conjunction with Mexican authorities. We need to bring those kids back home."

Thank God for that. At last there just might be hope for the women I saw being carried into that plane, as well as for the thousands of others smuggled south through dozens of deserted strips from south Texas to southern California.

They start to leave.

"Wait a moment," I say. "What about Gustavo? What about this casino connection…this Lisa Ang woman?"

Beckett and Marley grin. "Easy there," he says. "Please let us do our job."

"And you do yours," Jessica says, pointing at Nurse Retched, who is waving me over.

I don't even thank them as I take off in her direction, Margaret's condition overshadowing all other concerns.

"Yes?" I ask.

"You can go in, but only for a few minutes," she says. "She's conscious now but because of the sedative she's going in and out."

Before I step through those doors, I look back towards the reception area at the end of the hallway.

But Beckett, Marley, and Jessica are long gone.

CHAPTER 29

Everyone has defining moments in their lives, times that stick with you for years, decades…forever.

For me, most of those moments have been scenes from the darkest chapters of my life, perhaps with the exception of my wedding day and the day David was born.

Beyond that, I have a stack of bad memories that rivals Mount Everest, from my father's relentless beatings, the murder of my mother, and my foster home years, to the pure hell that Max Caporini and those pulling his strings put me through for the past seven years.

Defining moments.

I also remember starting Hill Country Haven, although during that time, so soon after the nightmare began, everything was a bit hazy, as if I were living someone else's life. Ryan did a lot of the heavy lifting then, carrying me along, giving me the figure head of HCH. I had limited duties back then, allowing me to drift away to distant places as I often used to do. It took me almost a full year before I began to get in the swing of things, before I began to steer, to guide, to take HCH as serious as such a noble cause deserved.

I remember the women. The countless faces that walked, limped, staggered, or were even carried through our doors. I remember their wet stares, their pleading eyes, their bruises, cuts, and broken bones. Each had a story filled with betrayal, fear, and shattered dreams. Each had her own reasons for coming to a place where we promised sanctuary.

A haven.

And for seven years we have taken them. We have sheltered them. We have helped them to not be afraid anymore—helped them gain the courage to be good again. We have taught them not just how to make a living, but how to live. And this, in the beginning at least, I did as my pathetic attempt to make amends, to atone for my sins, to seek forgiveness from a God whom my mother always portrayed as a merciful God.

For seven years I have tried to help others, have tried to help them heal, rise above the crushing fist of abuse. And in the process, I tried to also dig myself out of this dark hole I had dug through my own selfish actions.

As I push those double doors open and leave the past behind me in that stark hallway, I know what sins I did commit, and just as importantly, what sins I *didn't*.

I know what I'm guilty of, and what I'm not.

For the first time in a very long time, I stand on firm ground, sure of myself, ready to take on whatever fate throws my way.

Or so I think as I enter Margaret's room, as my legs start to tremble, as I see her laying there staring out the window, her bruised face and busted lips turning my new-found righteousness into mush.

She's saying something, whispering things I can't hear.

"Marge? It's me, Marge. It's David."

She continues to gaze at the trees beyond the large windowpanes—continues to move her lips, as if talking to someone else.

Dear God, what have they done to her?

My heart is crumbling as I stand here feeling impotent, like the night I watched my father deliver the final blow. I've failed my mother, my wife, and my son. And now I have failed Margaret. I've allowed the dark forces of our world to drag her back into their bowels. I've let them crush her fragile spirit just as she was finally stepping back into the light, just as the breath of dawn began to caress her face.

A hand taps me on the shoulder, and I jump.

Another nurse, this one much shorter than me and also much older, regards me with blue eyes encased by deeply wrinkled pale skin. Her lips are unusually pink. She has a stethoscope around her neck, and I realize she isn't a nurse but a doctor.

"Mr. Wallace?"

"David, please," I say, reaching deep in my tired and aching body for control as my legs keep quivering, as I'm feeling blood leaving my extremities.

"I'm Doctor Marcia Flanagan. I understand you're the closest individual she has to next of kin?"

I nod.

"Well, she's stable but heavily sedated. I'm afraid she's suffering from Post-Traumatic Stress Disorder."

I cringe, familiar with the diagnosis as it is quite common not just in the military but also at the shelter. And unfortunately, I'm also quite acquainted first hand with its many symptoms.

But being a doctor, she needs to tell me anyway, and given my current state of mind, I just stand there listening.

"I need to prepare you, David, as people with PTSD have persistent frightening thoughts and memories of their ordeal and feel emotionally numb. Margaret is likely to experience sleep problems, feel detached, as she is right now, or be very easily startled by anything from a loud voice to someone's touch. Although she has not told us what took place, we had to sedate her in order to examine her and also to treat her wounds. There is no permanent physical damage, but I'm afraid she was sexually assaulted. We were able to contact her therapist at HCH, and she emailed her case file. Given what she experienced some years back plus what she must have experienced in the past day, it certainly supports the PTSD diagnosis."

The room is growing opaque from my tears. I feel like reaching to the sky and crying out my frustration, my rage for what they have done to her. To us.

The doctor is still talking, still saying something about long recovery periods and successful treatments, and how PTSD victims can eventually go on to live very productive and emotionally stable lives.

But I'm barely listening, hardly paying any more attention to her. My eyes have shifted back to the still figure in that bed, to her slim arms, her fine hand resting on the bed's metal railing, her light brown hair against the white pillow, and her hazel eyes blinking while she continues to whisper something I can't make out.

Doctor Flanagan leaves us alone, and I approach the bed, pull up a chair, and sit beside her.

Watching closely as she continues to stare out the window, I finally recognize what she's mumbling.

My name.

She's calling out for me from the shadows of her nightmare while peering at the blue skies beyond the towering branches of a stately oak.

"Marge," I whisper back. "Marge, it's me, David. I'm here now. I'm here for you."

No response.

I try again. But she isn't even acknowledging my presence. It's as if I'm not here.

Slowly, I reach for her pale hand resting on the edge of the bed.

She jerks it away with a whimper, lips quivering, before slowly, she starts to mumble again.

So, I just sit there watching her lips moving steadily, her eyes fixated on the brightness beyond, begging for me to return.

Over the course of a few minutes, she drifts into deep sleep.

With great care, I reach for her hand again, slowly setting mine over hers, longing for her touch.

Her chest rises and falls steadily as the room sinks into silence, as my eyes drift from her profile to the branches gently swaying in the afternoon breeze.

I talk to her softly, telling her that it's going to be all right, that I will help her see this through.

Since she is just sleeping, and since I'm being quiet and appreciative, Nurse Retched allows me to stay here nearly two hours. Unfortunately, Margaret looks like she is done for the night, which according to Doctor Flanagan, who stops by at nine, the more she rests the better she will be at coping with her traumatic memories.

Thirty minutes later, under orders from Nurse Retched, I go for a walk, swinging by the cafeteria, where I grab a sandwich and a soda from vending machines. I eat them in silence while watching this massive black guy steering a floor polisher in rhythmic, almost hypnotic side-by-side sways.

He makes me think of Dana, and after wolfing down a borderline-palatable pastrami and Swiss on rye, I set off to find her.

It takes me a few minutes to reorient myself, go up one floor, and reach a long hallway of rooms. There I find a lone nurse at a station, identify myself as director of Hill Country Haven, show her my credentials, and she informs me that Dana is finally out of ICU and leads me to her room.

According to the nurse, Dana has been drifting in and out of consciousness due to heavy sedatives.

I always forget how large she is. Her six-four body barely fits in the bed, and her massive arms and legs require the side railings to keep everything on board. A bandage covers most of her head, and she has a cast on her lower left leg, which is elevated. Her torso is heavily bandaged as it took plenty of stab wounds. There are a few bruises on her arms and face, and she does have one heck of a black left eye. Very purple and very swollen.

I sit there staring at her **BE NOT AFRAID** tattoo while remembering the first time I saw her. How taken back I had been at the dramatic contrast of a person with the bubbly personality of someone like actress Meg Ryan trapped in a body that could challenge Arnold Schwarzenegger in his prime.

"Hey…Boss," she mumbles in her deep voice, flickering her eyelids, before opening them fully, zeroing in on me.

"Hey, Little Lady," I whisper.

Dana groans a half laugh before wincing in pain.

Pulling up a chair, I reach with my left hand for her large right hand, which she clasps while giving me a smile, showing the space in between her front teeth. "You know, you're damned lucky to be alive. And don't even think about telling me I should see the other guys."

She slowly nods, flinches in pain again, and says, "How...bad?"

I frown. "Has a doctor spoken to you yet?"

"Just...woke up," she says.

"Well, from what I've heard, you lost a kidney, your spleen, have a bunch of cracked ribs, have a fractured tibia, and a serious concussion. But the doctor says you'll be out of here in no time."

She turns serious, her bloodshot eyes locking with mine.

"Margaret?"

"Downstairs," I say. "Long story, but we got her back."

"How...is she?"

I just don't have the energy to lie, especially to Big Dana. She deserves the truth.

"Physically she'll be fine," I say. "But I'm not so sure up here." I press my right index finger against my temple. "She was sexually abused."

Dana closes her eyes momentarily, lets go of my left hand, and tightens her fists, which are massive. For a moment I think she is just going to rip everything off and get up.

"Last thing I remember was a gunshot from behind," she finally says. "Why am I still alive?"

"You have a thick skull, my friend," I say, tears also welling in my eyes. "Bullet deflected. You're lucky to be here."

"Don't feel...so lucky," she says with effort.

It was obvious she was going to drift away any moment.

"David...did you see who...who attacked us?"

I slowly shake my head. "The pepper spray. I was blinded. But I did hear them, and also you fighting them. They spoke Spanish. And...I did hear Margaret screaming for help."

She stares at me long and hard, grabs my hand again, tightening her grip, which even in her weakened state is nearly crushing. "David...before I passed out, before they shoved Margaret kicking and screaming in the van..."

"Yes, Dana?"

"I recognized someone. He was standing to the side... almost watching the attack."

"Who?"

"But...the thing is," she continues, her eyelids fluttering as she tries to remain conscious, "it makes no sense... why would he be there?"

"Who, Dana?" I ask, leaning closer. "Who did you see in that alley?"

"Ryan Horowitz."

CHAPTER 30

"Are you absolutely certain?"

I'm clutching my phone out by the smoking area near the helipad.

"Yes," I reply to Beckett Mar as I stand in the same spot where I had spoken to Ryan. "Dana saw him right before she was shot in the head."

I am angry but for reasons I can't explain, not as angry as I thought I was going to be. Ryan has already lied to me about the documents, about having been involved in the laundering scheme, which explained why Sheila didn't contact him. And now he has also not just lied but completely betrayed me by leaking to whoever he worked for that Dana, Margaret, and I went out to get Sheila during rounds.

I feel betrayed and also utterly confused. On the one hand he obviously wronged Dana and me, and especially Margaret. On the other hand, he also double-crossed the bad guys by releasing those documents to the cops, the FBI, and the media—effectively shooting himself in the foot, too. But if he had the ability to prevent Margaret from getting kidnapped and abused in the first place, and he just stood by...well, I don't believe I'll ever be able to forgive that.

"I'm not sure what to make of that," Beckett replies. "But you didn't see him, right?"

"No. I was completely blinded with pepper spray in my eyes."

"Well, all I can do is add this to the list of charges already piled up against him."

"I guess when you're that deep in the hole it may not matter much legally. But it sure as hell matters to me. In my book, it's one thing to have worked for the mob and then used that to try to keep him, and me, alive. But to harm innocent people like Dana and Margaret...damn."

"Listen," Beckett replies. "I know you've always looked up to him, but Ryan was the guy who devised the sexual-slavery scheme, so he's certainly used to putting innocent people in harm's way."

The good APD detective is, of course, correct.

He adds, "In any case, based on what we have, Ryan's going away for life multiple times, so adding one charge of kidnapping and battering isn't going to change the picture much. He's toast as far as Uncle Sam is concerned, though we would ask the judge for leniency because he was the one who fingered them. In the final analysis, I don't think that matters much because if I know him as good as I think I do, he's also very far away by now. Probably on some island well outside of our reach living under a different name. And if he is *really* smart, he would even get surgery to alter his face. He would disappear, and not just for our sake, but for the sake of those he fingered. In their eyes he is the ultimate rat. He made a deal with them to keep himself and you alive, and he just gave them all up. They'll hunt him down to the far reaches of the planet."

I have not gotten the chance to think about that. "I guess that would explain why he didn't try to make a deal with you guys in return for the evidence."

"You're learning," Beckett replies to my annoyance. "Even though we could have gotten him something better than leniency, perhaps even a connection to the Witness Protection Program of the U.S. Marshal Service, they still might have found him. Anyone willing to expend enough resources and money will get somebody to talk. If Ryan screwed them as much as it appears, I doubt WitPro would have helped him for very long, so I'm not surprised he took off, and now I know he didn't do it empty handed. Heck, if I'm going to piss off the mob, might as well use their funds to get away and *stay* away."

"Can he run forever?"

"No. Not even with unlimited funds, because even though he could pay his way to anonymity, there are those who would always pay more. Eventually they'll find him."

"So what he did in a way was suicidal?"

"Not entirely."

I'm confused again. "Why?"

"Because he is banking on us being able to use what he gave us to take down the whole operation, to put everyone away. And the best thing he gave us was their financials, their bank accounts."

"But, wait," I say. "Those accounts had to be at least seven years old. Are they still active?"

"You may look like shit, David, but you're still thinking. Yeah, they're old, but they also provide great starting points to track down their current accounts, and in this short time we've already located two pretty large ones.

We're freezing them as we speak. I'm sure we'll nail the rest by the end of the week. And frozen accounts mean they can't operate. They can't order hits. They can't bribe the people that would help them track down Ryan Horowitz. No money, no mob."

"Sounds like Ryan."

"He isn't dumb, but if you don't mind my saying, I think he did cross that personal line with what he did to your girlfriend. I hope she gets better soon."

"Thanks. And by the way, what does all of this mean for Margaret and me?"

Silence, followed by, "What do you mean?"

"My insurance is gone. Are Margaret and I sitting ducks?"

More silence, then, "I'll have to get back to you on that."

"That's not very comforting," I say.

"Listen, David. If you or Margaret were in any danger, I would be telling you that right now. And to be completely honest, you two would have been dead already if those bastards wanted you dead," he replies. "At the moment, thanks to Ryan, we got them all running for cover trying to leave the country and perhaps even the continent. I promise you that the last thing on their minds is a woman in a hospital and her banged up boyfriend. You're small fish. Now go look after her."

After I hang up, I stand here for a while watching the helipad under a blanket of stars realizing that Margaret and I will always be in danger as long as Bernard Wilson, Gustavo Salazar, and even this Lisa Ang are still alive.

But the orange windsock under the floodlights is as flat as my energy level. There is zero breeze this night in my personal engine, and I have to drag myself back into the hospital, past Nurse Retched, who has pity on me and lets me back in Margaret's room.

I take my seat by her side and somehow find solace in simply watching her sleep.

CHAPTER 31

I finally reach my apartment at six the following morning, having spent the night first in that uncomfortable chair, and later on a roll-away bed Nurse Retched brought into the room during a moment of kindness.

Although I managed to catch a few of hours of sleep, it isn't nearly enough to get me back up to marginal functional levels. So at the recommendation of Nurse Retched, who I'm beginning to suspect isn't human because I've yet to see her rest, I decided to come home, take an uninterrupted nap, then shower, grab a sandwich at the corner deli, and try to be back at the hospital by noon.

Damn. I feel terrible. My cheeks are on fire. My nose is still throbbing four days after Caporini—rest in peace—head-butted me. I'm now having difficulty swallowing solids from a nasty bruise forming around my neck.

I stare at my reflection in the small mirror in the foyer and nearly scare myself. And not just from my pathetic, Dawn-of-the-Dead appearance of cuts, bruises and Band-Aids, salt-and-pepper stubble, and bloodshot eyes, but especially from the long purple lines circling my neck.

I stare at them and stop breathing when remembering the strangulation marks around Heather's and Kate's necks.

And it's now my turn to wear this deadly necktie, though fortunately not while residing at the city morgue.

Joe and Sheila Castaneda spared me that fate, just as they provided me with the truth, with the reality that things were not as they seemed seven years ago.

It was because of them I now know what propelled me down this dark and crooked avenue of regrets was not real. It was fabricated by monsters who would go to any extreme to remain in the shadows, in the comfortable underworld of dark alleys, midnight flights, and overseas accounts.

But Joe and Sheila Castaneda, and Ryan Horowitz for that matter, dragged those beasts into the light. They had reached deep into the bowels of society, pulled them out of their murky dwellings, stripped them of their veneer, and exposed them for all to see.

And these purple bruises on my neck remind me of that ethereal artiste spraying terror on the white canvas of ordinary people trying to live ordinary lives; that monster that lives just beneath the surface of our fragile world.

I briefly close my eyes before locking the door and heading for the kitchen, where I plan to get a glass of water before going straight to bed.

I give the half-drunk bottle of Silver Oak a sideways glance, forcing myself not to think of her for just a few hours so I can rest. I'm no good to Margaret Black if I'm tired. She needs me at my best so I can help her through this, so I can be her rock, the one to reel her back from the shadows.

I down a Vicodin and four ibuprofens with a glass of tap water, and without even untying my shoes, I crash in bed, my mind going even before my head hit the pillow.

What feels like only an instant later, I shift in half sleep, trying to get comfortable when I glance at the clock on the nightstand and realize that just like that, I had slept almost five hours.

I blink, check my watch, confirming that it's almost eleven in the morning.

Time to head back.

Stripping naked, I step in the shower, but not without glancing in the mirror over the sink and frowning, not at my face or neck, but at the collection of purple blotches on my chest and my upper arms, where Caporini sat on me while pinning my arms with his knees. It even hurts to breathe and turn from side to side, which probably means he also bruised my ribs.

The hot shower stings at first, then it soothes as I wash thoroughly, trying to strip the last few days from my body and soul. In fact, I try to forget the pain and agony of the past seven years, letting the hot water wash it all away, feeling the regrets and anxiety swirling down the drain.

For the first time in a long time, I actually feel alive, ready to tackle my new life, my new mission. I'm ready for Hill Country Haven, and most importantly, I'm ready for Margaret. I'm ready to take her hand and help her through her cycle of mourning for what was taken from her during those fateful hours under the rule of monsters. But unlike Evelyn, David, Heather, Serrato, and Kate, Margaret survived. She managed to hang in there, and now I shall make it my life's mission to help her reach the light again.

Maybe not today or tomorrow, or the day after tomorrow, but soon.

One day.

I have to believe that deep within me, because that's the only way I can help *her* believe. I need to be her Gibraltar, her Samson, her pillar of strength.

And I'm ready.

I dress quickly, eager to head back to her side; fervent to hold her hand through her second journey around the block of abuse recovery she is being forced to travel.

But as I step into the kitchen, my world once more starts to collapse.

On the bar, just as I had left it, I see the half-drunk bottle of Silver Oak. And had it not been for the note standing on its side, I may have taken a quick trip down the boulevard of reminiscence.

Instead, I am propelled down the highway of startling disbelief because I know that note wasn't there five hours ago. I know I looked at that bottle of wine and did not see any message by it.

I'm as sure of it as I am of my love for Margaret Black.

And as I stare at it from a distance, as if it was a viper poised to strike and inject fear back into my life, I immediately recognize the handwriting.

Sheila.

THINGS WERE NOT AS THEY SEEMED YESTERDAY.

It is scribbled on the back of one of Ryan's HCH business cards.

EPILOGUE

Yesterday was very real to me—from nearly being choked to death by Caporini, to his own death as well as that of Preston Wilson at the hands of the crafty and unforgiving Joe Castaneda, to the amazing rescue of Margaret Black. I know what I saw and heard—from Ryan blowing up the skulls of two armed thugs to Dana's startling sight of Ryan in that alley before she was shot.

So as I stare at Sheila's handwriting on his business card while standing guard outside of Margaret's room, I can't help but wonder precisely what was *not* as it seemed yesterday.

According to the flat screen in the hospital's waiting room, Laurie Fox reported early this morning that the police released the news about the deaths of Caporini and Preston in association with organized crime. There are multiple stories running, one about the casino connection to Premier Imports and IBT and illegal accounts. There's another one about Gardner & Gardner and also about Mercer, Martinez & Salazar and their connection to money laundering schemes. There's even a scandal about the assassination of Sebastian Serrato. But the centerpiece is the incredible story about illegal prostitution rings in Mexico supplied by captured runaway teens forced into sexual slavery. That one has sent ripples not just across Texas and the nation, but across the world. Even the Vatican sent a communiqué condemning the actions of the multiple firms connected with this nightmarish practice.

And all of that is still very real to me.

I checked in on Dana early this morning, and as she ate a breakfast worthy of her size, she confirmed again that she had indeed seen Ryan Horowitz moments before she was shot in the head.

So that's also still very painfully real.

And by the way, so is Margaret, who I just touched on the face and shoulder to make sure I'm not dreaming. And there she was, still very real and sleeping from the sedatives, which they will start reducing throughout the day today to slowly bring her back to reality.

I'm hopeful, perhaps *foolishly* hopeful, that maybe, just maybe, her behavior yesterday was due more to the strong sedatives they administered, and less because of what she experienced.

One can only hope.

I stare at the card in my hands once more.

THINGS WERE NOT AS THEY SEEMED YESTERDAY.

Sorry, Sheila and Ryan—and also Joe—I just don't get it.

Although I have to admit that if it was Ryan who snuck into my apartment and dropped it off while I was sleeping, then he's either the dumbest, craziest son of a bitch on the planet, or maybe there is something I missed in all of the commotion yesterday.

And if the latter, then what was it?

I know what I saw. But I also have to admit that some of what I know I learned through other people, including Dana's sighting of Ryan, and the FBI and police's claim about the deaths of Caporini and Preston. For all I know those two monsters are alive and well in some witness protection program after giving the FBI and APD the farm while Ryan runs for cover.

As I consider that, I see Patricia Norton walking towards me in the hallway.

"Hey," I say.

"Hey, Boss," she replies, dressed in a pair of jeans and one of our T-shirts. "Things are pretty quiet at the shelter, so I figured I'd swing by. Dana said you were going to spend the day here."

"Where have you been? You guys dropped me off yesterday and—"

She slowly shakes her head, then says, "Stick to the script, Boss. It's in everyone's best interest, including the lady in that room."

THINGS WERE NOT AS THEY SEEMED YESTERDAY.

That message is suddenly echoing in my head as I stare at Amazon woman here with her broad shoulders and manly hands.

"I don't understand."

"There's nothing to understand. What's done is done. The people who are dead are not coming back, but those who are living need a chance to heal, including Margaret, Dana, *and* you. After what you've gone through, you deserve at least that. Leave it alone."

But I can't, and before I know it, I produce the business card and show it to her, explaining how I got it. And, I also tell her what Dana said about seeing Ryan in that alley before she was shot.

"So," I add, "I was willing to leave it alone, but apparently someone isn't."

"Truth is," she says, "you didn't see Ryan, and Dana was shot in the head, so any recollection has to be taken with a *serious* grain of salt. But say for the time being that Ryan was there. How do you know he was helping the kidnappers? How about if maybe—just maybe—he was actually trying to prevent them from taking Margaret?"

I have not thought about it from that perspective. Was Ryan there to help? Maybe he reached the alley too late? If so, why didn't he just tell me that?

She adds, "I couldn't tell you if it was Ryan or someone sent by Ryan who dropped off this business card today at your place. But I can tell you one thing: Ryan loved you like a brother. And while he may have cooperated with organized crime for reasons we may never know, he has cared for you all of your life, and it wouldn't be fair for you to think otherwise based on the vague and incomplete recollection of Dana Knox right before she was shot in the head. I wouldn't jump to conclusions so quickly. In fact, the only thing I would do *very* quickly is get Margaret out of here and back to HCH where we can all watch her and help her. If you want to focus your energy on something, that's certainly a worthwhile cause, as well as getting your ass back to work at the shelter where real people need real help. Any other questions, Boss?"

I slowly shake my head.

And just like that, without giving me any answers, without telling me what happened after they dropped me off yesterday morning, Patricia says, "See you at work, Boss." And she's gone.

And at that moment Nurse Retched calls me up to tell me that Margaret is awake.

Taking a deep breath, I muster all of my courage and step into her room.

She is once again staring at the window, but this time she isn't mumbling anything. This time her eyes drift in my direction as I approach her, pull up a chair, and sit next to her.

"Hey," I say.

She regards me with eyes that blink recognition but remain somewhat indifferent.

"Doctor says you're recovering nicely and will be able to come home very soon," I say. "It's very good seeing you again."

She gives me a barely imperceptible nod before returning her attention to the blue skies beyond the glass panes while keeping her hands to herself, signaling that she isn't ready for physical contact.

The days that follow are more of the same one-way conversation, making brief eye contact, receiving slight acknowledgements, but without uttering a single word.

Some of the girls from the shelter swung by with small gifts. Pat brought over Margaret's makeup case on the third day. I got her a new HCH T-shirt, some of her favorite magazines, and watched with satisfaction as her bruises receded, as color returned to her face, as she healed. Her body is still quite young and is rebounding nicely.

But after nearly a week, I still have not heard her voice.

Margaret Black is certainly recovering on the outside. But that's the easy part. I wonder how long it will take for the healing process inside that pretty head of hers.

I receive my answer the eighth day at Seton, just hours before she is scheduled to go home to HCH. I step out for about an hour to handle her release paperwork, and upon my return she has reverted to Goth.

Back is the black mascara, eyeliner, lipstick, and fingernail polish. She had cut up the lime-green T-shirt and turned it into a crop top, exposing her skull tattoo. And I knew that as soon as we returned to the shelter her pretty brown hair would also vanish in the dark wake of this mourning black tide.

The following morning, as I start to interview a few volunteer attorneys who have replied to Pat's online job posting, I see Margaret walking the hallway with black punkish hair. Although she is still not talking, she is getting around on her own, though keeping to herself.

My first official day back at HCH is quite busy between the interviews, a budget review with my accountant, a long discussion with facilities about what repairs can be postponed versus which are imminent, and making a couple of consulting appointments the following week, though all of them in town. Part of her recovery requires me to be a very consistent part of her daily routine, so no out-of-town trips for a while.

That evening, following my own rule, I head out and leave the all-female staff safely locked beyond the reach of any male predator.

In the weeks that follow we fall back into our routines, except for Margaret, who spends large amounts of time watching television in the break room or sitting on the small patio on the top floor overlooking the distant hill country beyond downtown Austin. She attends her therapy sessions religiously, but neither the two female doctors who see her regularly, nor Pat or Smith & Wesson—or even Big Dana who returned two weeks later—can get her to say a single word.

Margaret is neither friendly nor hostile. She doesn't smile but she also doesn't frown or cry. She is just... indifferent.

I make it a point to be consistent about having lunch and dinner every day with her in the cafeteria, where we just eat in silence while making occasional eye contact. As strangely as it sounds, I look forward each day to those few seconds when our eyes lock, when for a brief moment, I see a flicker of recognition, of gratitude for just being there.

One morning towards my second month since the incident I get an envelope from the Austin Police department. Imagine my surprise when I find an invitation for Beckett's retirement party in a week at a local bar.

Patricia Norton decides to be my date and we head for Maggie Mae's, a bar on Sixth Street, where we find ourselves surrounded by what appears to be the entire Austin Police Department, which makes us wonder who is watching our streets.

I tell this to Beckett as I shake hands with him.

"Not my problem anymore," he says, rubbing his basketball head while Patricia runs over to the bar to get us beers.

"So," I say. "This seems a bit sudden? I thought cracking the big case placed you back in good standing."

He nods. "It did, but over thirty-nine years with the force is long enough, and the case also got me an offer for early retirement with great benefits, so I took it."

"Good for you," I say with genuine honesty. In spite of the years I spent hating this man, it is ironic that in the end he actually saved my life by arresting me that Sunday morning. "What are you going to do now?"

He shrugs. "I have no family, no kids, deceased parents. Probably go travel around a bit. I've always wanted to see Alaska. See what I've been missing by spending almost four decades policing this town."

I nod. "If you get bored...I can always use a volunteer in our security department."

"I thought you only use women for that."

"I'm sure we can make an exception for retired APD officers with forty years of experience, and who also saved my ass."

He laughs again.

"How's Margaret?" he asks, turning serious.

"Day by day. But it's only been a couple of months," I say. "It's going to take time. But hell, what else have I got to do?"

"What little I saw suggested she's one special lady, David. Stick with her."

"I intend to," I reply as Pat hands me a beer.

She raises her cold mug and Beckett and I follow suit.

"To those who are still making their way out of the shadows of abuse," she says.

I can certainly drink to that.

As Patricia and I get ready to head back to the van, Beckett pulls me aside and hands me a newspaper clipping. "I'm not sure when your birthday is," he says, "but

I thought you would appreciate this. And check out the news tomorrow morning. You might like what you see."

He pats me on the shoulder, adds, "Maybe I'll look you up when I return from Alaska." He nods politely and leaves to rejoin his guests.

The clipping is from the international edition of the *New York Times*.

GEORGETOWN. GRAND CAYMAN. THE CAYMAN ISLANDS.

Gustavo Salazar, founder and senior partner of the consulting firm Mercer, Martinez, and Salazar, which became the subject of a Congressional investigative panel, was found dead at his mansion in the western carib-bean island, where he was believed to be in hiding after his firm was charged with money laundering and alleged connections with a decade-long network of sexual slavery. Also found dead was long-missing American industrialist Bernard Wilson, whose firm, Premier Imports, filed chap-ter 11 a month ago following a similar investigation.

The following morning I run over to the corner deli, get a cup of coffee, and catch a glimpse of the newsflash on the large flat screen behind the counter. Lisa Ang, former New Orleans casino owner currently at large, was found dead at her hotel in Geneva, Switzerland, this morning. Police are investigating.

I sip my latte while realizing that somewhere out there, three people are looking out for me, doing the job no one wants to do. They're not only making the world a better place but also giving me a chance to be good again, to live again.

I go straight for my office, where, to my surprise, I find Margaret Black sitting in one of the guest chairs by my desk.

"Good morning," I say, my heart skipping a beat even though my mind is telling me that her recovery will not be measured in months but in years.

And just as I feared, Margaret doesn't answer. She's just sitting there staring at the window, though her eyes do find mine for a moment before drifting away.

Rather than sit in my chair across from her, I decide to try the guest chair to her right while attempting to get some paperwork signed.

And at that moment, as I have my left hand on the armrest while leaning forward and reading a document, I feel her hand touching mine.

I look over and she is still gazing out the window, her Goth face impassive, her eyes fixated on the blue skies.

But I'll take it.

Just as dawn breaks slowly, with a faint trace of orange and yellow-gold dancing against the distant horizon at the end of the darkest night, perhaps I have just witnessed the first sign of her rising sun, her first step towards the light.

And I intend to be here, by her side, for as long as it takes, for better or for worse. Waiting. With open arms.

***

ACKNOWLEDGEMENTS

Matthew Bialer, my talented agent at Sanford J. Greenburger Associates, suggested a while back that I should consider a departure from my traditional military/computer thrillers that I've written for nearly three decades and try my hand at a domestic suspense mystery. It took a while before I finally got to it, but I'm glad I did. Thanks, Matt. You always have my back.

My sincere gratitude to Todd Barselow, president of Auspicious Apparatus Press, for taking me on and for going above and beyond the call of duty to make this possible. It's a pleasure working with such a pro.

A special thanks to Douglas Preston, Cheryl Kaye Tardif, and David Pennington for taking time from your busy schedules to review the manuscript.

Alan Graham, President of Mobile Loaves and Fishes, and Steve Fournier, Director of The Burke Center for Youth, for supporting this project.

Alice Frenk, for your awesome job at proofreading the book. Your attention to detail is truly a gift.

My beautiful and talented wife, Lory Anne, for your honest feedback during the writing process. Your amazing editorial eye is what keeps me from embarrassing myself. Every author should be as lucky.

And finally, St. Jude, Patron of Impossible Causes, for continuing to make it possible.

R.J. Pineiro
August, 2018

ABOUT THE AUTHOR

R.J. Pineiro is a 30-year veteran of the computer industry as well as the author of many internationally acclaimed novels, including *Without Mercy, Without Fear,* and *Ashes of Victory.* His new novel is *Avenue of Regrets.* He is an instrument-rated pilot, has a black belt in martial arts, and is a certified SCUBA diver. Pineiro makes his home in central Texas, where he lives with his wife, Lory Anne.

For more information on the author please visit:
www.rjpineiro.com
https://www.facebook.com/rjpineirobooks/

Made in the USA
Middletown, DE
06 January 2019